Skin Deep

Marissa Doyle

SKIN DEEP
Copyright 2016 © Marissa Doyle

This is a work of fiction. Names, characters, places, and incidents are a product of the author's imagination. Locales and public names are sometimes used for atmospheric purposes. Any resemblance to actual people, living or dead, or to businesses, companies, events, institutions, or locales is completely coincidental.

Cover by selfpubbookcovers.com/RavenandBlack
Book Layout ©2013 BookDesignTemplates.com

Skin Deep/ Marissa Doyle. -- 1st ed.
ISBN 978-1-944640-01-9

To Scott, for giving me my own
Happily Ever After

COLD MARCH SATURDAY mornings were made for sleeping late. Garland Durrell knew that. But here she was, snuggled under her down quilt, eyes resolutely shut against the coronas of light around her windows—and wide awake.

She would have been happily snoozing if it hadn't been for a freak storm that no one had predicted blowing in off the Atlantic during the night. She'd never heard the wind make sounds like that, shrieking and howling so fiercely that she'd half-dreamed it was trying to smash her windows and seize her. Not the best way to spend the first night of the rest of her life in Mattaquason, on Cape Cod's outer arm. If she believed in omens—but she didn't. Not anymore. Her wedding day had been gloriously sunny, and look how her marriage had ended up.

Though the storm had screamed itself back out to sea some time before dawn, she'd only been able to doze fitfully since then...and now, not at all. Well, if she couldn't sleep, then she might as well do something about unpacking all the boxes stacked around the house.

She threw aside the quilt and went to the bank of windows to open the curtains. Past the back lawn and a long, low dune the beach's creamy white sand spread enticingly before her. Maybe a walk would be a good idea before she began excavating her life out of moving boxes and reassembling it into its new form.

Garland yanked off her nightshirt and dressed quickly in jeans and a turtleneck sweater and a heavy, violet-colored flannel shirt on which she'd appliquéd a Compass Rose quilt square, along with a down vest. She almost ran down the stairs and through the garage where her little sailing dinghy sat on its trailer. Bigger sailboats were handsomer, but this one was so much closer to the wind and water, so much closer to what really mattered about sailing. Derek had always called it "Garland's toy boat." His own tastes ran to motorboats with more horsepower than was decent—and *damn* it, why did everything have to remind her of Derek? Had moving to this house been a mistake? Should she have sold it and gone someplace where memories wouldn't leap out at her unexpectedly like ugly Halloween spooks?

She slammed the garage door behind her and strode across the terrace to the back lawn. Once away from the protection of the house, the wind hit her like a fist to the stomach. But the sky was a soft, milky blue and the sunshine was so bright that instead of scooting back inside she paused to breathe deeply, expanding her chest as far as it would go.

Past the grass the beach was still damp and smooth from the receding tide. Off to her left, the long, narrow finger of Monomoyick Island poked into the ocean off the end of Cape Cod, pointing south toward Nantucket. The water was deep blue and choppy this morning but sparkling in the sun, making her squint as she stepped onto the sand.

Beachcombing after a storm was fun. Smashed lobster pots weren't uncommon, or broken oars, or other detritus tossed or lost off fishing boats. But sometimes the oddest things washed up. Once she'd found a waterlogged, two-foot long Winnie-the-Pooh half-buried in the sand, its red shirt faded to rose pink. And after another storm, a lacy, bright fuchsia bra from Victoria's Secret, size 46 DD. That find had sent her best friend in Mattaquason, Kathy Hayes, into gales of laughter, speculating whether any of the local fishermen had a secret lingerie fetish.

The memory made Garland smile. Kathy hadn't been home when she called last night. Out on a date, perhaps? Kathy often lamented the dearth of eligible men—whom she defined as "over six feet and without a substance abuse problem"—who lived year-round on the Cape, but maybe she'd found someone new. Hopefully she'd be in later, just in case Garland found the panties to match the bra.

Kathy had been delighted when she'd called to tell her that she'd be moving to the Cape. "Without Derek, I'm assuming," she'd said in the dry tone she always used when talking about Garland's husband. "It's about damn time. He was smothering you, Garland. Every year when you came down for the summer you looked a little paler and flatter. No, don't laugh. It was true. He was a mistake, and it was past time you cut your losses and started over. So when are you going to start quilting again? I told you, I'm keeping a space in the gallery for you, and Mrs. Feinberg asked again last summer if you'd made anything new."

Starting quilting again. She thought of the boxes of fabric and threads and the new long-arm quilting machine waiting for her at the house. She was free to create with cloth again—free of Derek's disapproval and his feigned dust allergies. She could festoon the house with fat quarters and leave pads of graph paper and piles of colored pencils in every room, and no one would care. It would be *wonderful.*

A sharp, barking call made her shade her eyes and stare out at the water. Was that a seal? Sometimes in summer she would see them a little way off the beach, lounging on the sandbar at low tide. Yes, there they were—three, no, four seals swimming parallel to the shore and looking at her with their liquid brown eyes. She'd always loved to watch them with their whiskery, inquiring faces, so at home in the water.

A houseguest had once given her a fancifully illustrated children's book about seals who could take off their skins and dance on the beach on moonlit nights in the form of beautiful men and women. Selkies, they were called. She often thought about them on the full moon nights in July and August, but Derek had never wanted to use them as a pretext for a romantic walk on to the beach. How well she remembered the patronizing smile he would give her as he told her to 'run along and enjoy herself' while he logged into his portfolio account.

One of the seals barked again. A gull, handsome in its sober gray and white feathers, cackled as it landed a few dozen yards up the beach before her. Something edible must have been tossed up in the storm, for another gull was already there.

Garland blinked away the tears in her eyes brought by the wind and squinted at the sand. There was something on the beach ahead—something large and pale, almost blending into the sand itself. The two gulls regarded it quizzically, as if wondering if it were tasty or not. She took three more steps, then froze.

The something was a naked body sprawled on its stomach, partly buried in the sand.

2

GARLAND'S KNEES felt like they'd been turned to water, and it was all she could do to keep standing. A thin voice in her head was screaming *Ohmygodohmygod adeadbodydeadbodydead—*

Another gull landed next to the first two and joined in the examination, creeping closer to what she realized was the figure's face, turned away from her. Abruptly, strength returned to her legs.

"Go away!" she shouted, and ran at them. The birds leapt into the air in an explosion of wings, one muttering what sounded like "Aw, jeez, lady!" in Seagull.

Garland knelt by the body. It was a child, probably no more than three or four years old, with shaggy light brown hair partly obscuring its face. How had a child ended up out here and in this condition? A network of deep cuts, purple with bruising and caked with dried blood and sand, crisscrossed its back.

She brushed the hair aside and pressed her fingertips to its throat. A faint but steady pulse beat there. Not dead! She scrambled out of her vest and took off her flannel shirt, then turned the child over…and gasped in horror. More cuts, punctuated with a few deeper gashes, covered his torso. She wrapped her shirt around him then rose and looked around wildly at the empty beach, sweating though she now only wore a turtleneck and jeans. The seals were still there, watching her. She hoped for an irrational second that they'd swim into shore, take off their skins, and help her deal with this. She knelt again, slipped her arms under him, and picked him up. He felt light and insubstantial as she cradled him against her, like a child made of air.

"Poor baby," she crooned. "You're going to be all right. We'll get you—"

"No!" a hoarse voice shouted.

Garland nearly dropped the boy as she whirled around. Twenty feet up the beach a man, equally naked and battered-looking, was climbing to his feet. She'd been so concerned about the boy that she hadn't even seen him.

The man stood for a second, swaying, then staggered toward her, grimacing as if in pain. The wind blew his hair, just like the boy's, around his face. "Give me back my son," he growled, reaching for the child.

"I'm sorry—I d-didn't see—I was just trying to help him," Garland stammered. His son! What had happened to the two of them? How had they ended up on her beach in this condition? The man's muscular body was cut and gashed in the same horrible pattern as the boy's, and patches of dried blood on his upper lip hinted at a freshly broken nose.

The man ignored her, his eyes narrowed fiercely above the purple bruises on his high cheekbones. But when his hands touched the flannel of her shirt wrapped around the boy's frail form he froze. A look of wonder replaced his anger, and his eyes opened wide as he stared at her so that she could see they were a light, almost golden brown, and unnaturally bright, as if he were feverish.

"What are you?" he whispered.

What was she? "Uh...I'm Garland Durrell. I live just up the beach." She nodded her head back toward her house. "I was out for a walk and found—"

"Conn. His name is Conn." The man still clutched the shirt and stared at her, not seeming to notice the fact that he was naked on a beach in forty-degree weather with a brisk wind. "Are you a man?"

She blinked. Couldn't he tell the difference? "Um, no. I'm a woman. A female."

He shrugged as if she were the one who'd misunderstood. "Yes. A female man. How did you know we were here? Did you hear..." He trailed into silence and glanced over his shoulder at the small waves slapping the sand.

"You're hurt. Can I help you?" She had to get this poor child out of the cold—and his father off his feet. Oh, *why* hadn't she grabbed her phone off her bedside table? She could have called 911 already and had help here in a few minutes.

"A healer. Conn must see a healer," he said.

"A healer? Do you mean a doctor? I think we need to get you both to the hospital." Maybe English wasn't his first language. Or might he be delirious?

"What is 'the hospital'? I want a healer." He frowned. "Don't your people have healers?"

Oh dear. "Yes, we have healers," she said carefully, and looked down again at the child in her arms. His pale, drawn face decided her. Strangers or not, he needed help. "If you're all right with coming to my house, I'll get one as quickly as I can."

"Wait." The man reached up and touched her cheek. "I think…you are not Mahtahdou's," he murmured, looking into her eyes. "I don't know what you are, but you aren't his." His shoulders drooped. "Rest, in a safe place—if only for a little while…"

Garland flinched but didn't move. His touch was like testing, like dipping a hand in bath water to check its temperature. Amazingly, his fingers were warm and supple. "Yes, rest," she agreed. "Will you let me carry Conn? Can you walk? It's not that far." Would he be able to make it back to her house without collapsing?

The man nodded and let his hand fall to touch a fold of her purple shirt. "You'll keep him safe in this."

His sudden trust was oddly touching, if bewildering. At least he'd decided to cooperate. "Of course I will. Speaking of which—that's my vest on the sand there. You can put it on. It might help a little."

"Help what?" He blinked and bent to pick up the down vest she'd stripped off.

Then he must be numb and couldn't feel the cold any more. But what about his hand when he'd touched her just now? "Um, never mind. But you can carry it for me." She hesitated, and looked at him. "By the way, what's your name?"

He hesitated too, just for a few seconds "Alasdair. My name is Alasdair."

She waited, but he didn't volunteer a last name. "All right, Alasdair. Let's go."

He walked just behind her, with one hand on her shoulder. Garland thought of a small child clinging to his mother's skirt. Except this child was well over six feet tall, solid and muscular under his injuries, with long limbs and straight, proud shoulders. Not that she'd been looking. Well, not much. She'd just gotten the man from hell out of her life and she didn't need another one in it, even if he looked like an angel home from the wars.

"Can you tell me what happened to you?" she asked, bracing herself for an explanation involving alien abduction, based on his earlier speeches. "Was there an accident?"

But Alasdair disappointed her "I'm not sure," he said slowly. "I can't remember. It was dark…"

"Were you on a boat? Did someone attack you?" she prompted when he trailed into silence. Only fishing boats ventured out this time of year. Who would take a small child out on a fishing boat in March?

The hand on her shoulder tightened at the word "attack," but all he said was, a little sullenly, "I don't remember."

"We can call your family, or the police. They must be looking for you—"

"No family. Not any more." He looked away, but not before she caught the anguish in his face.

She didn't persist. Maybe he'd remember more once he'd had a chance to recover a little. And surely he must have someone—a friend, at least—who might have some idea of what had happened.

But those cuts she'd seen on both of them…they'd been so evenly spaced, so cruelly precise, that it was hard not to conclude that they'd been deliberately inflicted. But by whom? Who could have done such a thing to a man and a small boy?

And why? And what—or who—was the Mah—Mahwhatever he'd said she didn't belong to that he seemed to fear so much?

Garland led him up her lawn and through the sliding doors on the terrace into the great room. She lay Conn on the couch and started to unwrap him from her shirt.

"No!" Alasdair said, putting a restraining hand on her arm.

"Hey, it's okay. I was going to wrap him in a blanket instead," she said, reaching for a thick fleece throw folded over the back of the couch.

"Leave him in it."

He looked so adamant that she left the boy wrapped in her shirt and tucked the blanket over him. "Uh, why don't I get something for you to wear, too?" Alasdair had sunk to the floor next to the couch and closed his eyes, breathing hard. The walk had evidently been nearly too much for him. "And I'll call nine—I mean, a healer."

He nodded, eyes still closed. "I can wait. Help Conn."

Garland ran upstairs to her room. Derek's belongings were mostly gone, of course, but he'd left a few things behind. Like the bathrobe she'd sewn for him a few years ago, made from indigo-dyed cloth she'd bought on their trip to Japan and appliquéd with Japanese ideograms. He'd never worn it. Alasdair was taller than Derek, and broader in the shoulders too, but it would be better than nothing. She took it from a hook on the back of the bedroom door, took the extra blanket from the foot of the bed, then snatched the phone from her bedside table and dialed 911 as she went back down the stairs.

"Mattaquason emergency services," said a male voice. It sounded beautifully calm and sane, unlike everything else that had happened this morning. She took a deep breath before speaking and tried hard to keep from rushing her words.

"I live on Eldredge Point in Mattaquason, and just found two people—a man and his son—unconscious on my beach—that is, the son was unconscious—they were naked and cut up pretty badly. I don't know who they are or how they got there, and the man doesn't seem to remember what happened. They must have fallen off a boat or something...." She took another deep breath. "They need medical attention—I think maybe the man's had a concussion, and the boy's still out cold..."

There was silence on the other end of the phone.

"Hello?" she said.

"On your beach? Jesus, I—oh, God, you're not joking, are you?"

The voice no longer sounded calm—instead, it sounded almost as flustered as she felt. She stopped halfway down the stairs. Something wasn't right here. "Of course I'm not joking. I need help!"

There was a sound of unintelligible urgent speech, as if the dispatcher had covered his mouthpiece and was talking to another person in the room. "Hello?" she said again.

Another few seconds of muffled speech, and then a different voice replied. Though it was calmer than the first, it still sounded distinctly strained. "Your name and address, please?"

Garland told him. "Is there anything wrong?" she added.

"No, not at all. It's just that we...we've had a lot of calls this morning and I don't know when we'll be able to get personnel out there, Mrs. Durrell—oh, there's a call on my other line—"

The connection went dead.

Garland stifled a curse. What had that been all about? She punched the three digits again.

Nothing. Not even a ring tone. Only a weird, buzzing hum.

She stared at the phone for a second, biting her lip, then shook her head and went back into the great room.

Alasdair hadn't moved. "I brought you this," she said softly, laying the robe across his knees. "Won't you put it on?"

His eyes flew open as the fabric touched his skin, and he grabbed at the robe and huddled under it as if it were a blanket.

"No—you're supposed to wear it—" She dropped to her knees and tried to show him, but he flinched away from her.

"Hey, I'm not trying to taking it from you," she soothed. "Here—it goes over your shoulders—and your arms go through here—" Holy cow, had he forgotten how to put on clothes?

As the fabric covered his back and arms, he stopped struggling and stared down at it in wonder. "What is it?" he murmured, stroking the fabric of an appliqué with one hesitant finger. "I can feel it…the power…just like the other…"

"It's just a robe I made for my husband."

"*You* made it?" He stared at her. "You are a magic-wielder?"

Damn those people at 911! She had an unconscious child and a possibly delirious man on her hands. "Look, I'm going to try to get that, uh, healer, okay?"

She climbed to her feet and tucked the other blanket over Conn, then headed toward the kitchen, glancing back at him. He was crouched next to the boy again, staring at his arms in the sleeves of the robe. She shook her head and went to the desk in the kitchen. In the top drawer was a business card listing the office and home numbers of Dr. Robert Mowbray, one of the town's newer physicians.

She'd met Dr. Mowbray at a couple of charity events for the Mattaquason Historical Society and the Friends of the Library and had liked him a lot. There was an aura of competence and integrity about him that was highly reassuring. She needed reassurance pretty badly just now, after that exchange with the 911 dispatcher.

The phone rang five, six, seven times. What if he'd gone away for the weekend or was tied up with whatever crisis seemed to be going on right now? Dr. Phelps, the town's other MD that she knew, was close to eighty and saw very few patients anymore. Would he be willing to come to the house and help? And there was the hospital in Hyannis, but that was so far away—

Then Garland heard the soft click of the receiver being lifted. She just had time for an inarticulate sigh of relief before a pleasant male voice said, "Hello?"

"Dr. Mowbray? This is Garland Durrell, on Eldredge Point. We've met at a few Historical Society events…"

He didn't pause more than half a second. "Mrs. Durrell—of course. Not another splinter, is it?"

Oh dear. She'd nearly forgotten about that incident two years ago, when she'd gotten an enormous splinter while going barefoot at a cocktail party on Amy Nickerson's deck. He'd been there too and had removed it for her, using a splash of his gin and tonic as disinfectant.

"No, not a splinter. It's—he's—I—" She forced herself to stop and take a deep breath. "I've just moved in, and went for a walk on my beach, and found…" She repeated what she'd told the 911 dispatcher and what had happened afterward, hoping Dr. Mowbray wouldn't have the same reaction.

He didn't. "Jesus Christ! Eldredge Point Road, isn't it? I'm leaving now. Keep them warm." The phone clicked off.

Garland sagged against the kitchen counter in relief. Thank heavens someone was coming. She set the phone down and went back into the great room. "The doctor—the healer is coming," she said, kneeling by Alasdair again. "Can I get you anything? Something hot to drink?"

He grimaced. "Hot? No." He stared out the sliding doors they'd come through. "Can you see in through those from the water?"

What an odd question. "Not very well, during the day. Only at night when the lights are on. I usually close the curtains then, unless it's summer."

"Good." He closed his eyes again and was silent. Garland felt awkward, sitting next to him doing nothing. She was afraid to touch any of Conn's scratches or wounds, even to clean them, lest she hurt him. Surely Dr. Mowbray would be here soon—

"Let me wash some of that blood off your face," she said to Alasdair, rising and going back to the kitchen.

She wrung out a few clean kitchen towels in warm water, then brought them back to the great room and carefully wiped the dried blood from his upper lip and cheeks. Darn, but he cleaned up well. Once those bruises faded and the swelling went down, he'd be gorgeous…those high cheekbones and that firm jaw with the little dimple in his chin. The long nose would be a little crooked now, it looked like, but it would only add a raffish charm to the symmetrical beauty of the rest of his face.

Alasdair sat quietly, eyes still closed, and let her work. "Thank you," he murmured when she was done. "Your hands feel powerful."

Garland was saved from having to reply by a knock at the front door. "That's the healer. I'll be right back." She scrambled to her feet and hurried into the front hall to open the door.

Dr. Mowbray carried a large black medical bag and that air

of quiet competence she'd remembered. "Where?" he said, without preamble.

"This way." Garland led him back to the couch in the great room.

Alasdair clambered to his feet when he saw them and stood protectively over the still form on the couch, the robe hanging loosely around him. "Are you the healer?" he demanded.

Dr. Mowbray didn't even blink. "I am. Will you let me help you and your son?"

Alasdair stared at him, swaying slightly, then turned and looked at Garland. She could feel the question in his eyes. "It's all right," she said, going to him and taking his arm. "He won't hurt Conn. Sit down before you fall down, okay?"

He leaned on her for a second, then nodded and let her lead him to a chair, watching closely as Dr. Mowbray knelt beside the couch and felt the pulse at Conn's throat, then retrieved a flashlight from his bag. He tensed as the doctor peeled back the boy's eyelids and shined the light into them.

"Well, that's good," he muttered. "Let's see what else we have here." He pulled away the blankets and opened the shirt. "Son of a bitch," he muttered, looking at the cuts crisscrossing the little body. "Can I have some more light here, Mrs. Durrell? And a big pot of water—hot but not too hot?"

Garland turned on the lamp by the couch and pulled the curtains all the way open, then hurried into the kitchen for the water. As she came back, trying not to slosh it on the floor from the soup pot she carried, she heard the beep of a thermometer and saw Dr. Mowbray staring at it, shaking his head. "Almost normal. For a small child who's spent hours on the beach in March with no clothes on, that's crazy. Oh, thanks. Let's get some of this sand off him and see what needs doing."

"Crazy" seemed to be the right word to describe everything she'd experienced that morning, except for Dr. Mowbray. She leaned over the back of the couch and watched him work. "Is it bad?" she murmured.

"It's not pretty, but he'll be all right. A couple of these might need suturing—I'll know better once I've…" he trailed into silence, concentrating on blotting away as much sand and blood as he could. "What happened to him?" he asked, very quietly. "What did the father say?"

Garland glanced at Alasdair, gripping the arms of his chair as he watched them. "That he doesn't remember—that it was dark. That's about it. Someone did this to them, didn't they? This wasn't an accident."

"No, it wasn't. Whoever did it was a sadistic bastard—who could do this to a child? Look."

With the worst of the blood and sand washed away, it was plain to see that the cuts on his body had been inflicted in a symmetrical pattern, from his collarbone down to the tops of his thighs. Not deep, but deep and frequent enough to hurt and bleed copiously. They were horrible in their cruel, surgical precision. She looked away, shivering. "I don't want to know who did this."

"And you found them like this on your beach? Lucky for them you were down for the weekend."

"Oh, I'm not just here for the weekend. I'm moving down here."

"Really?" His hands slowed ever so slightly. "Year round?"

"Yes."

"Hmm." He worked in silence for a moment. "No clothes, you said? No ID or anything?"

"Nothing. I found the boy first—he was lying face down in the sand. It had sort of drifted around him. I think they must have been caught in the storm last night and washed in on the tide. In fact they must have, because I walked there late yesterday afternoon after the movers left and they weren't there."

"Movers—so you really did just get here. Hell of a thing to find on your doorstep your first day here, Mrs. Durrell." He paused and glanced up at her. His eyes were blue, and had nice smile crinkles at their corners. She'd forgotten about those.

"It was a bit of a shock," she admitted. "But you don't have to call me Mrs. Durrell. I'm Garland."

"I know. And I'm Rob, okay?" More crinkles appeared. "Well, your driftwood theory might be right if they fell off a boat or were on one that went down in that storm last night. We'll call the Coast Guard when I'm done and see if they know anything. More water, please?"

Garland brought him more water and watched as he closed a few of the deepest cuts with Steri-Strips. He worked swiftly but carefully, and Garland couldn't help thinking that he would have made a deft quilter. "I'm amazed that he's not waking up," she whispered.

"I am too, even though I've given him a little topical anesthesia. He didn't seem to be concussed, but I should check again."

"What is it? What are you doing?" Alasdair demanded, wincing as he rose.

"It's all right." Garland hurried over and pressed him gently back down into the chair. "The doc—uh, healer is closing the deepest cuts so they'll heal properly. Conn will be fine. Now sit still till he's done, and then it's your turn."

Garland sat with Conn while Rob coaxed Alasdair to lie down on the floor to let him examine his injuries. It seemed wrong to leave the boy alone after what he had been through, and she fancied she could see some of the pain and distress lift from his sleeping features as she washed his face and stroked his salt-stiffened hair. Poor little thing—he wasn't much more than a baby, was he? His mother must be frantic—if he had a mother. What had Alasdair said? That they had no family?

Not surprisingly, Alasdair flinched at Rob's every touch. Something seemed to trouble him about Rob Mowbray despite the doctor's gentleness and calm. Was it the questions Rob asked him about where they'd come from and how they'd come to be on Garland's beach? Just as he had to her, Alasdair would only reply, in a monotone, *I don't remember. I don't know.*

"Well," Rob said after cleaning and bandaging Alasdair as much as he would allow. He wouldn't remove the robe she'd given him and seemed extremely dubious about the dressings Rob had put on his various wounds, including several deep and vicious ones on the bottoms of his feet. No wonder he'd had a hard time walking up to her house. "That'll do for now till you get to Hyannis. I don't know why 911 wasn't working, Garland, but I'm going to find out. In the meanwhile, I'd be glad to give them a lift to the hospital—if you don't mind coming with me, I can get them admitted pretty quickly—"

"We will not go anywhere," Alasdair said, struggling to sit up and frowning at Rob. "We shall stay here."

Rob blinked at his vehemence. "You and your son have, God knows how, just survived a horrific ordeal. I've done what I can for you here but you should both really go to the hospital for observation to make sure you don't have any internal injuries—if all goes well you'll be out of there by tonight, and that's a promise. But if you can't remember how you got into this condition or where you're from, that tells me you need to be admitted at least overnight to check for neurological—"

"No. We stay here."

"Have you discussed that with Mrs. Durrell?" Rob asked just as flatly.

"Hey," Garland broke in. Rob and Alasdair were scowling at each other so hard that their hair should have been on fire. "Why don't we bring Conn upstairs to the spare room and let you and him rest while the doctor and I think about what we can do to help you? You're in no condition to make decisions right now, and maybe after a nap you'll begin to remember something. Okay?"

"Garland," Rob muttered.

"It's *okay*." She looked at him meaningfully. "Come on. Is it all right if the doctor carries Conn?"

Alasdair glared a moment longer, then nodded. He let them help him up and watched Rob closely as he lifted Conn off the couch, then followed behind, leaning on Garland's arm. At the bottom of the stairs he paused and gazed up them. "So high," he said under his breath.

Garland motioned Rob ahead of them. "Left at the top, last room on the right," she directed. That was the room she'd planned on using for her quilting studio because of the splendid light from its east- and south-facing windows. It was also the only room with twin beds in it. Well, no matter. Alasdair and Conn would be long gone before she was ready to start work.

She turned to Alasdair. "I'll help you," she said, taking his arm. "I'm not surprised you're feeling dizzy."

Alasdair started to say something then closed his mouth again and let her lead him up the stairs. He climbed them one at a time like a small child, staring at his feet in concentration as he did. At the top he looked back down, blanched, and turned away.

Rob had already tucked Conn under the covers of one bed. They helped Alasdair ease down onto the other. He sighed, and she sensed the rigidity in his frame relax just a little bit. "Rest," she said. "I'll close the curtains, all right? Just shout if you need me."

"Garland." He stared up at her, and she got the feeling that he was actually seeing *her*, not just the person who'd found him. "You…" He fell silent and closed his eyes. Garland waited a few seconds but he didn't open them again. She pulled down the shades and drew the curtains, then tiptoed down the stairs after Rob.

"You make a very good surgical assistant, you know," Rob said quietly as they descended. "Not everyone can face the sight of more than a drop or two of blood."

"Oh, I didn't do much…" Was she blushing?

"May I make one more request, Nurse?"

"Um, sure."

He stopped on the bottom stair and grinned up at her. "Coffee, please?"

❧❧❧

"So you found them lying on the beach like that?" Rob took a sip of coffee. "Ah, that hits the spot. What a great way to start your first day here."

"It's certainly not what I expected." Garland leaned back in her kitchen chair and wrapped her hands around her mug. "What do you think happened to them?"

"I don't know. But it's obvious that it was intentional.

Torture, maybe. Then dumping them in the water and letting them slowly bleed to death." His voice was grim and controlled. "Did you see their wrists and ankles? They'd been tied up while this was done to them. Good thing they weren't left bound or they probably would have drowned."

"Dear God." The few sips of coffee she'd taken turned sour in her stomach.

"I'm sorry." He leaned forward and touched her arm. "You didn't need this today, did you?"

"My problems seem pretty small compared to theirs."

He smiled. "I'd forgotten how delightfully rational you are."

And she'd forgotten how charming his smile was. And how good-looking in a boyish sort of way, with thick, straight brown hair that had an endearing habit of falling over his forehead and clean-cut features. It felt strange to be contemplating another man's attractions.

She stole a peek at his left hand. Nicely groomed, capable-looking, and ringless. And she hadn't heard any gossip last summer that he'd been seeing anyone seriously. Young Doctor Mowbray was quite the darling of the town. He paid for it in charity bachelor auctions and the like, which he participated in with cheerful good humor. But evidently no one had managed to win him on a more permanent basis.

"So you've joined us year-rounders." His tone was light and casual—perhaps a little too much so. "Alone?"

"My husband and I are divorcing. It'll be final in a few months. I got the Cape house."

"Your choice?"

"Yes."

Rob looked around the bright, airy kitchen. She followed his gaze as it took in the top-of-the-line appliances and custom-made teak cabinetry. "Really?" he said. "This house is a showplace. Didn't you have it in the Mattaquason House and Garden Tour two years ago?"

"And the year before that. Actually, Derek was thrilled to be rid of it. He never liked it here very much. But having a summer place in a pricey and hard-to-get-to location was *de rigueur* in his office. Nantucket won the expensive and inaccessible contest, but the Cape ran a close second. He's keeping our house in Chestnut Hill for him and his new wife and the kids he's planning to have. That house makes this one look pretty humble." She tried to keep the bitterness out of her voice.

Rob shook his head. "Trophy house and a trophy wife? Some people have no clue about what's really important in life, do they?"

Garland poured herself more coffee. "Oh, I think he knew what was important to him. When I turned thirty-five last year, he decided it was time to divest some long-term holdings that hadn't performed up to expectations and check the market for growth stocks." She smiled wryly as she stirred milk into her cup. "My words, not his. But they tell the story pretty well. It's how he views the world."

"What are you going to do, now that you're here?"

"Aside from find bodies on my beach?" She smiled again, then glanced toward the stairs. Shouldn't she be up there, keeping an eye on them? Conn might waken and need comforting…she yanked her attention back to Rob Mowbray. "Quilting, I hope."

He raised an eyebrow. "That sounds interesting. Why quilting?"

Garland turned her mug so that she could see the "Quilters

Do It in the Ditch" logo on it. "I double-majored in history and art in college, and wanted to become a quilt artist. I'd been accepted into the fiber arts master's degree program at the Rhode Island School of Design when Derek proposed. But after we were married he discouraged me from pursuing the degree because we both thought I'd be too busy with our kids. Well, that didn't turn out to be an issue."

"I'm sorry," he said gently. "The whole infertility thing—"

"Oh, I wasn't infertile," she interrupted. "Neither was he. Believe me, he insisted we see the best fertility experts. We just couldn't get me pregnant. We even tried in vitro. Twice. I couldn't face it more than that."

She kept her eyes fixed on her mug. "He had his work, and I had my quilts. But when I did anything at all public with my quilts, especially selling them, it bothered him. I think he thought it reflected on his ability to support us. So then he developed 'allergies' and complained that my quilting raised too much dust, so eventually I just stopped. But I think I knew I'd come back to it someday. I'm hoping that being down here where it's quiet will help me find my way back to it. Kathy Hayes—you know, the Captain Hayes Gallery on Main Street—is an old friend, and she's promised me space in her shop if I choose to start exhibiting and selling. She sold a couple of my quilts years ago and Derek was furious. He wanted me to spend my time doing high-profile volunteer work to make him look good, not hiding in a studio sewing bits of fabric together."

Rob shook his head again. "I know he is—or was—your husband. But what a jerk. You can't demand that someone with a vocation stop doing what they love just to soothe your ego. I know I couldn't stop being a doctor if I tried. It must have been awful."

Garland looked up at him. Not all of her friends had understood what not being able to quilt had meant to her.

"I have to confess that I cheated," she said, toying with her mug again.

Rob cleared his throat and shifted in his chair.

She chuckled. "No, not like that. I started taking art classes again a couple of years ago when Derek thought I was going into Boston to do work for the Junior League. I managed to get a lot of the required classes out of the way, but it wasn't easy. I could only take one course at a time. Fortunately the school's been pretty understanding. So part of being down here is doing an independent study and finally making some quilts."

"Well, good for you." A slow smile spread across Rob's face as he in turn stared at his mug. "You know, I had no idea all this lurked under that attractive young society matron exterior when I first met you. But I hope you're not going to be all work and no play now that you're down here permanently."

Garland's stomach flip-flopped. Attractive? Young? Thirty-six wasn't exactly young but it wasn't middle-aged, was it? There might be a few lines at the corners of her eyes, but there wasn't a single strand of gray in her dark blonde hair. God knew she'd checked often enough when she first found out about Derek's girlfriend. Was Rob just being nice? Or was there something else behind his words?

A car door slammed in the driveway, then another. Rob glanced out the window. "Captain Howe," he commented. "About time someone responded to your 911 call."

"The police!" Garland sat up. "But I asked for medical assistance!"

"I know. I'm just as mystified—not to mention ticked off—

as you are, but I guess we'll have to take what we can get as far as emergency response goes." He rose and stretched. "Besides, considering the shape your guests are in, I would have suggested you call them anyway. The police'll do what they can to find out who they are—look at missing persons reports, check their prints, and start trying to figure who the hell did this to them."

Captain Edward Howe looked like he'd been hired from Central Casting, with his crew cut and big-man-slightly-gone-to-seed physique. The officer with him whose name badge said "Moniz" was a little less typecast, but looked like he was doing his best to catch up to his older colleague.

Rob greeted them with a nod. "Hello, Ed. How's the knee, Ben? You going to give it a break from the softball this spring?"

"It's better, thank you. I was kind of hoping you'd say I could play this season…" Officer Moniz glanced at his superior officer and trailed into silence.

"Come see me next week and we'll talk. Captain." Rob turned his attention back to the other man. "I'm assuming you're here because you got the message from the emergency dispatcher?"

Captain Howe's expression didn't alter, but his ears began to turn pink at the edges. "Uh, yeah. They're sorry 'bout that. Things were a little hectic over there—"

"It was inexcusable," Rob snapped, all affability gone. "You're just lucky I answered my phone this morning so I could help Mrs. Durrell out. We've got a father and son upstairs who look like a bunch of drugged-up trainee meatpackers had a field day with them then dumped them in the sound to drown. The son's unconscious and the father can't remember much more than his name."

The captain's ears were now bright red, but his face had gone oddly pale. Garland thought she heard him mutter a faint "Crap!" under his breath.

"Now, dammit, Ed, I want you to find out who the hell they are and who did this to them. And where they're from, so we can get them back to their family," Rob continued.

But Alasdair said that they had no family. Garland remembered the bleak look on his face when he'd told her that.

"And transport to Cape General Hospital might be appreciated, too," Rob finished. "I don't know what you folks were up to this morning, but now's your chance to stop screwing around and do your jobs."

Garland took a deep breath. "You don't have to do that."

"Huh?" All three men stared at her.

"You don't have to take them to the hospital. They can stay here until the police figure out who they are and where they belong."

Rob frowned. "Garland, I don't think that's a good idea—"

"I do. They're not just—just stray dogs that you send to the pound. How long could they stay at Cape General, Rob? You yourself said they'd probably only be there overnight. What then? A homeless shelter? They have nothing, and I have this big house."

"Garland, you *can't*. Ed, back me up." Rob turned to Captain Howe.

But the captain wouldn't meet his eyes. "I can't say I think it's a good idea, but I can't stop you, ma'am."

"You're not going along with this, are you?" Rob asked him incredulously.

"It's Mrs. Durrell's decision, not mine. If she wants to let them stay with her while we...look into this, I have nothing to say about it," Captain Howe replied. "Now, if that's settled, we'll be moving on—"

Rob looked as though he were barely restraining his temper. "Wouldn't a description and a victim's statement come in handy if you're going to try to find out who they are and what happened to them?"

Captain Howe shuffled his feet. "Well, I—"

"They're probably both asleep," Garland cut in. Something about Captain Howe bothered her. Was it the way he kept surreptitiously wiping his hands on his pants as if they were sweating? Whatever it was, she didn't want him upstairs in her house, looking at her poor defenseless castaways. "Can't we give you their description so you can get started on the identification, and you can come back tomorrow to take a statement?"

"Yes, ma'am, we can do that," Captain Howe agreed before Rob could say anything. "Officer?"

Officer Moniz pulled out his notebook and nodded. "Go ahead, doc."

Rob glowered at them all indiscriminately, but gave her an extra frown. "Fine. Father is an adult Caucasian male, age approximately thirty to forty, who states his name is Alasdair but did not seem to remember his surname. Height about six-three, build strong but a bit underweight, perhaps due to malnourishment. Brown shoulder-length hair. Eyes brown. Slight peculiarity in hands—"

Garland turned to him. "What?"

"Didn't you notice? He's got webs."

"Webs?"

Rob waggled his hands. "Just below the first knuckle of

each finger. It's rare, but it happens. Most people have them removed as children. The boy has them too."

This time there was no mistaking the captain's heartfelt expletive. Rob looked at him in puzzlement "Is anything wrong, Ed?"

Captain Howe's face had gone white again but he shook his head. "No. I, uh…I just remembered something I forgot to do this morning." He pulled his own notebook from his pocket and scribbled something in it. "Go on."

Garland could see his by the set of his jaw that his teeth were clenched. What had that been about? She looked at Rob.

He shrugged and shook his head at her very slightly, then continued. "No tattoos or other distinguishing marks noticed during rendition of medical attention. Extensive cuts and contusions recently inflicted, serious but not life-threatening, definitely intentional and possibly ritualistic."

The captain's pencil paused. "That's—that's a little hard to prove, don't you think?" he asked.

"Do you want to see them?"

"It's not necessary," he said quickly. "And the boy?"

Rob ran through a quick description of Conn. Captain Howe listened impassively while the junior officer scribbled away, then turned toward the front door. "Well, I think we've got what we need here. Moniz?"

"Can I offer you a cup of coffee before you go?" Garland asked. "I'd just made a fresh pot before you arrived."

The captain shook his head and continued edging toward the door. "Thank you, ma'am, but we need to get back to the station and start running some checks on this—on him." He jerked his head toward the stairs. "We'll get back to you as soon as we find anything out. See you later, Doc." He reached for the doorknob.

"I'll call this week," Moniz said to Rob. "Bye, Miz Durrell." He ducked his head and followed Captain Howe.

Rob shook his head as she closed the door behind the two officers. "I wish I knew you better, so I could spank you. Garland, are you nuts?"

"Why? Captain Howe obviously didn't want anything to do with them. And I can't just abandon them. You heard what I said."

"I heard you, and I'm going to use your words against you. You were right, this guy's not a stray dog that you can start feeding because he wandered into your yard. What if it turns out that he's an addict? Or fleeing the mob or something? Do you really want to get embroiled in this?"

"Does he look like an addict or a criminal to you?" she demanded. "Does the boy? He's just a baby, for God's sake. Somebody hurt them and abandoned them to die on a beach. Now somebody's got to help them, and I guess that's me."

"But damn it, Garland…"

"What?" She stood still and met his eyes, not blinking. "Who better? I already know a thing or two about being hurt and dumped."

He looked at her, ruffling his hair in agitation, then sighed. "All right. If you're not going to be reasonable, then you've got to let me help you. You've just moved to town after a nasty divorce and it sounds like you've got your own healing to do. Taking on someone else's healing as well is too much."

That stopped her. "I didn't mean to drag you into—that is, you've got your own patients to concern you—"

"And they aren't my patients now? Or you, for that matter?"

"I wasn't aware that I required a doctor's care." The coolness in her voice made her want to kick herself. Rob would think she was being a jerk.

"You're not under a doctor's care. You're under my care."

"There's a difference?"

"Yeah, there's a difference." He looked at her, his face stern. "I need to do some errands. I'll be back tonight to check on them around six. And I'll be bringing dinner and a bottle of wine with me. Now do you get what the difference is?"

Her stiffness melted away. "I get it," she said softly. "Six would be lovely."

His expression relaxed, and a hint of that boyish smile appeared at the corners of his mouth. "Good. If they start to feel feverish, or if the father seems more disoriented or confused, call me. Try to get some food—something light— and liquids into them. I'll leave you some painkillers, too. He might need them. Don't give the boy any. If he wakes and seems uncomfortable, call me." Rob briskly went to retrieve his medical bag, left her a couple of pills in an envelope, and shrugged on his jacket.

"Some rest for you might not be a bad idea, too. It's barely ten in the morning and you've already had a full day," he said at the door.

"Yes, Dr. Mowbray, sir." Garland made a face at him.

He snorted, and half-opened the door. "Oh, and by the way...Garland?"

"Yes?"

"Welcome to Mattaquason." He grinned at her, and left.

After Rob left, Garland wandered into the great room and began to slowly tidy up. What a strange morning it had been, finding Alasdair and Conn like that. And meeting Rob Mowbray again. She'd thought her new life would be quiet, a little lonely perhaps at first. Instead, she had two amnesiac houseguests and a date with the cutest guy in town. Welcome to Mattaquason indeed. If this was what the first twenty-four hours in town had brought her, what would next month be like?

She folded the blanket and plumped the cushions on the couch into fullness. Two people, father and son, wash up on a beach in early spring with no clothes and no memory of how they got there. She made a mental inventory of their injuries— the bruises, the blackened eyes—while trying not to think of the appalling brutality of the cuts. Ritualistic, Rob had called them. Who could have hurt a small child in such a deliberately cruel way? Had this Alasdair run afoul of some gang? Organized crime was everywhere, even on Cape Cod. Smuggling, drugs…all these existed under the wholesome, summer-paradise façade that Cape Cod liked to show the world.

One of her art teachers had maintained that it was possible to read personality in faces. She thought about Alasdair's, stern and unsmiling and haggard, and under it all, chiseled and beautiful. No, with a face like that, he wasn't a criminal any more than Rob was. Nor could she imagine that he would be involved with anything that might endanger his son—not if his anxiety over him just now was any indication.

She went to the kitchen, got the dustpan and brush from the closet, and went back into the great room to sweep up the sand they'd tracked in from the beach. Then there was Captain Howe. He'd been nervous, troubled, almost as if he'd known something about her castaways and didn't want to have to deal with them. But how could he? Or—or was there something not quite above-board going on in the Mattaquason police department? Was that why the 911 people had been so incoherent? But how could they—

A *thud-thud-a-thud-thud* sounded on the front door, followed by a muffled, "Hey, Garland! You home?"

Garland knew that knock. She dropped the dustpan and hurried to the door.

"There you are!" Her friend Kathy enveloped her in a hug. Paper crackled and something heavy bumped against Garland's shoulder blades.

"Oops!" Kathy laughed and let her go, displaying two gift

bags. "Forgot about these, I was so happy to see you."

Kathy Hayes was a tall, strongly built woman about fifteen years Garland's senior. When tourists asked her about the "Captain Hayes" her gallery was named after, expecting a romantic story of an East India trader ancestor or maybe a whaling captain, she'd smile and point to a small picture on the wall behind the counter: herself, in her Army uniform. She'd retired after tours of duty in Croatia and Iraq and three decorations and moved back to her family home on Cape Cod. Her gallery had a selection of crafts from the countries she'd been deployed in. "It's the least I can do to keep on helping those people," she always said.

Garland took the bags and led her into the kitchen. "You didn't have to, you know."

"Of course I did. One's a housewarming present, and one's got croissants from the bakery. They were hot when I bought 'em just now. Sorry I didn't call you last night—didn't get in till late." Kathy took off her brightly embroidered, quilted Afghani coat and tossed it over a chair.

"Date?" Garland piled the croissants on a plate.

Kathy grimaced. "I wish. No, my sister-in-law's birthday. We went down to the Daniel Webster Inn in Sandwich for dinner. Nice place—" She paused, looking at the used coffee cups on the kitchen table. "What? I'm not your first visitor?"

Garland smiled and brought clean cups and the croissants to the table. "No, you're the—umm—sixth. It's been a heck of a morning here."

"Sounds exciting. So who was it? Come on, spill." Kathy poured the coffee and looked bright-eyed and expectant.

Garland pretended to count on her fingers. "First there were the two people I found washed up on my beach. Then

Rob Mowbray who patched them up—God, Kathy, you should've seen it. And finally two of Mattaquason's finest…" She trailed into silence as Kathy's face changed. If she hadn't known better, she would have thought Kathy looked…well, frightened.

"People on the beach? Who? What happened?" Kathy stared at her over the top of her cup.

Garland explained about Alasdair and Conn and their injuries, 911's strange incompetence and Rob's gallantry, and Captain Howe and his peculiar behavior. "I really ought to go check on them," she concluded, glancing toward the stairs. "Do you want to come meet them? Maybe you'd know—"

"No, I don't. I saw enough semi-dead people in the service. Jesus, Garland!" Kathy set down her mug with a thud. Garland noticed her hands were shaking. "Why didn't you make the police take them to the hospital? Rob Mowbray was right. You can't be nursing total strangers back to health in this house all by yourself. You're the only person on Eldredge Point this time of year, aren't you? What if something happens? Even if these guys aren't dangerous, what if whoever left them for dead finds out they aren't and decides to come back and finish the job?"

She sounded almost angry now, but there was an edge of fear in her voice and words—Kathy, the decorated ex-soldier…Garland put those thoughts aside. "One of them is barely out of diapers, and neither of them are in any shape to hurt a fly. I couldn't just let them take them away. They need me—"

Kathy snorted. "No. Right now, *you* need you. Call the police back and tell that fat idiot Howe to get his butt over here and get them to the hospital already. You don't need to be mixed up in this."

"Mixed up in what?"

Kathy quickly took a gulp of coffee, but not before Garland saw her face redden. "Mixed up in what, Kathy?" she asked again.

"Mixed up in anything that isn't getting over your git of an ex-husband and working on your quilting again." Kathy leaned forward in her seat. "Garland, I'm serious. You could have an amazing career with your quilts. There's something about them—something...I don't know. Remember Sonja Feinberg, who's been bugging me about you? She says she loves inviting over people who've never been to her house, because they're always stopped dead by your sunset quilt that hangs in her foyer. They have to stare at it for several minutes before their legs will work again and their mouths will close. And then it's hard getting them out the door again at the end of the evening because they get stuck in front of it again. You put something into fabric and thread that turn them into another thing entirely. She says looking into that quilt is like looking into another world."

"You're making that up."

"No I'm not. C'mon, Garland. A few years of me selling your quilts in the gallery and we could both retire to a place that's a lot warmer than Mattaquason in the winter. Seriously. You've got a talent that's been hidden long enough because of one dumb guy. I don't want another dumb guy making you hide it any longer."

"Alasdair's not a dumb guy. And I doubt he and Conn'll be here more than a few days. Don't you think the police will find out who they are pretty quickly? They'll probably be gone by tomorrow. And besides, Rob's coming back tonight for dinner—"

"He is?" Kathy's tension seemed to lessen a little. "Well, that's better. Dinner, huh? Holy cow, she's here for less than twenty-four hours and already has a date with the best-looking guy in town?"

No he's not. Alasdair is. The thought flitted across Garland's mind before she knew it.

Kathy went on to list in delightfully scathing detail the women in town who'd been trying to angle dinner invitations from Rob Mowbray. Garland half-listened, but most of her mind was occupied with Kathy's strange reaction.

Kathy had always seemed utterly without fear. Garland had seen her almost single-handedly stop a riot at Mattaquason's annual Fourth of July parade four years ago after a cannon panicked a quartet of carriage horses. When she switched on her parade ground manner, people listened and did what she said. Nothing bothered Kathy.

But something bothered her now. Why else would she be trying to distract her with all this fluff about her quilts and gossip about people she'd never met?

"—plan to work on next?"

"Hmm?" Garland blinked.

"I said, so what do you plan to work on next? You know, quilts? Those fabric things your idiot ex-husband wouldn't let you make?" Kathy rolled her eyes.

"Cut me some slack, won't you? I just got here." Garland shook her head. "But I was looking at my fabric stash last night. There were a few pieces that were starting to talk to me."

"I'll take that as a good sign, though I'd love to know what bolts of fabric sound like when they talk."

Garland couldn't resist. "I'm not sure either. I keep losing the thread of the conversation."

Kathy groaned and pushed back her chair. "On that note, I'll let you get back to unpacking. Want to do lunch in a couple days, once you're moved in? The Captain's Bilge—sorry, Captain's Bridge Pub is open year-round this year, if you don't mind a touch of salmonella."

"Yummy. I hope they don't know you call it that."

"Everyone calls it that, including the wait staff. Fortunately a beer or two usually has an anti-bacterial effect, so no one's died yet."

Garland chuckled as she walked Kathy to the front door. "Lucky you're the president of the Chamber of Commerce, or they'd run you out of town on a rail."

"They're all too afraid of me to do that." Kathy paused at the door and looked hard at her. "I wasn't kidding before. You've got to get those two out of here." She shook her head. "I've got a bad feeling about this."

"You sound like someone in *Star Wars*," Garland teased. "What should I do, Obi-wan? The Force is—"

"It isn't funny, Garland!" Kathy slapped the doorframe with one hand. She looked so upset—and fearful—that Garland stared.

"Okay, okay," she soothed. "I'm sorry."

"Promise me they'll be out of your house by tomorrow."

Kathy wanted her to promise that she'd boot them out? Heck, *no*. "Kath, what's wrong? Why is this bothering you so much? Is there something you're not telling me? Do you know who these people are?"

"Of course I don't," Kathy said—too quickly. "It's just that you're here all alone in this house with a total stranger and no neighbors within half a mile. Isn't that enough for me to be concerned about? Look, I've gotta run. I'll call Monday and we'll see about that lunch."

Kathy gave her a quick hug and darted out the door. Garland waved as she backed her Prius down the driveway. If Kathy was hiding something, she wasn't going to talk about it. Not yet.

⚮⚮⚮

Alasdair lay on the soft platform Garland and the healer had brought him to and stared at his son who lay on the other platform a few feet away, unmoving except for the faint rise and fall of his chest.

Father had been killed twenty years ago. Mother, warrior that she was, fierce as a shark and wise as one of the great whales, had gone on a magnificently brave but foolhardy mission of vengeance and died in an ambush. His brothers had been picked off one by one over years of battles. Last of all was Finna, his sweet Finna who'd trusted him to protect her…all of them were gone now. He'd failed them all. Conn was all he had left, and he'd nearly lost him as well.

And even Conn had been saved by somebody else…by a human, no less. A bitter taste rose in his throat, and he swallowed it back. He should be grateful that his son was alive—and that *he* was alive. After all, selkies had been saved by humans before, if the old tales of their homeland were true. But it only seemed to be one more fish in his school of failures.

Conn stirred. Alasdair watched him carefully, but he did not waken. Thank Lir for that. Asleep he would not remember what had happened to them last night, attacked under cover of storm. Perhaps the gods had not forsaken them entirely if they could grant the mercy of dreamless sleep to an innocent child.

He shifted, feeling the deep ache of the long cuts in his

sides. The healer had been skillful and gentle and bound his wounds with care despite the mistrust he could sense radiating from him like heat from a fire. He would heal, thanks to the human called Garland who'd found him and Conn. Mahtahdou had underestimated their selkie toughness when he dumped them into the sea to slowly bleed to death, cold and alone, after their torture. But he'd known exactly what it meant to a selkie to have his sealskin taken from him. Seeing his skin—the other half of his being—clutched in Mahtahdou's claws had been far worse than feeling his knife slicing slowly and painfully through his flesh. And to know Conn was going through the same—his only son, who'd already lost so much—

A dull thud and footsteps, along with two new voices, joined the more familiar ones of Garland and the healer drifting up from down below. He lifted his head off the soft cushion and listened anxiously. No, they were not voices he knew. More importantly, neither of them was Mahtahdou's voice. At least no voice he'd ever heard Mahtahdou use. Mahtahdou could make his voice sound like whatever he wanted—but always underneath it had that otherworldly flat coldness, as if the words were edged with ice. Mahtahdou was not there. For now, they were still safe.

Safe. When had he and his people been safe, once Mahtahdou had broken his bonds?

Hundreds of years ago, when the selkies came to these shores hidden among the bearded Northmen and decided to stay in the New World, they had joined with the dark-eyed land-dwellers to vanquish the sea-demon they called Mahtahdou who had long troubled their lives on this sea-girt land. Together they had destroyed the body of the great shaman Mahtahdou had taken over so that he was once again a formless spirit, and then bound that spirit. Peace prevailed until the dark-eyed men were displaced from their lands by men from across the sea who had never known Mahtahdou, and memory of him went from the land.

But the selkies—his family—remembered. They continued to keep watch over Mahtahdou, maintaining the chains that bound him. All had been well through the long years; if the leader of the selkies did not possess the power to keep Mahtahdou chained, he or she would espouse one who did. Alasdair still remembered his grandmother's power, so tangible that she'd worn it like a second sealskin. Mahtahdou had been well fettered under her.

But when Grandmother had left this world and gone into the next, the bonds of her power that kept Mahtahdou restrained had weakened. Father had not been her equal, though he'd tried—

The voices below sounded closer now. He could hear Garland and the healer talking quietly just below. Would they come back up here? It would be good if she did, so he could try to figure out what she was. He stroked the smooth blue skin woven of thread that she'd given him and felt the magic running through it, strong magic speaking of love and caring and tenderness. It belonged to her mate, she had said. Lucky man, to be loved like this. Would he mind that she was allowing someone else to wear it?

He closed his eyes and saw again the picture on the beach this morning as he lay in the sand, fighting groggily to rouse himself from pain and weakness and despair: the sun gleaming on the hair of the human cradling Conn against her, her eyes— *blue* eyes! He'd heard some humans had them, but hadn't believed it—her blue eyes anxious but her voice soft and comforting. Then he'd panicked, dragging himself to his wounded feet to save his child—and had nearly been knocked over again when he touched the soft covering she'd wrapped around Conn and felt the power in it.

Who was this Garland? She was definitely human, but he had no idea that humans were capable of magic like this. He had thought that all their energy had been turned to harnessing the physical world so that they were incapable of even feeling magic. The fairy-folk—the Sidhe—had turned in the other direction, and were so wrapped in magic that they had mostly left the physical plane. His people, the selkies, occupied a place in the middle, embracing both the physical and magical worlds.

So was she a human who had somehow retained or re-learned magic? And if she was…

It had felt almost like his grandmother's magic. Wearing this skin he could probably march into Mahtahdou's hall—the hall that had once been the selkies'—and Mahtahdou would be unable to touch him. It was the first time since Grandmother's death that he'd felt really safe.

Safe. He closed his eyes and relaxed into the soft platform. How strange that humans liked to sleep on something so high instead of on a proper bed on the floor. Weren't they afraid of falling off? Once again he stroked the fabric of his—what had she called it? Robe? With this, he was probably even safe from that.

4

ROB ARRIVED AT six with a large pot of beef stroganoff and a bottle of dry red Spanish wine. Garland felt awkward greeting him; the instant intimacy forged between them this morning had faded. And she'd forgotten what it was like to be on a date: the butterflies in the stomach, the worry that she might say something dumb out of sheer nerves.

She put a pot of water on the stove to boil for noodles and watched Rob open the wine. He moved with a different rhythm from Derek, who'd never seemed to feel at home in his own skin. She'd often had the feeling that Derek was playing to an enormous, unseen audience, his smallest gesture or action just *so*, as if he were waiting for applause. Rob, on the other hand, moved with an easy grace that she found beguiling.

She smiled her thanks when he handed her a glass He'd

changed out of the slightly scruffy sweats he'd arrived in this morning and was wearing a navy blue cashmere sweater and khaki pants. Yum. She couldn't help wondering if he'd somehow divined that she was a sucker for a man in a cashmere sweater.

"So." Rob nodded toward the stairs. "How're our patients?"

"The little boy is still asleep. Alasdair slept a good part of the day as well. I gave him toast and tea just before you came." She chuckled and shook her head. "It was the weirdest thing—almost as if he'd never had toast before, or had forgotten what it tasted like. He told me very seriously that it tasted like the air off the land in summer, when the sun shines on it and warms the grasses."

Rob smiled too but didn't appear very amused. "I don't like the sound of that. Memories of basic things like taste and smell don't typically get lost in trauma-related amnesia. I have to wonder if his injuries aren't worse than I'd thought."

"He also made me eat some too—not because he thought it was poisoned or anything. He just said that he did not eat while others watched hungry. I tried to explain that I'd be eating later, but he just looked stern, so I ate it. He's—I don't know. I don't get the feeling there's much wrong with him physically, apart from those awful cuts. Mostly he seems…sad. Like he's missing something." Like somebody who'd lost something precious, something he'd never be able to regain. Had she worn a similar expression when she'd first learned that Derek was cheating on her?

Rob picked up his bag. "The stroganoff needs about fifteen minutes to warm up. That'll give me a chance to check on them. Coming?"

Alasdair pulled himself up, wincing, when they came in.

Garland saw the wariness in his eyes fade as he saw her enter behind Rob. Why was he so anxious? Rob had been more than gentle with him that morning. He responded in monosyllables to Rob's questions and let him examine and re-bandage his wounds, then watched closely while Rob surveyed Conn.

"Has he even moved?" he asked, frowning.

She came round the other side of the bed and knelt next to it. "No. Not that I've noticed. He did wet the bed, though I don't think he stirred while I cleaned him up."

"That's a good sign—at least he doesn't seem to be dehydrated—though I'm sorry you had to do that." He pulled out his flashlight and peeled back one of the child's eyelids. "I don't think he's concussed," he murmured. "But sleeping this long—"

"It is good that he sleeps," Alasdair said from his bed. "Would it be better for him to be awake and in pain?"

"I could give him something for the pain. Did he take any of the meds I left you?" He jerked his head back at Alasdair.

"No. He said that if it hurt, it meant he was still alive."

Rob grunted. Garland didn't comment further. Derek had kept a supply of prescription-strength ibuprofen around, in case of grievous injury like, say, a hangnail. It was refreshing to deal with someone a little less hypochondriacal.

Rob worked in silence after that, changing the bandages on Conn's wounds and treating the smaller ones with more topical antibiotic. She was again struck by the graceful economy of his movements. He loved being a doctor and healing people, didn't he? It was clear in his smallest action. There were people like him who were born to heal others. She looked back at Conn. It seemed that there might also be people out there who were born to hurt others.

The boy shifted and frowned, as if he had caught her thought.

"Easy, there," Rob murmured, pausing and glancing at his face. She reached out and took the boy's hand. He sighed and relaxed.

Rob pressed his lips together and went back to work.

⊷⊙⊙⊶

Garland had set the table in the dining room and built a fire in the fireplace there as well. The light gleamed on the cherry dining table and the antique brass candlesticks, and she reflected on how cozy it was as they sat down to dinner. Derek had never wanted to eat in here when they were alone. He'd preferred a tray in front of the TV so he could watch the financial talking heads on CNBC. She'd usually ended up in the kitchen by herself, reading.

The stroganoff was delicious. Wow. A compassionate, caring doctor who made house calls, wore cashmere sweaters, and was a wonderful cook to boot. Was Rob Mowbray too good to be true?

He topped off their wineglasses. "Did Captain Howe call?"

"Not yet. I guess that means there weren't any leads from the Coast Guard."

"No." Rob frowned down at his plate. "Did his behavior seem strange to you this morning?"

So she hadn't imagined that. "Yes, very. He couldn't seem to get out of here fast enough, once he'd seen Aragorn. And did—"

"Once he'd seen who?" Rob's fork, heaped with stroganoff, stopped in mid-air.

Drat. So much for not saying stupid things. "Oh, I,

uh…Alasdair sort of reminds me of Viggo Mortensen in *Lord of the Rings*, so I…you know…" She tried to shrug nonchalantly.

Rob's fork continued to his mouth, and he chewed in silence.

"Anyway, did you hear Captain Howe swear under his breath when you were talking about Alasdair? I wonder…" She paused and took a sip of wine, choosing her words carefully. "I wonder if maybe he knows him from somewhere, and wasn't happy to hear he's around. I've never heard any rumors about the Mattaquason police, but…" She let the rest of the sentence hang, for him to pick up if he chose.

Rob shook his head. "I thought of that. But I haven't heard any rumors either. As police departments go, ours seems to be fairly honest. Something personal, maybe?"

"Maybe. But then shouldn't he have said something if he knew them? Unless where he knew him from is something—"

"Something an officer of the law shouldn't be mixed up in," Rob finished for her. "In which case, we'd best not get involved and move this guy and his kid out of here as quickly as possible."

"But I can't just toss them out! What if Howe—"

"All the more reason to get them out and not get involved, then."

"Then you do think there's something going on?"

Rob sighed. "I have no idea, Garland. I'm still fairly new here myself. Two years in a town like Mattaquason don't make you an old-timer. Twenty years aren't enough, sometimes. All I'm saying is if there is something unsavory going on, I don't want you getting caught in it unawares."

"My friend Kathy Hayes was here this morning." Garland pursued a piece of mushroom around her nearly empty plate and speared it. "She said more or less the same thing but I got the feeling that she was hiding something too. She threatened to call Captain Howe and force him to bring them to the hospital." She shook her head impatiently. "I wish we knew who they are."

"That would make things easier, wouldn't it?" Rob commented dryly as they carried their plates into the kitchen.

They washed their few dishes in companionable silence then went to sit in front of the great room fireplace with brandies and a plate of exquisite truffles from the Candy Castle in downtown Mattaquason. "I cheated," Rob had said with a grin. "Their chocolate is light-years better than anything I could come up with for dessert."

They sat on the blue and white couch where Conn had lain earlier that day, not touching but not far apart. Garland curled her legs under her and stared out the sliding doors into the night, too relaxed to get up and pull the curtains shut. She was here. All the months of emotional upheaval and wrangling with lawyers over the petty details of the dissolution of her and Derek's marriage were over. She was ready to get on with the rest of her life.

"Tired?" Rob's voice was low and lazy. She looked up and saw that he was watching her reflection in the glass door.

"A bit. I was just thinking that it's been a long few months." She leaned her head back. "And now I'm here."

"And now you're here," Rob agreed. "Getting mixed up in Lord-knows-what when you ought to be taking a breather."

She smiled. "But I like Lord-knows-what. I wasn't able to get mixed up in it back in Chestnut Hill. Being the perfect corporate wife didn't leave much time for it."

"'Be careful what you wish for, because you might get it.'"

He held the plate of truffles out to her. She took one and bit into it, then took a sip of her cognac. The dark chocolate and brandy melted together on her tongue in a decadent blend.

"What about you?" she asked when the chocolate orgasm in her mouth faded. "Have you been less careful than you should have about wishing for things?"

"Not at all. I'm quite content with getting what I wished for." He raised one eyebrow at her suggestively, then laughed. "And not just right this minute."

"Behold, that rarest of creatures—a truly happy man."

"Well, yeah, I guess I am." He paused, staring into the fire, and stretched his arm out along the back of the couch, close to her head. "As long as I can remember I wanted to be a doctor, like one of my uncles. And I wanted to live by the ocean some day. My dad's a Patrick O'Brian fanatic, so I grew up reading about Captain Aubrey and Mr. Maturin. And the Captain Drinkwater novels. For a boy from Iowa, there wasn't anything more romantic than the thought of the deep blue sea. I actually thought about joining the navy, but decided that living next to it, rather than on it, was a better bet for an ex-farm boy."

"Farm boy? Really?"

The grin came back. "Okay, so I'm exaggerating a little. We did have a small flock of chickens in the backyard, though. And I belonged to 4-H in junior high. Does that count? I got my undergraduate degree in Indiana, went to med school in New York—all gradually heading eastward, toward the sea. I can't get much more east than Cape Cod, so I guess I'm finally where I want to be."

The humor in his voice ebbed, and his face grew thoughtful. "It was funny. When I first came here to look the town over, it was like I was coming home. I'd been missing the ocean all my life, without ever having seen it. Some people go to church on Sundays. I walk on the beach."

He began to toy absent-mindedly with a lock of her hair as he gazed into the fire. Garland held her breath as little electric shivers of pleasure ran over her scalp and down her back.

"Do you have a boat, so you can do more than walk?" she managed to say, after a moment.

"No. I've been too busy getting established in town. Summer's the crazy season here, as you know. No time for learning how to handle a boat. I'm not only taking care of my regular patients during prime boating season, but the summer folks too. Like the people who go barefoot at Amy Nickerson's cocktail parties and get splinters." He grinned.

Garland felt herself blush. "I had to take my shoes off that night. They were giving me blisters. Tell you what, Doctor Mowbray. If you'll promise not to tease me about that, I'll teach you how to sail this summer."

"It's a deal. But I wasn't teasing you. I couldn't help being glad that you got that splinter, even if saying so bends my Hippocratic Oath a little." He looked away. "You have no idea how disappointed I was that evening when your husband came up looking like thunder after I'd bandaged your foot with one of Amy's linen napkins. Only then did I realize that you were *Mrs.* Durrell. I'd been about two seconds from suggesting we blow off the party and go out for dinner when he arrived."

A warm glow spread through her. "Really?"

"Napkin-wrapped foot and all. So you see, I do get what I wish for. Eventually. Anyway, digging a splinter out of your foot was a great way to meet you without all the usual horrible small talk that I had to go through with everyone else. You did me a favor. So do I still get sailing lessons after that confession?"

"Well…" She pretended to consider the question.

"How about if I throw in that dinner afterwards?"

Garland smiled. "You drive a hard bargain, but I accept."

❧ ❦ ❧

After Rob left, Garland made sure the fires in the fireplaces were safely banked for the evening, turned out the lights, and went up to change into her favorite flannel pajamas, the blue ones with the black and white cartoon cows filing their hooves and applying lipstick.

So that had been her first date, post-Derek. In her wildest dreams she couldn't have had a better time. She and Rob had danced a careful, courteous conversational dance around each other, listening and learning, feeling each other out, testing— tasting, in a way. She liked his flavor very much, which made him sound like ice cream. She shook her head at herself in the mirror as she brushed her teeth. Ice cream was cold and could induce a headache. She didn't think Rob would ever do that. Well, she'd find out. It appeared that she would be seeing a lot of him from now on.

She looked at herself in the mirror again. There was a lift to the corners of her mouth and the tilt of her chin that hadn't been there for months. Maybe Rob's half-joke about being under a doctor's care wasn't so facetious after all.

Had he really been so attracted to her when they first met at that party? She remembered Derek's being sulky for the rest of that evening, so maybe Rob's interest had been obvious. Except to her. It had been so long since she'd thought of herself as a desirable woman that she hadn't even noticed. She turned off the light, pulled on her electric blue chenille robe and went to check on Alasdair and Conn before she went to bed.

Rob had looked in on them before leaving and left a lamp across the room turned on low. By its dim light she could just see Alasdair's form, long and straight, under the covers. He seemed to be sleeping peacefully. But Conn…he'd not wakened but was tossing and squirming on his bed, rolling his head fitfully from side to side on the pillow. As she bent over him he cried out weakly and then muttered something in a high, piping little boy's voice that sounded like pleading. The pitiful sound went straight to Garland's heart. Had his injuries started to hurt enough to rouse him from his sleep? Or was he dreaming about how he'd gotten them?

She carried the small yellow and blue toile wingback chair from the corner over to his bedside, careful not to let it drag on the floor and make a noise, and sat down. "Hey, it's okay," she murmured, smoothing his tangled hair off his forehead then laying her hand on it. No fever, which was amazing. Most people would have come down with pneumonia after spending a night in conditions not nearly as harsh as the ones he'd been in.

As her hand rested on his brow he stilled, and his whimpers faded into a sigh. She hesitated, then stroked his forehead again. He seemed to lean into her hand, like a plant following the light.

Something caught in her throat. Before she could remind herself that she was a failure in the maternity department and had no experience in comforting children, she bent over and scooped him onto her lap, still wrapped in her flannel shirt and the blankets from the bed. He turned toward her and buried his face in her neck, and the tension leached from him in a long, shuddering sigh. After a few minutes, his breathing was deep and even again and his little body was limp and relaxed.

She held him, hardly daring to breathe. Derek had needed her because she was presentable and socially well connected and could entertain his business associates. But this boy needed her because she cared. She'd been right not to send them to the hospital. Conn needed more than just doctoring. He needed someone to hold him when he cried in his sleep. Let Rob say what he wanted about strays. She'd taken responsibility for these two as soon as she'd seen them lying in the sand, and she wasn't going to abandon them now.

And maybe she needed them, too. Had she been adamant about keeping them here and nursing them herself because maybe *she* needed to be needed in this way? They all had their wounds to recover from, didn't they?

She lifted one of his hands and examined the odd webs of skin between his fingers that Rob had mentioned. Strange. She'd never seen anything like that before. And Alasdair had them too. She glanced across at him, asleep in the other bed and looking relaxed and absurdly like his son. His hands were hidden, one pillowed under his cheek and the other tucked against his chest, clutching the lapel of his robe. Maybe she'd get a better look at them tomorrow before he left. Surely by tomorrow Captain Howe would have found out who they were and where they belonged, and they could return home. And she—she could start rebuilding her life in earnest.

5

ALASDAIR AWOKE abruptly, called by the morning light
and an achy, all-over stiffness in his body that screeched into
downright pain in places. He groaned softly as he stretched,
then opened his eyes. Instead of sky, a blank, flat whiteness
spread above him, held up by soft yellow walls with long
windows divided into rectangles…walls?

Then memory returned. He was in a human dwelling, the
house of the blue-eyed human who'd found them on the beach.
And Mahtahdou had evidently not found them during the
night, for his sleep had been deep and restful. He'd been right
to go with her. With any luck her magic would shield them
from Mahtahdou for as long as they stayed.

He stretched again, taking inventory. The cuts in his feet
were the worst, sending intermittent stabbing pains up his legs.

It was hard to breathe through his broken nose but that would ease with time. The cuts on his body itched as much as they ached, which meant they'd begun to heal. Another few days and he could begin to plan his revenge—if his remaining warriors would still follow a selkie lord who'd lost his sealskin.

He closed his eyes as if he could escape the thought. The pain in his body was nothing compared to that. And Conn—he turned his head and looked at the platform where Conn had slept. It was empty.

He sat up in alarm, then fell back against his head-cushion. Conn, still wrapped in the soft purple skin that was full of magic, was cuddled in Garland's arms. She was sitting in a chair, and the two of them were soundly, peacefully asleep. Her hair, the same rich brownish gold as the kelp forests to the north of his home-waters, tumbled over Conn's darker head.

As he stared at them in astonishment, he saw her frown then open her eyes and blink a few times. She looked down at Conn, and he tried to decipher her expression. Surprise? Concern? Maybe even a hint of tenderness? Then she carefully rose and bent to put him on the platform again. As she did, he sighed and groped for her in his sleep.

She smiled and touched his cheek. "I won't go far," she murmured, then glanced up and met his eyes. And turned a deep pink color, like a delicate sea anemone.

"I'm sorry," she whispered, and pulled the coverings back over Conn. Then she came to kneel by him. "I—he was whimpering in his sleep last night when I came to check on him, and I—I thought maybe he needed comforting so I picked him up and held him, and them we both fell asleep. I didn't mean to…"

"You didn't mean to what?" he prompted when she trailed

into silence.

"To be inappropriate," she finished, and turned even pinker. It intensified the fascinating blue of her eyes. He wished he could reach out and hold her face still between his hands and gaze his fill at those eyes.

Then her words registered. Inappropriate? Did humans have some taboo about children? "Is it inappropriate to comfort a hurt child?"

"No…it's just that I don't want you to think I'm trying to"—she shrugged and looked even more uncomfortable—"to take anyone's place."

So that was what had troubled her. "Conn's mother is dead," he said, his voice hardening as it did whenever he had to speak of Finna. "You did him a kindness. He's known no woman's touch since he was very small."

"I'm sorry," she said again, then blinked. "You remember that? Do you remember your last name? Or your address or phone number?"

Shark's teeth, he had to be careful. "No, I don't remember anything else. But I could not forget losing my wife. Could you forget losing your husband?"

An odd change came over her face. "I'm trying to," she muttered.

A sudden loud sound, like a brief whir, came from the table next to him. He tensed, but she quickly rose as the sound came again and reached for something black on it.

"I've got to get a new phone for up here. The ring tone on this one is hideous," she said as she lifted an oblong object from it, poked at it with one finger—it made another short, peculiar noise—and held it to the side of her head. "Hello? Oh, good morning to you too, Rob. No, it's not too early. I'm awake, sort of."

Rob. That was the healer's name. Was she communicating with him through the little black oblong? He'd heard humans did things like that, just as they had boats that moved without the wind and silver metal birds that they flew through the air. It was fascinating to see some of their handiwork up close.

But what was even more interesting was Garland. She'd just said she was trying to forget her husband…might he be dead, too? He touched the skin she'd given him to wear. She must have loved him very much to judge by the feeling she'd woven into this. No wonder she had seemed so sad when she spoke of forgetting. By Lir, he had to remember that he wasn't the only creature in the world grieving for a lost love. How long ago had her husband died? Not very long ago, for surely other men would be eager to pay court to a beautiful widow like her. Perhaps one already was. He'd seen the way the healer had looked at her—

"No, the boy's still sleeping but Alasdair's awake. They spent a peaceful night as far as I can tell." Garland made a funny little face as she said that. She wasn't going to tell the healer about sitting up with Conn all night? Why not? "Of course you can. Boy Scouts? You're either very civic-minded or very crazy. Or both. See you in a few minutes."

She poked at the black thing again and stood looking at it with a little smile. "That was Dr. Mowbray. He wants to come check on you two now because he's doing a first aid class later with the local scout troop. He's really something, isn't he?"

"Yes," Alasdair said politely. Most of what she'd said made no sense but it seemed safe to agree.

"I'm going to go start some coffee. Call if you need me, okay?" She set the black thing back down on its platform, glanced again at Conn, then left. He heard her soft footfalls move away from him and counted them. This was a large place, with many rooms—large and lonely, if she lived here all alone. How sad for her.

He lay back against his cushions and winced as one of his cuts gave a twinge. He wished he could like the healer as much as Garland seemed to. But underneath that calm demeanor—all healers, selkie or human, seemed to have it—Alasdair could sense his suspicion, verging on hostility. He didn't want him and Conn here at Garland's house, that was certain. Why? Because he didn't want anyone getting between him and Garland? Too bad there was no way he could reassure the healer that he had no interest in her—not even one as lovely and compelling as she was. He was a warrior, and warriors must know only battle. After Finna had been killed—his hands clenched helplessly at his side. Never would he give Mahtahdou another opportunity to strike at him through a loved one. Someday, when Mahtahdou was again chained, when his people were safe and he'd regained his throne, there would be time for him to love again.

❧ ❧

Garland barely had time to make a pot of coffee before Rob arrived. He wore a tie and his white medical coat under his outdoor jacket and looked even more reassuring and competent in it, if that were possible. She resisted the urge to straighten his already straight tie, just for the sake of touching him. He smothered a grin as he looked at her.

"Wow. I'd pictured you as more the tailored silk pajama type."

Oh, hell. She'd forgotten that she was still in her cow

jammies and fuzzy blue bathrobe and slippers. She spread the skirt of her robe and pretended to curtsey. "I'm sorry to have disillusioned you. Now you've seen the worst of me."

"Oh, I don't know—I kind of like them." He came in then paused to consider her as he pulled off his jacket. "But you really need curlers and cold cream all over your face to complete the picture."

"Beast." She stuck out her tongue at him. "Next time I'm calling an acupuncturist when I get a splinter."

"The closest one's in Provincetown. And she wears clothes remarkably like your pajamas so you two might get on famously. But I'm not sure she makes house calls." He turned toward the stairs. "How are our guests?

"Rob, wait a minute." She reached out and touched his arm. "How common is amnesia?"

He paused on the bottom step and looked at her. "Outside of the movies? Not very. And not the global kind that you see in fiction all the time. Damn. I should have sent Alasdair to the hospital. Is he slurring words or showing signs of confusion or paralysis? What happened?"

"Nothing happened. It's just that—well, he still says he can't remember anything, but he was able to recall that his wife was dead. And he seems—I can't describe it. When you called just now, he jumped and stared at the phone as if he'd never heard one before. It's—"

"Yes?" Rob looked at her expectantly.

"I don't know," she finally admitted.

He frowned. "Are you afraid of him?"

"No, of course not. He'd never hurt me." *He needs me*, the thought popped into her mind, but she didn't say it aloud.

"How can you be so sure?"

"I don't know. But I'm sure."

"Hmmph. Let me have a look at him and then we can talk." He gave her a quick smile and headed up the stairs, but the smile hadn't quite made it to his eyes.

Alasdair's greeting was pleasant but subdued. He answered Rob's questions in monosyllables when possible. She again noted his wary scrutiny of Rob's stethoscope and his mystified reaction to the digital readout on the thermometer. Rob caught her eye when Alasdair flinched as his blood pressure was taken, but otherwise he maintained his cordial, reassuring manner, moving with exaggerated slowness as he checked and re-bandaged his wounds.

"Headache? Seeing any flashing lights or auras or doubling of images?" Rob peered into Alasdair's eyes and shone a small flashlight into one of his pupils, then did a few more assessments that Garland guessed were an impromptu neurological exam.

When he turned to Conn's bed, his cheerful smile faded. "I know you don't want to hear this," he said, gazing down at the sleeping boy, "but I strongly recommend we bring him to the hospital for observation. He should have woken up by now."

"Rob, are you sure? What about—"

"No," Alasdair cut in, pushing himself up. "We are not leaving this place. Garland, tell him."

"Garland, please explain to him." Rob glanced at Alasdair then turned back to her. "I'm worried about this kid. This sleepiness could be caused by anything from a physical blow to the head to meningitis or encephalitis. Do you want to risk him dying or being permanently disabled?"

"If you touch my son, you won't leave this dwelling alive." Alasdair now stood by his bed, swaying on his injured feet but clenching his hands into fists.

"Stop it!" She stepped between the two men and pushed Alasdair back down onto his bed. "Sit down before you fall. No one is going to hurt anyone in my house."

"I wasn't going to fall." He glowered at her.

"Yes, fine, you weren't going to fall. Don't you dare get up again."

"Thank you." Rob's voice was still quiet and even but edged with anger. "Will you please explain to this—"

"Rob, wait. Trust me." She led him a few paces away from Alasdair's bed then turned back to Alasdair. "I won't let anyone hurt Conn. You know I won't."

The fury faded from Alasdair's expression. "I know you won't. But you don't understand. We can't leave here. We can't leave *you*. Not yet."

"This is getting ridic—" Rob began.

She glanced at him and shook her head. "Why can't you leave?"

"When I am strong again, we will go." His voice was not much more than a whisper. "I promise. But not yet."

She met his gaze. It was unwavering, and there was something else in it too: despair, heavy enough to crush a grown man under its weight. And if it could crush him, what about a child?

She looked down at Conn then looked again, startled. Conn's eyes were open, and he was gazing up at her with wide golden-brown eyes exactly like Alasdair's. She fought down the impulse to exclaim out loud and channeled it instead into a smile. "Well, hello little sleepyhead," she said, and sat down next to him. "How are you this morning?"

"He's awake?" Rob was there in an instant.

"Conn," Alasdair breathed, and rose again.

Conn didn't react to either of them. He kept his eyes fastened on her face for a few seconds longer then squirmed up and wrapped his thin arms around her neck, burying his face in her shoulder.

"Okay, okay." She lifted him up and settled him back on her lap, just as they'd sat last night. "I'm not going anywhere."

"Umm, right," Rob said. He squatted next to the chair and tried to catch the boy's eye. "Hello, Conn. How do you feel?"

"He's not going to your hospital," Alasdair said. He staggered the two paces to Conn's bed, sank down on it, and leaned toward him stiffly. "Conn, *ciamar a tha thu?*" he murmured.

The boy didn't respond aloud but made a small motion with his head and snuggled even closer to her.

"It's all right," she said to him gently. "I'm not going to put you down if you don't want me to." What had Alasdair said? What language had it been? If they were from a foreign country it might explain some of Alasdair's unfamiliarity with everyday things, but not entirely. "How are you, Conn? Can you tell the doctor?"

He didn't move.

"Does he understand what I'm saying?" she asked Alasdair. "Does he speak English?"

"Enough of it," he said shortly, as if unwilling to reveal any more. "But he does not speak much in any language."

"Look," Rob said. "If you could just put him down on the bed, I can make sure he's—"

"He's…he's in some pain, but not a lot," Garland found herself saying as she peered down at Conn's face. He looked back up at her from under his long eyelashes. "The bandage feel funny and the deeper cuts ache, especially the one under his ribs on the right side. Mostly he's confused and scared. And he'd rather I didn't put him down just now."

There was a silence, broken only when Rob cleared his throat. She looked up. Both men stared at her, Alasdair looking shocked and Rob dubious.

"Garland, what's going on?" he said. "How do you know that?"

"I don't know. I just do." She leaned back slightly so that she could see full into the boy's face. "Conn, if I hold you, will you let the doc—er, the healer look at you? He needs to make sure your hurts are healing properly."

He looked at her. And she could *feel* his thoughts, feel their shape and color if not their exact meaning, and knew that right now she was the only thing keeping him from dropping back into that trance-like sleep again—that somehow, she'd come to represent safety to him. His little body, still tense, relaxed against her. She looked up at Rob and nodded.

Conn kept his eyes scrunched tightly shut the entire time but let Rob remove the old bandages, check the Steri-Stripped cuts, and reapply fresh dressings. She kept up a quiet litany of reassurance and explanation while Rob worked, aware as she did that Alasdair did not take his eyes from her, even to watch Rob. She wished she could decipher what his gaze meant.

"All set, Conn," Rob said heartily when he was done. "You're one brave little boy, you know."

"He knows," Alasdair said. He was still looking at her.

Rob didn't reply but packed up his bag quickly. "I'll be back to check on you tomorrow," he said when he was done. "Garland?" He nodded at the door. "The scouts are expecting me at one and I have to finish getting ready."

"Can I give you to your daddy for a minute while I say good-bye to the doctor?" she asked Conn. "It'll just be for a few minutes. I promise."

His grip on her robe tightened and he buried his face in her neck again.

"Conn," Alasdair said, and then spoke again in that strange, liquid language. The boy held on stubbornly for a few more seconds, then loosened his grip and let her put him into Alasdair's arms.

"I'll be right back," she said, touching Conn's hair. She could feel his eyes on her as she left the room behind Rob.

Rob was silent all the way down the stairs. He put on his jacket and said, "Come out to the car with me."

She glanced toward the stairs. "But—"

His jaw tightened. "They'll be fine for five minutes. Please, Garland."

Garland pulled her jacket on over her robe and followed him outside. He put his bag in his car then leaned against the door and looked at her. "I don't like this," he said flatly.

"What?"

"Any of it. Alasdair knows more than he's telling, and there's something wrong with that child. And both of them seem awfully fixated on you."

Garland leaned against his car too and sighed. "What did you expect? The poor kid was attacked and left for dead, is confused and frightened, and has decided he can trust me. How would you feel if you were in his condition?"

"Probably the same. But I still don't like it. And I don't like the way Alasdair looks at you." His face was closed, all boyishness fled.

A light bulb turned on in Garland's brain. "Rob, he can

barely get out of that bed without help. You don't *have* to trust him. In another day or two I'm sure he'll start to remember who he is and we can send them home to their family or whatever. I feel sorry for them. I know what's it's like to be hurt and tossed aside." She gave a self-deprecatory shrug and looked down at her feet.

"Hey." Rob straightened and turned to face her, tilting her chin up with one finger. "I'm sorry. I'm being a jerk." He smiled ruefully. "For a minute, I was jealous. I hope he realizes how goddamned lucky they are that you found them."

"Oh, anyone would have—"

"Would have taken them into their house and stood over them like a dragon with a nursing degree? I don't think so." He glanced toward the house. "I see what you meant by the amnesia question. I thought Alasdair would jump out of his skin every time I tried to use any instrument on him."

"So how is he?"

"I wasn't lying. He's healing amazingly fast considering what he went through. At least physically. I couldn't find any signs of actual brain trauma that would explain the memory loss—no weakness or paralysis, or lack of alertness, or aversion to light. You'll have to keep an eye on him, though—some injuries can take days to manifest themselves. And be very careful helping him when he's up and walking. Further head injury could be fatal."

"But you don't think it's a physical injury, do you?"

"No, not really. An accident—or whatever he's been through—can certainly trigger amnesia. It can be the mind's self-defense against something that's too much to handle at the time. As he recuperates, his memory will probably return. And the sooner the better as far as I'm concerned." He frowned.

"Look, this is too much to expect you to handle. Why don't I call the hospital—"

"No." Even in her own ears, her tone sounded final.

Rob looked at her. "All right," he said after a moment "But I'm going to call Captain Howe and try to light a fire under him. And I'm going to ask you about calling the hospital at least twice tomorrow and again the day after that. I think you've bitten off more than anyone should chew, but that's your right. However, it's my right to keep on asking you."

Garland exhaled. "That's fair."

"Good. Forgive me?"

"Forgive you for what?"

"Even better." His smile turned sunny. "So will you say yes if I ask you to come out for dinner with me later in the week? Like Friday?"

Garland hesitated. Conn and Alasdair might need her—

But surely the police would have found out who they were and sent them home by then. "Yes," she replied.

He looked at her for a swift second, then put one hand on her shoulder, drew her slightly toward him, and kissed her— nothing that he couldn't have done in public, but definitely more than a peck. She liked the feeling of his lips on hers, firm and steady, just like him.

"That's good." He squeezed her shoulder. "I wish I didn't have to leave, but the scouts really want this badge."

"Go. Have fun." She stepped back from the car. Her lips still felt the warmth of his.

"I'll stop in this evening for a second and check on them, if I can." Rob climbed in the car, smiled at her again, and backed out of the driveway.

Conn liked toast as much as Alasdair had. If they stayed in the house much longer she'd have to start buying loaves of bread in triplicate. He drank three glasses of milk and licked the dribbles of butter and strawberry jelly off his plate after he'd eaten his fourth piece, then sighed and crawled onto her lap.

Garland smiled and smoothed her purple flannel shirt over his shoulder. She'd have to find him something to wear other than it—a quick trip downtown might be a good idea in the next day or two. Unless Captain Howe had found out who they were and where they belonged. Even so, it would be nice to send him home clothed.

"I have some work to do," she said, looking down at him. "Do you want to watch me?"

He blinked at her.

"I'll take that as a yes." She stood up, then set him back down on the chair and wrapped a blanket around him. He clung to her neck but she gently detached his arms. "Wait a moment, little limpet," she told him. "We're going to do something fun."

"'Little limpet'," Alasdair repeated, and looked at her strangely.

On the other side of the room was the worktable she'd planned to use for cutting her fabric. Right now it was piled with plastic storage bins of fabric and quilting supplies and a rainbow pile of fabric draped haphazardly over it all, thanks to a clumsy moving man who'd dropped one of the boxes on the stairs. She could fold it and maybe begin to think about work, yet still keep close to Conn.

She dragged the toile armchair with him in it over to the

table. He clutched the arms and smiled—in fact, she was sure she heard a very small giggle escape him. Maybe he wasn't as damaged as she'd feared.

"This is what I do," she told him, picking up a piece of yellow fabric. "I cut out shapes from pieces of cloth and sew them back together in patterns, and then make layers of cloth with more stitching to hold them together. They're called quilts. I haven't made any for a long time, but I used to be good at it."

She shook out the cotton lengths—mostly the tone-on-tone batiks she loved, in rich, vibrant colors—and folded them quickly and neatly. They'd have to be ironed again before she worked with them, of course. It had driven Derek crazy when she ironed. "That's what the housekeeper's for, you silly darling," he'd always said when he found her pressing fabric lengths. The words "silly darling" had never sounded as loving and patient as they should have. "Why do you think we're paying her?"

A piece of fabric ripped as she shook it out. She stared at it gripped in her fists, then relaxed her tensed shoulders and smiled ruefully at herself. She wasn't married to him anymore—at least, she wouldn't be come May when the divorce would be final. It was high time she put him out of her mind and picked up the pieces of her life, just like the fabric the movers had dropped. Picked them up and ironed them smooth so that she could rearrange them into a new pattern. Look at this turquoise, printed with waves and swirls like the grain of wood from a fairy tale tree. It had made her think of a summer storm when she bought it, the color rich and beautiful but electric with energy. And this dark blue batik, printed in a spatter pattern that reminded her of raindrops on a quiet pond. The truer blue made the greenish turquoise sing when she set them side-by-side. Could it be that after a year of barely touching fabric she was feeling the urge to create again?

Something touched her shoulder. She whirled. Alasdair stood there in his robe, looking pale but very determined.

"What—?" She stared up at him. God, he was tall. She'd been so distracted yesterday on the beach that she hadn't noticed. The top of her head would probably just tickle his chin. He'd have to bend to kiss her properly, and she'd have to lean back, far back, to meet his lips, her body stretching and open to him—

"I wanted to see your—this," he said, reaching a tentative hand toward the pile of fabric.

Garland tore her gaze away from his mouth and hoped he couldn't read minds. "You could have asked. What if you'd fainted or something? Back into bed with you. And don't do that again till the doctor says you can."

"One moment, please." He touched the topmost piece of fabric with the tip of a finger, as if he were afraid it would burn him. Then he stroked it, and finally ran his hand down the whole pile, touching each piece. He frowned at them for a few seconds then ran his fingers down the front of his robe, over the appliquéd symbols.

"It's not the same," he murmured, then looked at her keenly. "So it must be you."

What must be her? "You mean the *kanji* on the robe? Yes, I sewed them on—they're not part of the fabric."

"You made the...the—" He seemed to be groping for words. "What are they? Do they have...are they—?"

"*Kanji*—Japanese ideograms. They have—or had—meaning. This one"—she pointed at a symbol on the left side of his chest—"is love. This one is longevity. These are protection, devotion, and companionship. And here are honesty and fidelity." Ha. Maybe that was why Derek never wore the robe. Even if he couldn't read the symbols, maybe their meaning still came through. Honesty and fidelity were definitely concepts he'd struggled with.

Alasdair looked solemn. "I can feel them."

"Oops, did I leave a pin or two in there?" She couldn't help smiling at his seriousness. He was looking at her again with that strange expression, as if he wanted to say something further but didn't quite know how. It was disconcerting. "Come on," she said. "You shouldn't be on those feet."

"One moment," he said again, and lurched toward the window.

"Is he always this stubborn?" she asked Conn, who stared up at them from his chair.

"Not stubborn. Persistent," Alasdair said. But he let her take his arm and put it over her shoulders, and leaned on her heavily as they went to the window. He was warm, even under just the thin cotton robe. But he didn't smell rank or sweaty. Salty, yes. If she were to touch her tongue to his skin she knew exactly how he'd taste—like a still summer evening just before a fog swept in off the ocean, damp and briny and mysterious—

Oh, stop it, Garland! Why did she keep getting these thoughts about him? He was a temporary guest, someone who would figure in her life for no more than another day or two. If she were going to think about anyone in that way, it should be Rob. And honestly, even Rob was probably too much just yet. She needed more time to let Derek air out of her psyche, like a bad smell.

At the window Alasdair clung to the sill and stared out through the glass at the scene below. She followed his gaze along the horizon, where Monomoyick sat just offshore. The winter-dead lawn and the sand below it made a dramatic contrast with sparkling dark-blue water beyond, tinged with purple this morning. Just then a vibrant red cardinal flew past, followed a second later by its more sober-hued mate.

An idea nudged at the back of Garland's mind. She stepped back, not taking her eyes off the scene, and groped on the table behind her for the pad of graph paper she'd been doodling on the day before yesterday. Those colors, in that landscape arrangement, but pieced with a traditional block design, one with a lot of smaller components so that the colors could be shaded to follow the landscape—a sort of hybrid between a traditional and an art quilt. Small—a wall quilt, so that it could be viewed from a distance, where color would make the first impact… She scribbled notes, nodding to herself as she wrote, then looked up and saw that Alasdair was watching her with a look of great concentration.

"What's wrong?" she asked.

A shutter seemed to come down over his eyes. "Nothing. I—I am sorry if I was intruding."

"Intruding? No, I just got an idea for a quilt and wanted to get it down before I forgot it—oh God, you're exhausted, aren't you? I'm sorry—let me help you back to bed."

He sighed and shifted on his feet. "Thank you."

Slowly and carefully, she led him back to bed. He lay against the pillows looking white and tired, his robe open over his chest. It was a good thing she'd remembered it hanging on her door—helping a gorgeous naked man in and out of bed several times a day would have been difficult. Even with the yards of gauze bandage on him and the scrapes and bruises he was beautiful. She tried to picture him in jeans, or in a jacket and tie, and couldn't. A body that beautifully formed shouldn't have to wear clothes. She tore her gaze away and pulled the sheet up over him, chastising herself for ogling a sick man. "Do your wounds hurt?"

He shrugged, then looked at her and nodded.

"Are you sure you don't want something to stop the pain?"

He shook his head.

Persistent, hell. He was just plain stubborn. "All right." She hesitated, and looked back at her quilt table. "Would it bother you if I did a little work? If you want to nap I can do it later—"

"No." He sat up again "I want to see your work."

"Fine. But stay there, okay?"

She felt Alasdair watching her as she took the pictures off the wall closest to the window and tacked a king-size flannel sheet to it in their place, stretched it taut, then set up spot lamps to shine on it.

"What is that for?" he asked, pulling himself up to sit a little higher against his pillows.

"It's my design wall. Small pieces of fabric will stick to the flannel so that I can lay out quilt designs and look at them from different distances to see if they work. The lights have full spectrum bulbs in them."

"What are full spec—what you said?"

"They mimic sunlight so that you can see colors as they truly are. Most indoor lights are limited spectrum, so you get a distorted view of color."

"Like little suns," he said, looking impressed, "trapped in glass."

Garland smiled at this image, but her heart sank. She wanted to jump right into this quilt idea now, while the picture in her mind was fresh. Was he going to ask what she was doing every time she picked up a tool or sewed together two pieces of fabric?

She went to her box of blue fabrics—one of three, actually, because she was unable to pass up blue fabric—and started pulling out pieces for the water. Conn had drifted back to sleep curled in the chair; Alasdair remained silent, though she knew that he still watched her. After a few moments, she felt herself slide into her "color trance"—the slightly altered state she entered in the beginning stages of a quilt, a universe where only color existed, and where it occupied its own form of dimensional space. Usually the floor would be paved with fabric by the time she came blinking back into reality.

Oh, it felt good to be working again!

⁂

Somewhat to her surprise, Garland finished laying out most of her new quilt that afternoon and got all the pieces cut. Alasdair didn't ask more questions, but whenever she came out of her color trance long enough to notice him he was always watching her closely. Nor did he interrupt her to ask for anything, which made her feel guilty when she happened to glance at her watch and saw that it was after three.

"Why didn't you tell me it was so late?" she asked him, clicking her rotary cutter shut and stretching. Even with her cutting table made to her height, cutting still made her shoulders ache.

"Late for what?" Alasdair replied, looking honestly puzzled.

"Lunch, for one thing."

He shrugged. "You were busy, and I wanted to watch you do your—your—" He gestured at the fabric on the floor. "What are the words you say to yourself as you are working?

Are they the same for each thing that you make, or do they change depending on the purpose?"

She stopped and stared up at him. "What are you talking about?"

To her surprise, he flushed. "I'm sorry. I should not have asked that. Your—you speak quietly as you work. I thought perhaps it was a ritual to give what you make its power. It was rude of me to—"

Garland wasn't sure whether to laugh or blush. "No, it's all right. I guess I do talk to myself as I'm working. I'd never noticed before. It's not a ritual or anything. It's just thinking out loud."

He looked relieved but not convinced. She went downstairs to make lunch, shaking her head. Power? A ritual? What an odd conclusion to have drawn.

ON TUESDAY afternoon Garland emerged from her creative fog long enough to remember that Captain Howe hadn't called yet. Contrary to her fears, Alasdair and Conn's presence hadn't kept her from working—in fact, most of the time she forgot they were there. But when she'd look up, they'd be watching her: Conn eagerly, waiting for her to come and snuggle him on her lap, and Alasdair—well, she'd yet to decipher what his expression meant.

But surely the police must have found out something about them by now. She waited until they'd had lunch—both of them seemed to find tomato soup as entrancing as toast had been—then went downstairs into Derek's old office to call the captain.

"Mattaquason Police Department," said a bored-sounding voice.

"May I speak with Captain Howe, please?" She used her best Junior League manner. "This is Garland Durrell, on Eldredge Point. He—" She stopped. Had she just heard a muffled hiss of indrawn breath on the other end of the line?

"I'll, um…I'm not sure if he's at his desk, Mrs. Durrell. I think I might have seen him leave earlier, but…but it's been a little…that is, he's—" The voice sounded anything but bored now. Instead, it sounded disconcerted. Scared, almost. "It might take me a few minutes to track him down. Wouldn't you rather have him call you back?"

The way he was supposed to have yesterday? "That's very considerate of you, but I think I'll wait," she said firmly.

There was a click, and then the low hum of on-hold limbo. She leaned back in Derek's tufted leather chair and got through nine quietly whistled repetitions of the theme from "Jeopardy" before someone finally picked up the line again.

"Howe here." The captain's voice was clipped and wary.

Garland switched to the soothing tone once reserved for Derek's former boss, who chewed through two rolls of antacid tablets daily. "Captain Howe, it's Garland Durrell. I promise I won't take more than a minute of your time. I was just wondering if you'd found any leads on Alasdair and Conn."

There was a silence. Then, "Who?"

She mentally hummed a few more bars while fighting down the urge to shriek. "The people I found on my beach on Saturday?"

A faint sound of shuffling paper could be heard on the other end of the line. "Er, no, I'm afraid we haven't. No Coast Guard reports of lost vessels or persons, and no matches for missing person reports. I'm sorry, Mrs. Durrell." He sounded like he was about to hang up.

"So that's it? There are no other channels for us to pursue? Isn't there somewhere we can report a found person or something?"

"This isn't the Rescue League, ma'am."

She took a couple of deep, centering breaths. "I apologize, captain. I thought that since Alasdair's feeling a little stronger, someone from the police department might want to talk to him. I'm sure you'd be able to do a much better job questioning him than I would."

"We're not the Gestapo, either, Mrs. Durrell."

Was he going to twist everything she said? She turned back on the Junior League Steel Magnolia. "I assumed—perhaps wrongly—that you would want to speak with him yourself to complete any formal reporting requirements that you might have, or to satisfy yourself that he's not a possible fugitive from justice. And if it does turn out that he has a family searching for him, it would not reflect well on the town if the utmost had not been done to identify him."

Captain Howe sounded like he was taking his own deep, centering breaths. She couldn't help being glad.

"I didn't say that we wouldn't be following up, Mrs. Durrell," he finally said. "But cases that impact the town as a whole take priority. We don't have an unlimited number of uniformed personnel nor an unlimited budget to cover overtime, and so far this week we've seen some fairly nasty vandalism at two summer houses in your neighborhood and a fisherman who went out clamming Sunday morning and never came home. When we have a chance, an officer will be out to speak with—with the man."

"His name is Alasdair. Thank you very much, captain. I'll look forward to that." She hung up and sat frowning at the phone. He couldn't be lying about being overextended. It would be far too easy for her to verify that houses near her had been vandalized, and surely the town would be abuzz about a missing fisherman.

Buzz. If she wanted to hear what was going on in town, it was time to call Kathy and take her up on that lunch offer.

⁖⁖⁖

"Well, you're looking pleased with yourself," said Kathy, eyeing Garland as she spooned up her quahog chowder the following day. Her joking put-downs notwithstanding, the Captain's Bridge Inn made the best chowder in Mattaquason. "Positively glowing, in fact. Let me guess—did Rob Mowbray get lucky this week?"

"Kathy!" Garland looked around the crowded restaurant. The Mattaquason Women's Club was having its monthly luncheon today and every table in the room was filled. "I barely know him, for Pete's sake."

A couple of women at nearby tables glanced over at them. Kathy gave them a wide, false smile and turned back to Garland. "Crap. If I'd known the Mattaquason Sewing Circle and Terrorist Society was lunching here today, we'd have gone somewhere else. So come on, what are you looking so pleased about? Let me guess again—Rob Mowbray's *going to* get lucky?"

Garland stuck out her tongue. Someone at the next table coughed slightly. "Get your mind out of the gutter," she murmured. "For your information, Rob Mowbray is right now spending his lunch hour checking Alasdair and Conn while I endure personal abuse from my dearest friend."

"In that case, you'd better make it worth his while." But the humor had drained from Kathy's sparkling eyes. "Alasdair, huh? Why is he still there? Haven't you found whoever he belongs to?"

"No, we haven't. He's had some memory loss and can't remember much apart from that name. Believe me, I've tried to find out where he's from, but the police have been about as helpful as a bushel of rocks. Poor Conn. He—"

"Shh!" All traces of a smile had thoroughly vanished from Kathy's face.

"What's wrong?" Garland asked her in a lower voice.

"The whole room doesn't have to know about this—these people."

"Why not? Wouldn't it be better if the whole town knew about them so we can find out where they're from? In fact, Rob suggested just today that we call the Mattaquason *Mariner* and get them to do an article."

Kathy put down her spoon and began drumming her fingers on the table. "Someone needs to have a talk with Rob Mowbray, and soon," she muttered darkly. "Garland, this is ridiculous. What are you going to do, keep them like a couple of stray puppies you found by the roadside? You don't need this."

"C'mon, Kath, they're still swathed in bandages like Lon Chaney, Jr. Somebody has to help them."

"I don't see why it has to be you. Get *rid* of them. This is serious. All I'm thinking about is your well-being." Kathy's voice was angry, but her eyes were wide and…yes, there it was again. Anxious. Scared.

"Okay, okay," she said. "Maybe Rob can find some social service network that can take them in or something. I'll ask him later—"

"Tomorrow, Garland. They should be out of there by

tomorrow."

It was time to change the subject. "So don't you want to know why I'm looking pleased with myself?"

Kathy sighed and turned to her chowder again. "By all means. Though I still wish Rob Mowbray had something to do with it."

"Give me a chance, Kathy. I'm not even formally divorced yet."

"That didn't stop Derek."

"I'm not Derek, in case you hadn't noticed." Garland bent to pull a plastic bag from her handbag and handed it to Kathy. "Now you can't whine at me about not quilting anymore."

Kathy raised one eyebrow and pulled out a bundle of fabric. She held it up to let it unroll and gasped. It was the landscape Garland had created the other morning.

"It's just the quilt top," Garland explained. "I'm going to set up my new long-arm quilting machine today, and I'll need a day or two to play with it and get a feel for how it works before I quilt this. So do you like it?"

She hardly needed to ask. Kathy was gaping at the square of piecework in her hands as if it had hypnotized her. Garland leaned sideways in her chair and regarded it as well.

"Urgh. Now that I look at it in here, I don't much care for the fabric I used for the islands on the horizon. Sorry, Kathy, I guess I'm a little rusty yet. Or maybe a lot rusty." Garland held her hand out for the quilt top and noticed that the restaurant had gone almost totally silent. She glanced up and saw that all eyes in the room were on her quilt. Several women had even left their seats to get a better look at it.

"Garland, it's perfect," Kathy finally whispered. "It's the view from your house. I can see it…jeez, look—you used a piece of blue fabric that had a green streak in it, right where that green buoy is off your beach."

"Did you make that?" asked a tall woman, coming to stand behind Kathy. Four or five others joined her, and then it was as if the entire dining room, wait staff included, was clustering around their table and straining to get a look at her quilt top.

"Yes, she did." Kathy seemed to snap out of her spell. She rose, then climbed on her chair and held the quilt top up, slowly turning. More murmurs arose as she made a slow circle.

"Kathy, get down from there before you fall." Garland was sure that her face was crimson.

"This is Garland Durrell, ladies, and she's just moved down Cape from the Boston area. Her quilts will be in my gallery later in the spring and summer after she gets settled in. I hope you'll all come and see them," Kathy called out in ringing tones. Her face, permanently tanned from her years in exotic locales, was pink with excitement. "Captain Hayes Gallery, across Main Street—but you all know that."

"When will *that* quilt be there?" called a voice from somewhere to Garland's left.

Kathy looked down at Garland and cocked an inquiring eyebrow at her. Garland tried to answer, but her voice had been snatched away by shock.

"Soon," Kathy replied. "Give the poor woman a chance to finish unpacking. She hasn't even been here a week, after all. Come on, Garland, stand up and say hello." She gestured with her head.

Garland would have preferred to dive under the table. But Kathy wouldn't be gainsaid. She glared at Garland while still managing to smile sweetly at everyone else, so Garland reluctantly climbed up on her chair and gave the room a tentative smile.

"Oh, I know you," said another voice. "You're down on Eldredge Point, aren't you? I see you in the summer at the library."

Murmurs of agreement rose around her.

"Garland has been an active supporter of the Mattaquason Historical Society and the Friends of the Library for several years," Kathy affirmed. "She's just getting through an unpleasant divorce and is making a new life for herself here. I hope you'll all welcome her and join us for her first one-woman quilt show in August."

Garland nearly fell off her chair. What was Kathy doing, telling everyone about her divorce? And *what* quilt show in August? "Kath!" she muttered urgently.

"Well, I'm sure you'll all want to get back to your lunches before they get cold. Thank you for welcoming my friend, and if you stop in at the gallery next week you might see the completed quilt." She shot a look at Garland, who nodded meekly.

The crowd of ladies resumed their seats, a few stopping to greet Garland as if they were old acquaintances. She recognized several volunteers from the library and the Historical Society, and even remembered a name or two. Kathy beamed at her like a proud parent till everyone had sat down again.

"That was terrific! I couldn't have planned it any better if I'd tried." She was nearly dancing in her chair with glee as she rolled the quilt top back up. "That was practically the entire female half of the population that matters in this town. Two of them were selectmen's wives, and one *is* a selectman. You've just gotten the Mattaquason equivalent of a two-page spread in the *New York Times* for your work."

Garland accepted her quilt top back with a glare. "What did you do that for? I felt like I was on display up there."

"Deal with it. If you want your quilts to sell, you've got to be visible. But mostly I expect your quilts will sell themselves. Oh, wait till I call Sonya Feinberg in New York. Or better yet, those two friends of hers who came in and told me they wanted the next Garland Durrell quilt, no matter what color or design. Ooh, I can just *taste* that winter home on Antigua. Or maybe St. Croix—it's less crowded, I hear—"

"Hey—earth to Kathy. What quilt show in August? What black hole did you pull that idea out of?" Garland wasn't sure whether she wanted to laugh or throttle her friend.

"What do you think? A show in the gallery in August is perfect—it's peak tourist season. All the really filthy rich ones come in August. You'll get maximum visibility."

"Oh, sure. There's just the teensy little fact that I haven't even finished one quilt yet."

"Don't get sarcastic with grandma. August is years away. You'll have plenty of time to make—let's say, a dozen quilts? Eighteen would be better, of course. I'll schedule it for the end of August, rather than the beginning. Will that help?"

"No problem. I'll just give up sleeping till then."

Kathy snorted. "You can sleep when you're dead. Look how quickly this top went together. And if you've gotten yourself a quilt machine, that'll make them go even faster. I know you like to hand-quilt but you can save that for next winter when you've got more time. Just make some more wall-sized beauties like this one, and we'll be golden. Literally."

"Kathy—"

"Oh, look, here's our lunch. Hey, Sandy, did the chef actually cook this or just stare at it really hard?" she asked as the waitress set her blue-cheese-and-bacon burger down on the table. "I like my burgers rare, not just stunned and left to die of blood loss like the one he served me last week."

"Well, it's not trying to crawl off your plate and escape, Ms. Hayes." Sandy grinned and put Garland's smoked turkey Reuben in front of her. "Boy, Mrs. Durrell, that quilt you made is gorgeous. You can, like, really feel the waves in the water. I can't wait for your show."

"Um, thanks."

Across from her Kathy sang the chorus from "Kokomo" under her breath as she sprinkled salt and vinegar on her fries. Now that she was in a better mood, maybe it was time to find out if Howe had been lying. "So, uh, Kathy. What's this I hear about a missing fisherman?"

Kathy stopped singing and put down the bottle of vinegar. "Who told you about that?"

"Captain Howe, when I called yesterday. What happened? Did he—"

Kathy glanced around her at the other tables. "Look, let's not talk about that right now. The guy's wife is beside herself, and most everyone in this room knows her. It's not...it's not something to discuss in public."

"What do they think happened to him? He was clamming, right? What about his tools? Are they gone too? Do they think he ran away with another woman or something?"

"Drop it, Garland."

The rest of their lunch was quiet.

❧❧ ❧❧

Garland was grateful that her dinner with Rob on Friday was less public than her lunch with Kathy. But only slightly less.

She could feel the eyes of everyone in the room on them as the hostess ushered her and Rob to a fishnet-shrouded alcove in Jason's, one of the few upscale restaurants in Mattaquason that stayed open in the off-season. Most of the groups at the tables they passed called out greetings to Rob. Garland herself recognized one woman who had been in the Captain's Bridge yesterday. She returned her greeting, then watched from the corner of her eye as the woman turned to her companions and began to relate something in a low-pitched but animated voice.

"Small town life," Rob commented. Garland looked up and saw that he too was watching the woman. "They didn't warn us about this in med school. I never thought I'd find myself a local celebrity just because I'm the new doc in town." His tone was wondering and slightly sheepish.

He really thought everyone idolized him just because he was a doctor. Garland smiled inwardly. Being extremely personable, civic-minded, good-looking, and unmarried had nothing to do with it, of course.

"At least there aren't any paparazzi shoving cameras in our faces," she said aloud.

"Thank God for that." He smiled and nodded as a waiter brought a free-standing ice bucket with a bottle of champagne and two flutes to the table. "I hope I didn't mistakenly assume you liked champagne."

"I don't think you're capable of making mistakes, Rob Mowbray." She caught a glimpse of the label on the bottle. "Oh, my. So what's the occasion?"

The *pop!* of the cork once more focused the eyes of the entire dining room on them. Rob ignored them and leaned forward, lifting his flute to hers. "Oh, I don't know. Just because. Because I like champagne. Because I like you."

For a fleeting second, tears started to her eyes. Just because. She had spent the last fourteen years of her life with a man who viewed everything in life as items on a balance sheet to be totted up as credits and debits. And now she sat across from another man who'd ordered a bottle of hundred-and-fifty-dollar champagne "just because."

"I like you, too," she whispered, and touched her glass to his.

He smiled a slow, sweet smile. "I'd hoped you say that."

A soft wind seemed to blow through the room. Without looking up, Garland was able to guess what it was: the whispers of the other diners, watching them.

"Don't look now, but I think I saw a camera," she said, hoping her tone was light.

He glanced around the room. There was an abrupt clatter of cutlery as everyone suddenly remembered the plates of rapidly cooling food in front of them. "You were joking, right?" he asked, smiling uncertainly.

She sat back and took a sip of champagne. "Mostly. Do you think Alasdair and Conn will be okay?"

Rob's smile faded. "They're fine. Don't worry about them."

Their waiter arrived then to take their orders. Garland was glad for the interruption. Why was she brooding about Alasdair, when Rob was here plying her with Veuve Clicquot Reserve and telling her he liked her a lot? Then again, being part of the evening's entertainment for everyone else in the restaurant wasn't helping matters. She felt stiff and uncomfortable suddenly.

Rob cleared his throat. "Speaking of Alasdair, I got hold of the guy I know at the Mattaquason *Mariner* and told him about you. His name is Jim Barnes, and he's one of the staff writers.

One of two." He smiled wryly.

"You told him about me?" Garland had a flashback of Kathy making her stand on her chair at the Captain's Bridge.

"You and finding Alasdair and Conn on the beach. Jim was shocked that he hadn't heard about it. Anyway, he said of course he wanted the story and that he's free tomorrow morning if that's all right with you. I'm kind of surprised that they haven't been sniffing around already—something like this should be big news in off-season Mattaquason. Hell, the middle school spelling bee was on the front page last week." He shook his head. "The only thing is, I've got office hours on alternate Saturdays till twelve-thirty. Do you mind if I'm not there when Barnes comes?"

Here was a chance to recapture the evening's earlier mood. "Of course I'll mind," she said. "But I'll let you make it up to me."

Rob's grin flashed as he refilled their flutes. "I'll have to see about that."

৵৩৫ ৩৫৵

Alasdair had not been happy when Garland said that she was going somewhere with the healer and would be leaving him and Conn alone that evening. Even though she promised she'd lock everything and showed him how to press a button on the "phone" that would make it so that he could talk to her on the tiny one she carried with her, he was still uneasy. He turned every light in the bedroom on, even her special sunshine lights and the tiny lights on her sewing and quilting machines. He thought about taking the coverings off the lamps but wasn't sure if that would annoy her when she returned.

Conn was not happy either; he'd clung to Garland while the

healer checked his wounds and could hardly be convinced to let her go. Alasdair tried yet again to talk to him after she left, to ask what he was feeling and why he was so drawn to her. And as he had every other time, Conn only stared at him in silence. The boy had rarely spoken even before the attack—hiding from Mahtahdou, he'd learned silence early. It was no life for a small child and Alasdair had known that. Several times in the last few seasons he had come close to sending Conn out to foster among the selkies scattered across the waters north of here, but had never had the courage to do so. And his cowardice had nearly killed his son.

Was that why Conn clung to Garland? Because he knew she could protect him when his own father could not? And wasn't he doing the same thing, hiding behind this human who had no idea of what power she wielded?

He shifted in his bed, straining to look out the narrow gap between the coverings on the window. With all the lights in the room on it was hard to see anything in the darkness outside, and the various hums and rumbles that a human house made drowned any sounds as well. He glanced over at Conn and saw that he slept, clinging to the stuffed figure with large ears Garland had sewn for him from some soft brown cloth. Good.

He put aside the covering on his bed and set his feet on the floor. They throbbed and shot needles of pain up his calves as they always did when he'd tried to walk this week, but he knew about living with pain. Carefully, so that he did not stumble and fall and wake Conn, he shuffled over to the window where Garland had placed a chair and knelt stiffly on it, then peered around the edge of the curtain, cupping his hand to block out the light. He might not be in any shape to defend himself or his son, but he could at least keep vigil until Garland returned.

Outside, a fog had begun to roll in off the water. Alasdair stared at it suspiciously; it was early in the season for fog though the day had been warm. It crept in long tendrils up from the beach, feeling its way along the ground, and he stiffened. Though there was not much wind tonight, what little there was blew off the land, toward the sea. Nevertheless the fog progressed steadily against it, creeping crab-like toward the houses along the shore. As it swirled it seemed to shimmer with a faint, sickly-green phosphorescence.

The back of Alasdair's neck prickled as if the cold mist had touched it.

He squinted into the darkness and saw the mist pause, then race up the beach toward the house nearest Garland's. For a moment the house was obscured, and he heard a strange tinkling, crashing noise come from it. The sound happened several times more, then stopped.

Alasdair turned away from the window and tottered over to Garland's work table, where the cloth picture she'd made waited to be completed with more stitching. He snatched it up and moved as quickly as his feet would let him to Conn's bed. He draped it over him, then staggered back to the window and peered outside again.

There was nothing to see. Fog swirled over the clear material of the window, casting a faint greenish glow. It seemed to be probing it, as if trying to get inside, and he realized what the sound he'd heard from the other house had been. The fog had smashed the windows, and he could guess why.

It was looking for something.

He clutched Garland's robe tighter at his throat and watched in horrified fascination as the fog thickened into an opaque mass and pressed against the window. The frame creaked in protest, but the glass did not break. He heard a flurry of sounds from around the house and knew that the fog assailed the other windows and doors, but no crashes followed. For some reason, the fog could not penetrate Garland's house.

It drew back a little and hovered outside the window. Was it thinking about what to do? Did it even think? Could it harm him and Conn if it managed to break the window? Or was it just a scout, searching blindly and reporting back to its master when it found something suspicious…like a house that it could not enter?

The fog thickened and assaulted the windows again. Alasdair was sure he could see the glass deforming under its pressure, but it held firm. Were they of better quality than the glass in other houses or was something else keeping it out? He couldn't be sure, but he could guess. This was the dwelling of a magic wielder. Nothing could enter it without her permission.

He smiled grimly and settled himself more comfortably in the chair to watch the fog curl uncertainly around the house. It had to be something of Mahtahdou's who was master of the insubstantial and ghostly, of images and shadows. Let it search all night if it wanted. It would never find him. And when Garland came home—

He sat up quickly, ignoring the pain in his sides. Lir's breath! Garland was out somewhere in this. It could not touch her house, but to be out there in the very thick of it, surrounded by Mahtahdou's foul air…

He looked at Conn, still sleeping peacefully under Garland's cloth picture. Then, step by painful step, he left the room and inched his way down the stairs to the front door. Garland had saved him. The least he could do was try to help her.

To Garland's relief, the rest of their dinner went smoothly. Since they showed no signs of doing anything more titillating than talking a great deal, the other diners finally seemed to forget they were there. Garland kept her concern for Alasdair under control though she very nearly called him from her cell phone in the ladies' room. The food was delicious, far better now than in summer when the chefs were more rushed. Likewise, the noise level was more tolerable and the service friendlier and more relaxed.

"I can begin to see why the year-round population has such a love-hate relationship with the summer people," Garland commented as they walked back to Rob's car. It was a warm evening for March. She lifted her head and took a deep breath of the soft, moist air. A faint mist swirled in the glare of the parking lot's lights.

"It's true. They bring lots of money, but they bring themselves too. Most businesses on Cape Cod earn three-quarters of their income between mid-June and early September. But we get the best to ourselves during spring and fall. There's nothing more beautiful than September in Mattaquason. I can't wait to show you." He smiled that slow smile again as he opened the car door for her, and Garland felt a flutter of anticipation.

The mist thickened into fog as they rolled out of downtown and toward Eldredge Point. Her house shimmered as Rob pulled into her driveway, every window spilling light into the moist night air so that it looked like it had a halo.

"I promised Alasdair I'd leave all the lights on," she explained. How had he and Conn done without her? Had they gone to sleep the way she'd told them to?

"Oh. Well." Rob put the car into park and turned to her, his face half-lit from the bright post lights on either side of the front walk. "Thank you for a lovely evening."

"Thank you, Rob. It—" She suddenly felt tongue-tied.

He made a small move toward her—just a small one—and she realized he was letting her decide if she wanted to kiss him goodnight.

Of course she did. Why else had she ordered sesame-crusted tuna instead of garlicky shrimp scampi at dinner? She leaned toward him, and his hand reached up to cradle her cheek. His quick kiss the other day had been a promissory note for this one, she knew. It was going to be good.

It was good. Rob's lips took hers gently but eagerly, with just enough heat to let her know what he wanted from her some day. Garland closed her eyes, waiting for the warm glow of anticipation in her midsection to build into excitement.

But nothing happened.

"Wow," Rob murmured a few minutes later, coming up for air. "That was even better than I'd dreamed it would be."

She smiled self-consciously. "Had you been dreaming about it?"

"All week." He ran a finger down her cheek. "Can I do that one more time, and then I'll be a good boy and go home?"

Garland lifted her face to his again. Surely this time the spark would ignite inside her. Though he kissed her as well as she'd ever been kissed—certainly better than Derek—there was something missing. She broke the kiss suddenly.

"Garland…" Rob dropped kisses on her eyelids, her cheeks, her jaw, then rested his cheek against hers. She reached up to stroke his hair. But her internal thermostat never as much as flickered.

He turned his face to kiss her hand. "I'm sorry. Was that too much, too soon?"

Relief flooded her. That had to be it. She wasn't responding to him the way she ought to, the way she wanted to, because she wasn't ready yet. Surely that was why kissing him had been nice, but had somehow felt wrong? "Maybe. I liked it, but—"

"But you're still a little tender as far as the heart goes. I understand, Garland."

"I'm sorry, Rob, I really am."

"Sorry for what? I shouldn't have rushed things. I didn't lie, back at the restaurant. I do like you. A lot. Maybe more than a lot. But it *is* early days yet, isn't it? You've just moved here, after all, and you're just getting used to being a single woman again." He kissed her again, quick and gentle like the other day. "I'll be over tomorrow to see how it went with Jim Barnes, okay?"

"Okay. Thank you for a lovely evening. It was wonderful— all of it." Garland smiled into his eyes as she reached for the door, then climbed out into the swirling fog. Rob waited while she unlocked the door and went inside. She heard the crunch of his tires on the crushed shell driveway as he drove away.

❧❧❧

A new sound—not breaking glass but a scratchy, grinding noise—brought Alasdair to his feet from where he perched on the bottom stair. Another sound, this time from the door itself, made him tense. Then the door opened and Garland stepped inside. She didn't look harried or frightened, as if she'd been fleeing or fighting anything. Instead, her face looked thoughtful and maybe even slightly sad. She did something to the metal doorknob, then turned and saw him.

"Alasdair! What are you doing down here? Your feet…" She dropped the small bag she carried and hurried across the polished wood floor to him. "You shouldn't be out of bed. Are you all right? Is something wrong with Conn?"

"Nothing's wrong," he said. Not any more. "I was afraid…but you're safe." Was it relief at seeing her unharmed that made him suddenly sway on his feet, or just the pain of spending so much time on them?

"Of course I'm safe," she said, reaching her arm around his waist to steady him.

"Garland…" Before he could stop himself he'd pulled her against him and held her tightly, burying his face in her hair and ignoring the faint protest of his wounds. She was safe, and so were he and Conn. Mahtahdou had not gotten them this time.

"Hey! What are you doing?" Her voice was muffled against his throat, sounding astonished and maybe a little shocked. But her body spoke with different words, softening and molding itself against him with little movements as her free hand slid slowly up his chest. He closed his eyes and let sensations almost forgotten wash over him. This was what it was like to hold a beautiful woman in his arms again, to feel her breath quicken and her body respond to his—

He pushed her away and nearly collapsed, groping for the railing that lined the stairs to hold him up. It took him a moment to master his breath and pounding heart before he could look up and meet her blue eyes. They were dazed and wide, and her cheeks bloomed red as she looked at him.

"I'm sorry…I was afraid…" he mumbled. That's all it had been, hadn't it? He'd been afraid for her, and was relieved that she was safe. That was the only reason he'd wanted to hold her. It had to be.

JIM BARNES WAS a tall, shambling teddy bear of a man. He shuffled into Garland's kitchen the next morning and gave her a wide smile as he shook her hand. Only after they had been chatting for a few minutes did she notice that the smile never reached his eyes. He refused coffee and pulled out a battered notebook.

"Your fame precedes you, Mrs. Durrell. My wife—"

Garland sighed. "She belongs to the Mattaquason Women's Club, right?"

He chuckled. "She did say you looked pretty embarrassed standing on that chair. So tell me about your quilting. Do you have formal training or is it a hobby? I hear the show in August will be your first."

"I'm working on a Master of Fine Arts degree, but quilting's my hobby as well. I'd love to talk about it with you, Mr. Barnes, but I had thought you were here to learn about the people I found on the beach. At least, that's why Rob Mowbray called you. Isn't that a more important story than my quilts?"

He cleared his throat. "Oh, absolutely. I just thought I'd…you know, get facts for both stories. Can we finish up the quilting first, so I don't get my notes mixed up? Where are you getting the MFA? I didn't know you could get a degree in quilting."

Garland simmered but let him ask her questions about her quilting, down to what model of sewing machine she used. This was not why they had called him. She wanted Alasdair's story out there, not hers. But he seemed determined not to stray from the subject of her quilts. Then a thought occurred to her.

"I'm sorry you didn't bring a camera"—and how was he supposed to take a picture of Alasdair and Conn for his article to get readers to help identify them, without one?—"but would you like to see what I'm currently working on anyway?" she asked him. "I spent the morning fiddling with my new quilting machine." Alasdair and Conn had watched in fascination while she prepared the ten-foot-wide frame that held quilts taut and a free-moving sewing machine apparatus that could be moved across the frame to sew together the layers of a quilt with decorative stitching patterns. If all went well, she'd get the first wall quilt done for Kathy today.

He brightened. "Sure! My wife said the piece she saw the other day blew her socks off. Darn it, I should have grabbed the camera before I left."

Of course he should have, the slime. Garland plastered a smile on her face and led the way up the stairs.

"It's quite convenient," she said, pausing in front of

Alasdair's door and politely gesturing him in ahead of her. "You can see my quilts and have a chance to meet Alasdair and Conn, too. Alasdair, here's the man I told you about." She herded Jim Barnes into the room.

Conn looked up from his bed where he was playing with the scraps of fabric she'd given him, laying them out in patterns, and gave her a sunny smile. Alasdair set down the copy of *National Geographic* he'd been leafing through. His posture was tense until he saw her. "Hello," he said politely.

Jim Barnes froze. Garland had never seen anyone go as rigid as he did then, as if he might shatter if she poked him.

"Dr. Mowbray wants them to stay in bed a few days longer till they're over the blood loss and the worst of their wounds have had a chance to heal," she said. "But you can talk to them for a few minutes."

For a moment, she felt almost sorry for the man. Barnes's mouth opened and closed, rather like an asphyxiating fish's. He'd also turned an interesting shade of pasty white. "Uhh— I—"

Garland steered him to the chair next to Alasdair's bed. He seemed to be engaged in an internal struggle over whether to actually sit down, but manners and what looked like rubbery legs won out. He dropped into the chair but managed to shift it slightly away. She waited for him to say something, to introduce himself further. Instead, he stared dumbly down at his hands, over at the windows or at her quilting materials, but never at Alasdair or Conn.

"Mr. Barnes?" she prompted.

"What? Oh, er, yes…my pen—I seem to have left it downstairs…" He fumbled in a pocket.

"I've got one here." Garland went to her worktable for a

pencil and turned back to Barnes. A loud, electronic version of "La Cucaracha" stopped her.

"Darn! Now who could that be? 'Scuse me for a sec, won't you?" Barnes pulled a cell phone out of his pocket. Conn's eyes widened as he tapped the screen and barked, "Barnes here."

A pause. "Right now? I'm kinda in the middle of an interview, Joe. Can't you take care of it?"

Another pause. "Oh. I'd forgotten about that. Well, wish her a happy birthday for me. I'll get over there right away. Bye."

Garland had already guessed what his next speech would be by the time he'd put his phone away. "I'm sorry, Mrs. Durrell, That was my editor. I don't know why he schedules things for Saturday delivery, but I've gotta get down to the office pronto to let the delivery guy in, because he's got his daughter's birthday party starting in a few minutes—my editor, that is."

She wasn't more than four words off. "I'm sorry too. You didn't even get to talk to Alasdair."

"Yeah, well, maybe we can take care of the rest of this on the phone." He glanced around the room again, and his eyes fell on the landscape quilt set in the big frame. A look of wonderment made his face even more teddy-bearish.

"Is that...? My wife said it was...holy crow, Mrs. Durrell." He edged toward the quilt top, staring.

He looked at it so long that Garland couldn't help taking a little malicious pleasure in saying, "I'm sure the delivery man won't want to be kept waiting."

"Oh, uh, you're right." He looked at it a second longer, then turned on his heel and almost sprinted for the door. She showed him out, just managing not to slam the front door behind him, and stomped back into the kitchen.

What had the point of that been? Yes, it was nice everyone

in town seemed to like her quilts. But she'd assumed Barnes had been here to cover the far more important story of Alasdair and Conn. Because if they didn't find Alasdair's home and family soon, she didn't know what she would do.

What had gotten into her last night? Poor Alasdair had been frightened and had come down to wait for her, then hugged her in his relief that she was home. And her traitorous body had interpreted that embrace in an entirely different way, so that she'd been about a heartbeat away from—well, never mind that. Darn it, it was Rob she was ought to be getting hot and bothered for, especially after the way he'd kissed her goodnight. She'd responded to Alasdair's innocent hug the way she should have to Rob's hot kisses. It was utterly ridiculous.

Rob arrived a little after one. "I brought sandwiches from Pete's. Best roast beef in town," he said, handing her a bag.

Garland sniffed it. "You didn't have to do that. Ooh, lots of horseradish. Yum. I wonder if Alasdair likes horseradish?"

Rob looked embarrassed. "I only brought two."

Oh Lord. Could she have put her foot through it any harder? "That's probably a good thing. He's already had nearly half a loaf's worth of toast this morning. He'd eat it round the clock if I let him," she said.

Rob listened to her indignant description of Jim Barnes's visit without much comment, and ate only about a third of his sandwich. Nor did his grin make an appearance, even briefly. "Are you all right?" she finally asked him.

"I'm fine," he said shortly, then frowned. "No. I mean, I'm fine, but..." He shook his head.

"What?"

"It's—well, Ben Moniz came in this morning to see me. You know, the officer who came with Captain Howe last

Saturday?"

"With the knee trouble. I remember." Garland sat up straighter. "Did he have any news about Alasdair?"

"I wish he had." Rob's mouth twisted. "It's nothing to do with Alasdair. Or maybe it is—I don't know. Dammit, I don't like this."

Garland touched his hand. "What is it?"

He sighed and scrunched his napkin into a ball, then smoothed it out again on the table. "Strictly speaking, I shouldn't be telling you this. Ben swore me to secrecy, but…you heard about the guy who went clamming last weekend and never came back—they found his rake and his baskets, but no sign of him?"

"I remember. Let me guess—they found him in Atlantic City with his girlfriend?"

"I wish to God they had. They found him all right—early this morning, washed up on Harbor Beach. Or what was left of him."

"Oh my God."

"Poor Ben was just coming off duty when the call came in, so he went along to help. It was—he said they had to use bags. A lot of them."

No wonder Rob hadn't wanted his sandwich. She swallowed hard and took a gulp of the ginger beer he'd brought. "What do they think happened? Could he have had a heart attack and then gotten washed out to sea and—and sharks or whatever found him?"

"Maybe. I don't know. All I can say is that I'm glad I'm not the M.E. around here." He sighed again and rubbed his forehead. "I should leave in a minute and stop by the widow's house and see if she needs anything."

That was right, the man had been married. "Kids?"

"No. Thank heavens for small mercies." He drummed his fingers on the table, then looked up at her. "Garland, I know I don't have any right to say this, but I want you to send Alasdair and Conn to the hospital to finish recuperating. Now. What if these attacks are connected—and personal?"

"You don't have any way of knowing that—"

He went on as if she hadn't spoken. "What if whoever did this finds out Alasdair is here and comes back to finish the job? This is for his protection as much as yours. Though I have to admit I'm more concerned about your safety."

Garland stared down at her empty plate. What if Rob was right? What if whoever attacked Alasdair came back? Whoever had been capable of such savagery on three people probably wouldn't think twice about removing her to finish his job.

Besides, here was her chance. Hadn't she just been telling herself that having Alasdair here was dangerous for other reasons?

But it wasn't just Alasdair. It was Conn, too. She couldn't abandon him. "Do the police think he's in danger or not? Is there any official word?"

"Ben didn't say. He wasn't even supposed to mention this to me."

"Why not? Why keep it so hush-hush? Shouldn't this be public knowledge—" Public knowledge...oh, no. She'd just had a newspaper reporter in here to talk about Alasdair. If Alasdair really were in danger from someone, having an article about him in the local paper would *not* be a good idea. Not that she and Jim Barnes had actually exchanged more than a word or two about him, but still...

Rob seemed to read her thoughts. "I wonder if maybe we

should give Jim Barnes a call and ask him to hold off on an article about Alasdair."

"He'd want to know why, and what would we say? But he hardly asked any questions about Alasdair. I told you, I had to trick him into going upstairs, and then he faked a phone call that he was urgently needed elsewhere. All he wanted to hear about was my quilting. He'd even heard about Kathy's plans for a show in August. It was pretty strange."

Rob raised his eyebrows. "He was all gung-ho about doing an article about Alasdair yesterday. I got the impression he was going to call the police and give Captain Howe the third degree as soon as he got off the phone with me."

"Maybe he did, and caught Howe's allergy to Alasdair." Garland sat back in her chair. "I know you want me to ask Alasdair to leave, but I can't do that to him, and I even more can't do it to Conn. It doesn't look like anyone else wants to help them."

"Maybe that's the best way to help them."

"Who else would take them in? No. They stay here until—"

"Until what?"

Garland gave a non-committal shrug. "At least until they're healed and can take care of themselves. You would do the same if you were me, and you know it."

"Yes, but I don't live half a mile from my nearest neighbor." He glanced at his watch and stood up. "I should go see that poor woman."

At the door he took her face in his hands and looked at her earnestly. "Keep your doors locked, and call the police if you see anything funny. I don't like the thought of you here all alone."

"I'm not alone. I've got our friends upstairs."

Evidently her light tone had fallen short, for his mouth tightened. "There's something else. Ben said that there's been a lot of vandalism around beach houses over the last week—broken windows, trashed houses. They're stepping up patrols, but…be careful, Garland. If anything happened to you, I'd—"

She put her hands over his. "I'll be all right, Rob. Promise. I've taken all kinds of self-defense and strength training classes. I could probably have you flat on the floor in about five seconds if I tried."

"Yeah, well, you wouldn't have to try very hard to get me on the floor, you know." He smiled—really smiled—and kissed her quickly. "Just be careful, huh? I'll call you later."

❧❧❧

After Rob left Garland made lunch for Alasdair and Conn—plain tuna on toast, with not even a dollop of mayo or a drift of ground pepper on it—and brought it upstairs. Conn abandoned his scraps of fabric and made her sit beside him while he ate. She smoothed his hair back from his forehead and smiled as he wiggled closer, still crunching happily on his toast. Little cuddle-bug. She'd gone so many years without snuggling—even longer than without sex. And snuggling a child was totally different, anyway. Conn snuggled consciously, purposefully, just as he played or ate his lunch or settled for sleep.

"That man did not stay long," Alasdair observed, breaking the silence.

"Who, Jim Barnes? No, he didn't." She stared pensively at the rainbow of triangles and squares on the bed. Rob's horrible story had pushed him out of her mind for a while, but—

Her gaze focused on a group of scraps. Conn had taken a

square and some triangles, and made—"Hey, it's a fish," she said, sitting up. "That's very good, Conn. I like it. In fact—"

She swept up more of the scraps and assembled another one like it, with different proportions, and set it next to the first. "That could be fun. Do you want to help me make a quilt? If you make me more fish like this, I can sew them together and make them into a little quilt."

He looked at her solemnly, stuffed the rest of his tuna and toast into his mouth, handed her his plate, and turned to the fabric. She laughed.

"Oh no you don't, buddy. Wash hands first, and then we'll make a quilt. Hold on." She brought a warm washcloth to wipe his face and hands, then got out her scrap box full of odd bits and handed it to him. "So long as you don't get them all over the room, you can look for pieces in here too. Make me lots and lots of fish, okay?"

He took the box, and she got the impression that if he'd known how, he would have saluted.

For the rest of the afternoon she sewed Conn's fish, big ones and little ones and a few highly peculiar ones. She resisted her impulse to fiddle with his designs but took them as he gave them to her. He became so engrossed that he didn't take his usual nap, and she became so engrossed that she didn't even notice. Only now and again did she sense Alasdair silently watching them from his bed, which was fine with her. The less direct interaction they had for a day or two, the better.

She pieced Conn's fish together with odds and ends of vibrant blue batik that reminded her of the color of the water outside her window. When the last light had faded from the sky she had a small quilt top, maybe thirty inches square, that shimmered with slightly lopsided but recognizable and very colorful fish. She brought it to Conn's bed and laid it out so they could survey it together.

"Not bad for an afternoon's work," she told him, ruffling his hair. Maybe it wasn't high art, but it had made a small boy happy. Besides, it was appropriate for Mattaquason, where a sizeable part of the year-round population was involved in fishing or marine-related—*that* was it!

"What?" Alasdair said, as if she'd spoken aloud.

"You'll see." She found the box labeled "thread"—one of these days she really had to unpack—and rummaged inside it till she found a roll of thin gold cord. She cut several lengths, pinned them across the top of the quilt in rows, then began to knot them together at inch-and-a-half intervals. The metallic cord stood out against the dark blue fabric and enhanced the multi-hued fish like a setting for jewels while drawing the whole image together.

"A net," Alasdair said, craning his head to watch.

"Of course. This is a fishing town. What else should there be?" She smiled down at her work as the fishnet took shape. All she'd have to do is layer it with the batting and backing and catch-stitch it at each knot to quilt it. It would be quick and, better yet, perfect.

Conn leaned over the quilt top and intently watched her. He stroked an end of the shiny gold cord, then wiggled a finger under the corner of net she'd completed.

"Don't tug on it, please, big boy. It's only held down by pins. You wouldn't want the fabric to get torn, would you?" She cut the end of the cord and started on another row. Conn didn't move.

"Please, Conn?"

He waggled his hand but didn't remove it. The little scamp!

He was pretending he'd been caught in the net. She chuckled. "Looks like I caught another fish for the quilt, didn't I? Are you a big fish or a little—" she broke off as she glanced up at him.

He wasn't smiling. Instead, there was disbelief swiftly shifting into shock in his eyes as he tried, more frantically, to yank his fingers out from under the net. They didn't budge.

For a few seconds she stared at him in bemusement. Was it self-hypnosis? Had he convinced himself that this was a real net and that it would catch everything, even a curious finger?

"Conn," she said, and gently tugged his wrist. Just as gently, his fingers slipped out from under the cords. But for a fleeting second she'd felt them resist, as if they really were trapped by some enormous, unseen force.

Self-hypnosis. It had to be. She caught him up and carried him over to the chair. He buried his face in her neck and though he didn't cry, he drew a few ragged, sniffly breaths.

"It's okay, Conn. You're all right," she murmured, over and over.

He lifted his head and glanced back at the quilt on the bed. She followed his look. "It's just a quilt. It can't hurt you."

He shivered and squirmed closer, if that were possible. Well, that was too bad. She'd already decided to give it to him when it was done. That probably wouldn't be a good idea now. "I'm sorry," she said to Alasdair. "I didn't mean to frighten him."

On his bed, Alasdair still watched her thoughtfully. "When that quilt is done, may I have it?"

Garland blinked and wanted to laugh. "Um, are you sure? I'm not sure somebody here likes it anymore. Unless you want to use it to keep him in line."

"No. I want to see if…" He looked at her, then shrugged carelessly. "As you wish. But I would be most honored if you would make one for me."

"You want me to make you a quilt?"

"Yes," he said simply.

An odd sensation, part schoolgirl bashfulness and part pleasure, coursed through her. After so many years of stifling her creativity, people actually wanted her quilts.

"I'd be happy to," she said, then laughed. "I even know the design." She rose and carried Conn over to him, then fetched her graph pad and shaded in a pattern of squares, diamonds, and triangles. "It's called 'Storm at Sea.' I've always wanted to make one, and it would be perfect for you, under the circumstances."

"I suppose it would." He looked at the design, then at her, his face solemn. "Will I be able to bear it?"

Sometimes he said the oddest things. "I'm sure you will."

She went to her boxes. Where were those batiks she'd been looking at? In a few minutes she had slipped into her color trance, and blues of all shades and intensities filled her awareness. But even while she sorted and chose, and hearing and touch all seemed in some strange way to become different ways of seeing, she was aware of Alasdair watching her.

On Thursday Rob appeared at Garland's house in a cold driving rain. As she opened the door he stepped inside and produced a copy of the Mattaquason *Mariner* with a flourish.

"Here you are, hot off the press. Ink's still wet, even," he said as he handed it to her and took off his streaming coat. Water puddled on the floor at his feet.

"That's just rain, silly." Garland hung his coat on the Shaker coat rack and turned eagerly to read what Jim Barnes had decided to write.

Rob followed her into the great room. "Hey—is that all the greeting I get?"

Garland dropped the paper on the table behind the couch and turned to him. Even when he pouted he was adorable. "I'm sorry. I'm just dying to see what actually made it in here." She put her hands on his shoulders and kissed him.

"That's better. I think I'll be demanding more often." He wrapped his arms around her and held her against him. "You're damned huggable, you know."

"So are you." But she couldn't keep her eyes from straying to the newspaper on the table. He laughed and let her go.

The *Mariner* was a typical small town paper: news in the first section, special interest stories in the middle, and advertisements in the third. Garland unfolded it and laid out the front page so they could both read the main headline:

VANDALISM EPIDEMIC STRIKES SUMMER HOMES
Police investigating, no leads

Garland chuckled mirthlessly. "I guess I owe Captain Howe an apology. He wasn't stonewalling after all."

" 'A rash of destruction over the last ten days in unoccupied summer homes on Bethlehem Neck and Eldredge Point have Mattaquason Police stymied,' " Rob read aloud. " 'Altogether, six residences have been attacked'—where's 56 Point Road?"

"That's Don Grenham's house, I think. Three houses down. Boy, I'll bet he's hopping mad. He doesn't even like birds trespassing in his trees. Are you done reading?" She bent to turn the page.

"Number 64 too, Garland. That's right next door. Doesn't that bother you?" His voice was incredulous.

She looked up at him. "Well, of course it does. Poor Mrs. Lufford. I hope they didn't mess things up too badly. She collects porcelain figures of hippopotamuses, you know. Has at least a hundred. I didn't realize there were so many of them in the world. Now that I think of it, though, if I were a vandal, it would have been sorely tempting to see just how aerodynamic some of those little hippos actually were—"

Rob made an exasperated sound. "That's not what I meant."

He wouldn't let himself be distracted, would he? "I'm sorry, Rob. But truly, I'm not worried. Vandals only go after empty houses—it's probably a bunch of bored kids. They're not going to risk getting caught breaking windows in an occupied house. Look—nothing about Alasdair here, either. I don't know whether to be mad as hell or relieved." She turned the next page and skimmed it. "Oh, here's the police log…nothing there, either. I was sure there would be at least a mention." She turned the page again and sighed. "Editorial and op ed. It won't be there. Let's see the second section."

The top half of the front page was taken up by an article about the plans for the upcoming celebrations to mark the hundred-and-twenty-fifth anniversary of the Mattaquason Public Library. But under that…

ARTIST IN RESIDENCE: Quilter Captures
Mattaquason with Needle and Thread
by Jim Barnes

"A little more saccharine than I'd like. Well, at least it was below the fold, and he didn't have his camera." Garland squinted at the column. "He's calling me a 'summer resident made good.' That's a little much, don't you think?"

There was nothing on the next page or the page after that. Garland gathered up the paper in disgust and tossed it into the basket by the fireplace. "The Mattaquason Congregational Church's bake sale got more coverage than Alasdair."

"Garland, you just finished saying that it might be better if there were nothing there," Rob said patiently.

She slumped against the edge of the table. "I know I did. In a way, it is. It's just that it feels like no one wants to help them but me. Why? Why won't anyone else even look at him, much less help him?"

"*I* helped him."

"I know you did. I didn't mean you." Garland turned to him and put her hands on his shoulders. "I meant everyone else."

He pulled her against him. "I don't understand it either, if it makes you feel better. If you'd like, I'll give Jim Barnes a call and see what's up with him."

"Oh, thank you, Rob." She rested her head on his shoulder. "You're one pretty terrific guy."

Rob's arms tightened around her. "Not really. It's pure selfishness. All I want is to finally find where Alasdair belongs and send him there, so we can concentrate on what's really important. I started to fall for you two years ago, remember. It's hard to be patient that long." He bent and kissed her.

Garland closed her eyes and cooperated with the kiss. Mmm, nice, but no fireworks…not yet, she hastily amended. Surely they would come soon.

8

GARLAND MENTALLY ran through her list as she pulled into a parking place on Main Street in Mattaquason. The grocery shopping was done. Now it was the library, Vernon's Five and Ten for thread, Kathy's gallery, and the Purser's Shop, for clothes for Alasdair.

Rob had given Alasdair and Conn the go-ahead to spend more time up and out of bed. Which meant that no matter how handsome Alasdair looked in the robe she'd given him—rather like a figure from a medieval illumination—he needed real clothes.

When he'd come downstairs for the first time, Garland had felt a little like Mrs. Van Winkle introducing Rip to the wonders of modern technology that he'd missed out on during his twenty-year snooze. Even the refrigerator had surprised and confused him though oddly enough, cars and passing airplanes had not. She puzzled over his bizarrely selective technical amnesia as she reminded him not to stand in front of the freezer with the door open when he wanted to cool off. She had measured him because she wasn't sure that he could handle a shopping trip, even to quiet, off-season Mattaquason.

The sun was finally out after two days of rain that had culminated in a ferocious storm last night. Garland lifted her face to it as she walked. Well, the equinox would be here in a few days. Winter couldn't last forever. Not even this one.

The woman behind the counter at Vernon's Five and Ten peered at Garland from behind a pair of enormous glasses. "All-cotton thread? I think so. You'll have to look. All the dry goods are in aisle three, 'bout halfway down. Say, are you the lady that's moved into town with the quilts? I saw that story on you in the paper. My sister-in-law's a quilter, too. There's a quilt guild in Brewster she belongs to. You oughtta check it out some time. I'll tell her you were in here."

After Garland had found and paid for her thread the clerk gave her a radiant smile and fished out her cell phone. As the door swung shut, Garland could just hear her say, "Maureen? Guess who I just met?"

In the library, Garland returned a book that had somehow been overlooked last August and spent the winter on her bedside table. The volunteer behind the desk looked at the due date stamped in the back and raised her eyebrows.

"Things were a little hectic when I left last summer," Garland explained defensively.

"Mm-hmm." The woman scanned the barcode on the book and glanced at the screen on the circulation desk's computer. "Well, after ten weeks we have a maximum late fine of—oh my goodness, you're Garland Durrell! You're on the board of the Friends of the Library, aren't you? No late fees for you, Mrs. Durrell." The woman patted her blue-rinsed hair and beamed at her.

"Actually, I'm not on the board any more. I resigned last fall." Garland dug her wallet out of her handbag to pay the late fee. She'd given up all the board positions she'd formerly held. There would be enough alimony from Derek to live on until she hopefully started selling quilts but not enough to maintain the high level of charitable giving that being on boards usually entailed.

"I was so sorry to hear that. The library will miss your generosity, especially just now with the anniversary plans heating up for next fall. But your quilting, now—I did enjoy the story in the paper. After I read it I told my husband, 'I *did* have to go and have an appointment down in Hyannis with the podiatrist on the day of the Women's Club meeting and miss seeing Mrs. Durrell's quilt, didn't I?' I suppose I'll just have to wait for your show this summer."

"Er, thank you—"

But the woman hadn't finished. "Aren't you down on Eldredge Point? How did you weather the storm last night?" She leaned on the counter and spoke in lower tones. "Did you hear about what happened down near Uncle Eb's Beach? Seems like the wind was just in the right quarter with the waves, and dug the bank on the northern end out in a matter of hours. The Swains' house went right into the drink. Mr. Swain got out all right but they're still looking for his wife. They're both in their eighties and she was dreadfully crippled with arthritis. Just terrible. I've always said that building so close to the water is a bad idea. But that house was over a hundred and fifty years old.

You would have thought that if something like that were going to happen, it would have happened already. Just terrible," she said again.

Garland finally escaped after another five minutes of being enthusiastically talked at by the volunteer ("My name's Shirley. Actually, both of them are. Shirley Shirley. I almost didn't marry my husband because of it, but I'm used to it now.") and after having her fourth attempt to pay the late fee refused. She took a few deep breaths on the library steps, then headed for the Purser's Shop (*Fine Gentlemen's Clothing, est. 1921.*)

Garland found herself drifting to the soft, handsomely tailored designer-label khakis and pinpoint-weave button-down shirts rather than the more utilitarian athletic pants and sweatshirts she'd intended to buy. Somehow sweats and Alasdair just didn't go together. He was too elegant, too unconsciously dignified, even when peering in amazement at the toaster as it popped his sixth piece of toast into the air.

In the end, she bought the khakis and oxfords, some soft cotton shirts and pants for Conn and, after much internal argument, a deep green cashmere sweater. She soothed her conscience with the fact that it had been marked down substantially in preparation for the summer season and tried not to think too much about a cashmere-covered Alasdair as she handed the sales clerk her credit card.

The elderly clerk swiped her card through the slot in the register and glanced at it as she handed it back to her. "Thank you, er—oh, Mrs. Durrell! How nice to meet you."

Garland smiled, groaning inwardly. There wouldn't be any escaping that *Mariner* article, would there? She put the shopping bags in her car and fished a different bag out of the back seat, then turned down the hill toward the Captain Hayes Gallery.

The pale sun warmed the salt-weathered, soft gray cedar shingles of the town's buildings, making them shine like old silver. Here and there withered Christmas greenery, brown and shedding its needles, looped around the windows and doors of shops that had closed for the winter after New Year's. But in other windows, signs proclaiming "winter clearance sale—must make room for summer merchandise—BIG savings!" blossomed, as sure an indicator of approaching spring on Cape Cod as robins and crocuses.

Just ahead, three slightly swaying figures stood on the sidewalk in front of the Captain's Bridge, waiting for the pub part of it to begin serving at noon. Fishermen, most likely, come to drink—and in the men's room, snort or inject—up their paychecks until their next trip out. It wasn't surprising that one of the most popular bumper stickers in town read *"Mattaquason…a Quaint Drinking Village with a Fishing Problem."* Garland hurried past them, crossed the street, and blew into the Captain Hayes Gallery on a gust of chilly wind.

"Where's your winter clearance sale sign?" she asked as the chain of Indian brass bells on the door that announced her arrival shivered into silence.

Kathy looked up from the box of pottery she'd been unpacking. Bits of straw were scattered on the floor around her, making the large white room with pickled wood beams look like an upscale horse barn. "Right there by the door, but it's written in Farsi," she said, nodding at a small sign written in flowing, curly script and illuminated with geometric designs in gold, turquoise, and umber.

"Is that what it really says?" Garland put down her bag and studied it.

Kathy rested her elbows on the edge of the box. "No. It

actually says, 'This space intentionally left blank.' I once had a translator overseas who shared my sense of humor. She had her uncle make it for me. So have you been hitting the boutiques, you crazy shopping diva?"

Garland hated shopping, and Kathy knew it. "Not particularly, unless the Five and Ten counts as a boutique," she replied lightly. Hopefully no one would tell Kathy she'd been buying men's and boys' clothes at the Purser's Shop. "Honestly, Kathy, I couldn't so much as poke my head in a shop without someone saying, 'Oh, you're Mrs. Durrell.' That darned article in the paper."

Kathy chuckled. "Local girl makes good. What did you expect?"

"I'm not local. I'm a lowly summer resident."

"Not any more you aren't. People know you from the Historical Society and library. Being successful automatically makes you a local. So what's in the bag, if you didn't shop till you dropped?"

"Some new summer merchandise you aren't having a sale to make room for."

Kathy jumped up from the floor and dusted the bits of straw from her jeans and Peruvian sweater, eyeing Garland's bag. "Ah! Some merchandise? You have more than one?"

Garland smiled and held the bag out to her, then sat down on one of the old church benches scattered around the gallery. Kathy made little sounds like a contented hen as she held up the now quilted and bound landscape quilt.

"I see you figured out how to use your quilt machine pretty quickly. Dammit, Garland, how did you manage to quilt wind into this thing?" Kathy made her stand holding up the quilt and backed several paces away. "Just amazing. Guess I can put the sign up, then."

"What sign?" Garland peered around the edge of the quilt.

"This one. Much better than 'winter clearance', don't you think?" Kathy went over to the old desk that served as her sales counter. She held up a small, discreetly lettered sign that read "Quilts by Garland Durrell."

Garland stared at it until the letters started to blur and look like they spelled something else. That was her. Her name. Her quilts. People wanted to come see her quilts. The ones that she'd made. They weren't sulking that her quilting took up too much time or clogged their sinuses with dust. They liked them.

Kathy was still talking. "—must say, it was nice of Helen Foster to agree to let the quilt hang here for a couple of weeks before she comes to get it. It's hard to advertise if I've got nothing to advertise with."

Garland came back to reality. "You mean you already sold it?"

"I told you that I had a standing order from Sonya Feinberg's friend in New York. And from her friend what's-her-name as well. Lord, I'll have to call her and let her know she's got a quilt if she wants it. *If* she wants it." Kathy snorted. "Agreeing to pay a thousand dollars for a quilt she hadn't even seen yet—I'll guess she wants it. She knows someone else will be looking over her shoulder ready to snap it up if she doesn't."

"*A thousand dollars?*" Garland let the quilt slide to the ground and groped for the bench.

"That was the price both of 'em suggested. Who was I to disagree? Hey, careful with that thing. That's the first payment on our condos in Maui." Kathy snatched the quilt from her and folded it carefully. "You heard me, sweetie. You turned some fabric from your stash and a few hours' work into two quilts and two grand. Now let's have a look at the rest." She stepped back, looking expectant.

Garland bent automatically and lifted the second quilt from the bag. Her brain was spinning, trying to take in Kathy's words. Two thousand dollars? Kathy had sold two forty-by-forty wall quilts for two thousand dollars? "Are you sure about this?" she said from behind the second quilt. "Surely they must have meant a hundred dollars."

Kathy didn't answer.

"Kathy?"

"God damn it," said Kathy's voice, a moment later. She sounded distinctly shaky. "I should have asked for *five* thousand dollars each."

Garland lowered the quilt and looked down at it. She'd used the same idea and scene as the first quilt, but this time the weather was different. Instead of sparkling, dancing waves, fog drifted across the landscape in moist, gray billows. The islands in the background loomed ominously out of the mist. "I like the silver thread I used to quilt some of it with," she said. "It adds a nice touch."

"Nice touch," Kathy echoed weakly. "It's a damned good thing this isn't a bed quilt, because whoever slept under it would wake up sopping wet and with galloping rheumatism. My God, Garland, don't ever make a quilt of hell or we'll have the pope himself knocking on our door wanting to do an exorcism."

Garland laughed. "Oh, come on. It's just fabric. Aren't you getting a little carried away?"

"Me and the entire Mattaquason Women's Club and three extremely knowledgeable New York art collectors? I know they're just fabric, Garland. It's how you choose the colors of the fabric and put them together and—I don't know. They're something else too. They're like a window into the essence of what they depict." She stepped forward and touched the surface of the quilt, then rubbed her fingers together. "I could almost swear it was wet."

"Then you may want scuba gear for this one." Garland put the fog quilt down and bent to the bag again.

"Another? Busy little bee, aren't you?" Kathy's voice was light, but her expression was avid as Garland rose and unfolded the last quilt.

"And?" she asked, holding up Conn's fish quilt.

This time, Kathy laughed out loud. "Well, that does it. You've just gone and guaranteed your popularity in this town."

Garland smiled to herself above the quilt. "I did it mostly for fun."

Kathy shook her head. "Watch this." She took the quilt, went to the window by the door, and pinned it to the display board there, right over a selection of Indonesian carved teak plaques. Then she went out the door, leaving it open.

"Hey, you!" Garland heard her call to the clump of men still standing in front of the Captain's Bridge. "Come tell me if this is straight."

Garland thought about stepping out and murmuring to Kathy that from the look of them, they wouldn't be able to tell vertical from diagonal. But the men had already shuffled across the street and were peering obediently in the window.

"Mother o' God," one of them muttered. "Will you look at that."

"Wouldn't mind seein' the nets look like that, next trip out," marveled another, rubbing his unshaven chin.

"Is it…does it *smell?*" asked a third man, rather the worse for drink than the others. He reached under his orange watch cap, scratched, and blinked owlishly at the quilt.

"Probably better than you do!" crowed another. His companions laughed and jostled him, but kept glancing back at the quilt as if they too would have liked to ask the same question.

"Do you think maybe we could borrow that thing when we go out tomorrow?" said the stubble-chinned man to Kathy when the laughter had died away. "It…well, it looks like it would bring the fish into the nets. I could use a lucky trip just now."

"Ain't there someone else you should be askin' about that?" said the orange-capped man with a wink.

An uncomfortable silence met this remark. "You shut your mouth, Joe, and don't be talking about things you shouldn't," the first man who'd spoken finally said. "Is this one of those quilt things my wife was talking about, Miz Hayes? Guess I can see what had her all excited."

"Oh." The man who'd asked to borrow it looked crestfallen. "I suppose you ain't lendin' it out. But will you leave it up so we can come and look at it, sometimes?"

Kathy's voice was grave, but Garland could hear the laughter behind it. "I'll be happy to, gentlemen. Now, if you'll excuse me—" She came back into the shop, grinning from ear to ear.

"That's probably the first time most of those men have so much as looked in my window. Now they'll probably be here every day," she said. The little llamas on her sweater looked as if they were dancing as she laughed.

"Why aren't they out fishing?" Garland watched as another pair of flannel-shirted men joined the group at the window, their eyes wide.

"Storm last night, remember? Too rough out there till the waves subside. Come on, help me move some things so I can hang the other quilts and clean up this dump. Things are going to get busy once word gets out."

"Speaking of the storm, did you hear about those people whose house fell in the water?" Garland followed Kathy and held a small ladder steady while she climbed it, then accepted the baskets Kathy took off the wall and handed down to her. "What an awful thing to have happened. That poor woman."

Kathy dropped a basket and cursed under her breath. Garland picked it up and set it with the others. "This is getting kind of spooky, don't you think? First Alasdair and Conn wash up on my beach, then that guy who'd been clamming, and now this, all in the space of a few weeks—"

"Forget about it." Kathy's voice was tight and low.

Garland looked up at her in surprise. "What?"

"I said, forget about it. Don't talk about it. Don't even think about it." Kathy climbed down from the stepladder. The llamas on her sweater were no longer dancing.

"But why—"

"Look. Most of the town makes its living through the sea, one way or another, or is closely related to someone who does. They're a superstitious bunch. They don't like to talk about things like that. You'll make enemies if you bring it up, even in passing."

"Then why did the woman at the library—Mrs. Shirley—"

"She's only been here a couple years, since they retired down here. She doesn't know any better." Kathy hesitated. "Especially don't talk about your—your former houseguests."

Garland thought about the bags of clothes in her car and bit back the rest of the questions she had. "All right," was all she said.

Kathy's relief was apparent. "Good. So let's get these babies up on the wall."

࿊࿊࿊

Alasdair stood by the window of his room, staring out at the sky and whitecap-edged water spread before him. There had been a storm last night and he had lain in bed listening to it, sensing the cries and shouts of Mahtahdou's creatures that blended with the wind. It had sounded like the night he and Conn…but no. He was in Garland's house now. As long as they were here within her walls they were safe. Thank Lir she hadn't been out in that storm last night, dining with the healer.

But maybe it wouldn't have mattered. Not even his grandmother had possessed stronger magic. Some magicians used magical wands or rings. His grandmother had knotted a circle of beach grass that had kept Mahtahdou safely enchained for a century. Garland took thread and cloth and turned them into objects of power.

He and Conn had been beyond fortunate to land on her beach. When they were healed they could slip out of Garland's house and be back in their world in seconds. He would find his scattered people in their hiding places and resume their fight. There were only three problems: Garland, Conn, and himself.

Mahtahdou had left him for dead but kept his sealskin, no doubt as a symbol of victory over the selkies. Without his skin, how could he return to his people and live a selkie's life? Without it he was only half a selkie—and only half a lord. Would his people even want him back, lacking as he was?

Then there was Conn. He looked behind him at the child,

wrapped as always in his purple shirt, curled in a chair and absorbed in one of the books with colored pictures that Garland had given him. She and his son had formed some mysterious bond that he couldn't fully understand. What would happen if he took Conn back to the selkie world? With Garland he did things he'd rarely done before—smiling and laughing and…and being a child. Mahtahdou had not only taken Conn's birthright—he had also stolen his childhood.

He hugged Garland's robe closer to him. It made him feel less naked, less incomplete. He could feel it—her power, not as strong as when he touched her but there nonetheless, like a cloak. Like…his breath caught. Like a new skin, to shield him in place of his lost one. Garland possessed a power that defied description. Was there some way he could convince her to use it to help him defeat Mahtahdou and free the selkies? Would she believe that Mahtahdou existed if he told her the truth? And even if she believed him, how could she help? How could they harness the power of her quilts?

He gazed out at the long slender island that men called Monomoyick and shifted his weight uncomfortably. His body ached, but not because of his healing wounds. He ached to feel Garland again as he had the other night, all her softness and her warmth under his hands and pressed so lusciously against him. But he never would again—not if he could help it. He must not—*must* not—let this unexpected desire for her get the better of him. How could he betray the memory of his dead Finna?

Surely when he was stronger, Conn would be able to let go of Garland. And by then he himself would have figured out how to use her power. Then, when Mahtahdou was defeated and he was back in his rightful place, Conn would again be the happy little boy he should be. And he could again take lovers, selkie females who would ease his body's needs. But never love. Not again. And *never* the love of a human—

Downstairs, a door closed. A few seconds later Garland practically danced into the room, her eyes shining, and dropped several large paper containers on the floor near him. Conn set his book carefully down, then held his arms out to her.

"Kathy loved the quilts! In fact, she'd already sold two of them sight unseen! A thousand dollars each!" she announced.

Alasdair felt suddenly ill. "Sold them?" he asked. "Did she have to?"

"Yes, she did. Hello, sweetheart. Do you like that book?" She sat on the edge of Conn's bed and gathered him onto her lap. He wiggled into his favorite position, with his head tucked against her throat. Alasdair had begun to envy him being able to do that.

"You don't understand," she continued. "I've never really earned any money on my own since college. My husband wouldn't let me. And he didn't like my quilting, either. Now that he's gone I can quilt, and it seems like I'll be able to quilt and make money at the same time. It means…it means—"

He held out a hand to her. "I'm sorry, Garland. I didn't understand. With your husband dead, you must find a way to support yourself."

She laughed a bitter-sounding laugh. "Oh, he's not dead."

Not dead? "But you said he was gone."

"We got a divorce. He left me for another—well, I'll be honest—a younger woman."

"He *left* you?" He stared at her clear sea-colored eyes and smooth brow and generous mouth that tilted up at the corners and sturdy, curvaceous body. How could any man have left Garland?

Garland's laugh this time was much less bitter. "Thank you. That's probably the nicest thing anyone's said to me since Rob…well, since the day I found you, anyway." She smiled. "Now I'll go unpack the groceries, and then let's try on the clothes I bought you. You too, pumpkin," she said, bouncing Conn on her knee then setting him back on the bed and rising. "I want to get busy on another quilt before I leave for dinner."

"Are you going out again with the healer?" Alasdair hadn't been able to call him "Rob" the way Garland encouraged him to. He knew that the healer was in love with Garland and didn't like his continued presence in Garland's house.

"Yes, I am." She patted his arm and turned toward the door. She looked so pleased at the thought of spending the evening with the healer. Was she beginning to return his feelings? And why not? She deserved to be loved, really loved, after the way her first mate had treated her.

Garland came back upstairs after a little while and unpacked the paper bundles she'd brought in. He watched her unfasten the little white discs up the front of one of the clothes and hoped his fingers could repeat the action as dexterously. He hadn't really cared about clothes, but she'd been adamant about getting them for him. "You can't wander around practically naked all the time," she'd said to him before she left this morning.

"Why not?" he'd asked, and seen immediately that that was a mistake when her eyes widened in surprise. It had been a good thing he hadn't asked her why she didn't go naked as well in this warm house, which had been the next thing he was going to say.

She'd turned pink and looked away. "It's…I suppose you don't remember, but it's just what we do. We wear clothes."

It was convenient, her attributing his strangeness to a loss of memory. He'd meekly agreed with her, and now he stood, letting her slide the tubes—no, they were called sleeves—over his arms and slip the little discs through holes, so that the short robe stayed closed across his chest. The fabric was cool and smooth on his shoulders as he moved them experimentally.

"Well, I got the shirt right," she said. "Let's try the pants."

She made him put on a strange garment that covered just his nether region, and then something that covered him all the way down to his ankles. He was delighted to see that it had a zipper. He had discovered the one on the edge of his pillow and loved to slide it up and down, marveling at the faint whizzing sound the tiny teeth made as they meshed.

Now Garland stepped back and examined him. He stood still and returned her gaze. She smiled, her head to one side.

"Am I all right?"

"You're perfect." She turned to unpack the other parcels, and he heard her say under her breath, "Even though I think it was a crime to cover you up."

Lir knew he'd rather be in his own skin, too. But he only said, "Thank you, Garland."

He sat back on his bed and watched her help a bewildered but cooperative Conn into his clothes then go over to her quilt tables. He liked to watch and try to see just at what point the power started seeping into the quilts she made, but it was too subtle a process. First there were pieces of cloth, full of striking colors but otherwise ordinary. Then there was a design up on her cloth wall, beautiful but only hinting at what would come. Finally, as she sewed, the power shone through the pieces of fabric, stronger and stronger, until she was done and held up to his astonished view the glowing webs of magic trapped in cloth.

She set aside the pieces she'd already cut for the quilt she'd promised him—all triangles and diamonds and squares that, when set together, created the illusion of curves in restless motion. He'd been excited when she showed him part of the design on her fabric wall. But clearly her mind was on something else today.

She'd chosen a fabric that she'd explained to him was called batik, made in a far-away place called Bali. He liked that they came from an island. They had a faint background magic all their own, woven of color and sheer exuberance. They also seemed to complement her power, to focus it somehow. She'd used almost all batiks in his quilt.

This batik was a rich spring green, the color of trees in mid-May. Little splashes of magenta here and there made the green sing louder, and the pattern was short and spiky, like the wild cedars that grew close to the shore.

"I thought I'd do something different with this one," she said out loud, half to him. She'd started doing that a few days ago, and he liked it. It drew him closer into her world, and he hoped he'd get a glimpse of how she did her magic.

"Not a landscape. Just color and pattern. It's harder to do because then the fabric is the boss, not the picture in your mind. You've got to listen to what it says to do." She studied the fabric a minute longer, then smiled and turned to her storage boxes. Now was when she usually began to—well, not quite sing, and not quite talk, and not quite hum, either, but some odd combination of the three. It reminded him a little of the ground-nesting bees that sometimes made their hives in sand dunes—a gentle, busy sound, made up of differing tones.

Soon several shades of green cloth, from palest yellow-green to deep pine but all harmonizing with the first batik, surrounded her. She added a few pieces of the magenta, nodded, and turned to her cutting board and picked up her little rolling knife with the blade that was a circle, and which cut through layers of fabric like lightning. Some of men's inventions were so simple yet so clever that it was impossible not to admire them.

After a few minutes of watching her cut fabric his attention tended to wander. She didn't make her little sound when she cut the fabric but stared at it, leaning against the long, clear ruler so that her cutting ran straight and true. Today it occurred to him that perhaps the concentration she used in cutting fabric was when the magic began to enter it. So he watched her closely as she lined up her edges and rolled her little knife across the green cloth. But try as he might, he couldn't quite see it—only sense the growing aura around the pieces.

It was almost an hour later before she clicked the cover back over her knife and straightened her back with a sigh.

"That's my least favorite part," she said, collapsing into the chair at her sewing machine and reaching up with both hands to rub her neck. "I always end up feeling like a piece of rope that's been twisted till it kinks."

To Alasdair's surprise Conn sidled over to her, walking stiffly in his clothes. He reached up and began to rub her back.

Garland smiled and let her hands fall. "Mmm. How did you get to be so good at that?" she asked him. "You can rub my back any day you want."

Before he could stop himself, Alasdair was behind her. He touched Conn's shoulder and nodded him back to his chair, then took over.

Garland sat up straighter as his hands settled on her shoulders. "I'll be all right—you don't have to do that," she said, sounding suddenly breathless.

"It is no trouble." Her tight muscles warmed and softened as he worked them, and gradually she relaxed back against her chair. She felt so warm and solid and good under his hands. "Unless you would rather I didn't?" he asked, pausing in mid-knead, suddenly uncertain.

"Tease." She made a soft, amused sound deep in her throat. "Don't you dare stop. No one's done that since…since I can't remember when."

He rubbed lower, just under her shoulder blades, and she groaned and leaned forward over the sewing table. "Not even your husband?" he asked.

She snorted. "*Give* a massage? Derek? I don't think so."

"He did not give much, did he?"

"Not unless he could get a receipt and write it off his taxes."

Sometimes she said perplexing things like that, but he thought he understood the spirit of it. "May I ask…he didn't approve of you making quilts, you said. Why not?"

Garland was silent for a moment. "I'm not sure," she said at last. "A lot of reasons, I expect. Derek didn't like the idea of making things if he could buy them. People might get the idea that he couldn't afford something if he made it. I think that went back to being poor as a kid and wearing made-over clothes from the Salvation Army instead of brand-name jeans."

"He couldn't overcome his past," Malcolm said. "But what about your quilts?"

She sighed. "I wasn't supposed to attract attention away from him, and having a career of my own might do that. For a while that was okay because I didn't know any better and because Derek was so charming and I loved him. Only after a while it began to wear a little thin. I have to make quilts. I have to create things, or else I shrivel up inside. So I made a few, and attracted some attention with them, and Derek smiled and said how proud he was of me in front of everyone, but inside I knew he was seething."

"He was jealous." He pulled her back up and went to work on the muscles at the base of her skull.

"God, that's so good…he was jealous of anyone who stole his limelight. He developed an allergy to dust, and got his doctor to tell me that having too much fabric and working with it in the house was making his condition worse."

"He didn't have the courage to tell you himself he didn't like your quilt-making?"

"Of course not. Why do something unpleasant when you can get someone else to do it for you? That was Derek's motto. Do you know who told me he wanted a divorce?" She leaned her head further back and opened her eyes, fixing him with her blue gaze. "His mother, if you can believe it. Of course, that was after his girlfriend told me in the middle of an aerobics class that he was moving in with her and could I have the cleaner send his shirts to her apartment from now on."

She had every right to be bitter. With all that magic within her, needing an outlet and not finding one, it was amazing that she hadn't exploded. And then to be discarded like that— "He did not deserve you. He did not understand what he had when you were his," he said fiercely.

"Alasdair." Garland shifted in her chair, and he realized that he had stopped rubbing her shoulders and was gripping them tightly. Possessively.

"I'm sorry," he muttered, and forced his hands to relax.

9

"DRAT THAT phone anyway," Garland took her foot off the pedal of the sewing machine and pushed her chair back.

"Would you like me to answer it?" Alasdair set the iron down and turned to her.

"No, that's all right. I need to put a phone back in here one of these days." She hurried out of the room and down the hall to her bedroom, smiling to herself. Alasdair had come a long way, from being terrified of the telephone's ring to being willing to answer it. And not only that. Now that he didn't need to spend all his time resting in bed, she'd taught him how to press the seams of pieces of quilt as she sewed them.

She'd found, to her surprise, that she liked having Alasdair and Conn around while she worked. Conn was her cheering section, gazing with rapt awe at every seam she completed. And

Alasdair seemed to know intuitively when it was all right for him to ask questions and when not to distract her. She realized that she enjoyed discussing her designs and choices with him and teaching him about color theory and how to create the illusion of movement and weight and light with design. Quilt piecing was usually a solitary activity, unlike quilting a completed top in a quilting bee. It was nice to have company for a change—company that she felt so relaxed and at home with. Company that she didn't have to perform for or be perfect for.

Some days when she was in her color trance she wouldn't say a word to either of them for hours, and it didn't matter. She'd emerge from her trance and find Alasdair still there, patiently watching her with his glowing brown eyes. His presence was like a…oh, like a safety net. Somehow she felt better knowing he was there.

The phone was still ringing. She sat down on the edge of her bed and answered it.

"Garland? It's Elizabeth Souza, from the library."

Elizabeth Souza—never Betty or Liz—was the president of the Friends of the Mattaquason Library. She was all of four feet eleven inches, with a personal dignity in inverse proportion to her height. Even Derek had deferred to her. "Elizabeth, how nice to hear from you. How are you?"

"Very well, thank you. Shirley Shirley said you were in the library the other day."

Garland decided not to mention the seven-months-overdue book that had brought her there. "I was. And I'd love to volunteer again, once I'm a little more settled—"

"Oh, I'm sure you will. We've had some trouble with filling in volunteer staff for the Circulation Desk on Friday afternoons if that would suit you. But that's not what I'm calling about. As you know, the library celebrates its hundred-and-twenty-fifth anniversary this coming fall."

Garland closed her eyes. "I know it, Elizabeth. I'm afraid that I can't make as generous a contribution to the annual fund as I have in the past. My circumstances have changed—"

"Yes, yes, my dear. I know all about that. Contributions of any size are always appreciated. But I'm not calling about that, either."

"You're not?" she blurted before she could stop herself.

Elizabeth actually sounded amused. "No. Several of the trustees have come to me over the last week with a proposition. They've seen your quilts and think it would be an excellent idea if we commissioned one from you for the library's anniversary. It would hang in the lobby, above the front door. Something colorful but restrained, of course, in keeping with a library atmosphere. I brought a stepladder in this morning and measured the space, and a piece about six feet square would do nicely. We can't offer payment in keeping with what they say Ms. Hayes is charging for your work"—she gave a slight indignant sniff. Garland wasn't sure if it was for the trustees or for Kathy—"but we hoped that perhaps, in view of your years of commitment to the library as an institution and your past generosity, that you'd take a smaller fee and consider the rest as a donation."

Garland was glad that she was sitting down. "You're commissioning me to make a quilt for the library?"

"I've not yet had the pleasure of seeing your work, but when five trustees independently suggest it, I feel I must listen. Jeanette Sims threatened to not give to the anniversary fund if I didn't call you and ask if you'd be interested in doing this for us."

"She didn't!" That must have caught Elizabeth's attention. Mrs. Sims was both very rich and very under Elizabeth's thumb.

Another sniff. "I'd like to be able to present a design to the Board for its approval at our meeting in May, if that's possible." It was not a question.

"I, uh…that will be fine, Elizabeth." Garland's head was spinning too fast to think of any possible objections.

"Good. We have a tentative date of the second weekend in November for our Friends celebration. I trust you can be finished by then?" Elizabeth didn't wait for her confirmation. "I'm glad it's settled. It will be nice to have something done by someone who's a part of the town rather than an outsider. I'll call you in a few days, shall I, to see how you're coming along?"

Elizabeth must have been satisfied with her reply, for she hung up a moment later still sounding content. Garland sat staring at the phone. She'd hoped to sell one or two quilts in Kathy's shop over the course of the summer, and instead she was selling quilts that hadn't even been made yet for thousands of dollars and getting commissions from public institutions. And not just any public institution. What had Elizabeth said? That it was nice that a local person, not an outsider, was doing this? Even the thought of having to listen to artistic input from Elizabeth Souza couldn't take the shine off that.

oge geo

She was still feeling sufficiently buoyant two nights later to invite Rob over for dinner to eat her cooking. She and Derek had spent so much time entertaining and going out to eat that she felt inadequate in a kitchen from sheer lack of practice.

Alasdair and Conn never complained about anything she made for them, but then they never complained period.

"Why don't you come down and join us for dinner tonight? You're already coming down for meals anyway," she asked Alasdair as she gathered up the Storm at Sea blocks she'd pieced earlier that day. He'd hung over her like an anxious parent watching her work, breathing soft exclamations of astonishment when she showed him how the triangles and diamonds created gentle curves.

He didn't look at her. "I think I would be in the way."

"I don't," she protested. "Rob would be delighted to see you strong enough to come down. Come on, Conn. What about you?"

Conn looked mournful and shook his head, then picked up a book and hid his face in it. Alasdair smiled politely and turned back to gazing out the rain-speckled window, and she wondered if he knew about Rob's occasionally-voiced hopes that he and Conn would find another home soon. She knew that Rob had checked back at least four times with Captain Howe, most recently this morning, as to whether they'd found any leads about Alasdair's identity, and received no satisfactory reply. Alasdair had not looked surprised when she told him but had merely shrugged, which surprised her. "Don't you want to know who you are and what happened to you?" she'd asked.

He'd been silent for a moment then said, "You can see what happened to me."

"I mean, find your famil—er, that is, find your home and your friends. And yes, find out who hurt you so they can be brought to justice."

"Justice? Do you think such a thing really exists in this world?" He sounded very tired all of a sudden.

Did she? If there were justice, Derek wouldn't have divorced her and they'd have adopted four orphans from an underdeveloped nation and lavished love and a happy home on them. If there were justice, Captain Howe would have taken charge of Alasdair and Conn instead of scuttling out of her house as if it contained the plague. If there were justice, none of this would have happened to any of them in the first place.

"No, I guess I don't," she finally said. "But that doesn't mean I can't try to achieve it in my little corner, does it? What else can I do?"

He'd looked at her and then over at the Storm at Sea blocks hanging on her design wall, and said softly, "If anyone can achieve justice here, it's you."

The doorbell rang, interrupting her thoughts. "Oops, there's Rob. I wish you'd come down for a minute to say hello." She put her hand on his shoulder and squeezed it gently, then hurried away to let Rob in.

"How's the quilt queen of Mattaquason?" Rob said cheerfully as he blew in on a gust of wind, shaking the water from his jacket before he hung it up. "If this rain and wind keep up, you'll need to teach me how to sail now just so I can make it to the office."

Garland took the bottle of wine he handed her. "Happy first day of spring to you, too. For your information, it often rains like this around the equinoxes. Don't you read the Old Farmer's Almanac?"

"Since I'm not an old farmer, no."

"Ha. Some farm boy you are."

"Ex-farm boy, remember." He gave her a quick kiss. "Something smells awfully good."

"Robert Mowbray, you are without a doubt the sweetest guy

on the planet. But I'd better warn you now that I've not had much chance to cook before." She lead the way into the kitchen.

"That's all right. I'm a doctor."

"And what's that supposed to mean?" She frowned at him in mock indignation.

"Whatever you want it to." He grinned his naughty boy grin and Garland couldn't help melting a little. There was something forever seventeen about his smile, something lighthearted and carefree.

"So what's this I hear?" he asked, going to the drawer for the corkscrew. "You're going to slipcover the entire town in quilts and life in Mattaquason will come to a standstill while everyone stands about and gawks? That might be bad for business in summer, you know."

She made a face at him. "Funny man."

"I'm serious. Elizabeth Souza from the Friends of the Library was in to have a wart removed this morning, and I needn't have bothered with anesthetic because she was still dazed and starry-eyed from stopping in at Kathy Hayes's gallery to see your quilts. She said you're doing one for the library and was nearly beside herself with excitement."

Garland paused. "You're kidding. Elizabeth?"

"I nearly had to sit on her to keep her still, or I might have frozen something else off beside her wart." He chuckled as he uncorked the wine. "So I went down there myself at lunch to have a look."

"And?"

The bantering tone left his voice. "They're something, Garland. They—" He stared at the wine that he'd just poured into their glasses, a faraway look in his eyes. "I can see, in a sort of twisted way, why Derek didn't like you making them. He'd be about as significant as an ant next to them. They're beautiful. No, magical."

Garland busied herself with checking the baking chicken breasts that she'd carefully stuffed with chopped apples and brie. To have other people say such things about her quilts was one thing. To have Rob say them—

"Kathy Hayes couldn't say enough about you and the quilts," he continued in a slightly more normal voice. "I hadn't really ever had a chance to talk to her before. She said she's too healthy to see a doctor."

Garland smiled. "That sounds like Kath."

"She…well, I'm afraid I nearly put my foot in it."

A faint warning chill stiffened her shoulders. "Oh?"

"She seemed to think our friends upstairs were long gone."

Garland went to the refrigerator to get the antipasto platter she'd arranged earlier in the afternoon. "I'm sorry, Rob. I sort of…all right, I lied and told her they were gone. She seemed awfully disturbed about my having them here." An olive rolled off the tray as she lifted it out, and she realized that her hands shook slightly. "What did you say?"

"What could I say?" Rob sighed. "She went on for a minute about not liking the idea of someone taking advantage of your soft heart. I can't help agreeing with her."

Garland put the plate down on the counter. "I'm not doing this because of my so-called 'soft heart,' which by the way is not as soft as you might think. Honestly, what will Alasdair and Conn do if I kick them out now? They're not ill enough to go into the hospital but they're too disoriented to take care of themselves. Alasdair can barely navigate how common household appliances work, never mind searching for his past life."

Rob held up a hand. "Peace. I know he couldn't handle going out on his own yet. But if he's still having that hard a time we could maybe place him in a psych unit somewhere. Cape General Hospital has one, and it's not too far away so that you could visit him whenever—"

"He's not mentally ill!" Garland retorted. "And what about Conn? What will you do with him—stick him in a foster home somewhere? I'm not going to have them put away just because you and Kathy think I can't run my own life—" She turned her back on him and hugged her arms around herself. Damn it, it was up to her whether or not she let Alasdair stay with her. Why did it bother everyone so much?

"Hey." A clink told her Rob had put his glass down on the granite countertop. He came around to where she stood, peeled her arms away and slid his own around her. "I didn't mean to get you upset. We're worried about you, that's all."

She stood stiffly in his embrace for a moment, then relaxed. It was impossible to stay miffed with Rob, especially when he looked at her with that contrite puppy-dog expression. "I'm a big girl, you know," she said. "Despite those years with Derek, I didn't lose all capacity to take care of myself."

"I know you didn't. But Kathy was right. You *are* very kind-hearted. I just don't want it leading you into making mistakes." He reached up to tuck her hair behind her ears.

"My heart's quite well acquainted with the rigors of life, thank you very much," Garland returned tartly.

"So maybe we should be glad that you've stayed kind instead of turning bitter." He ducked his head and brushed his lips across hers. "You know what? It's not just your heart that's soft."

A quick shiver ran through her. "Is that so?"

"Uh huh." He kissed her again, more decisively that time. "Most definitely. And…" He slid his hands slowly down her back. "Mmm. Soft here, too."

His lips skimmed the side of her neck before settling again on her mouth in a firmer, more demanding kiss. She shivered again and her knees went wobbly. Was this it? Had she finally made up her mind to let Rob love her? He'd been so patient, not forcing himself on her. He was another kind man, like Alasdair—

(his warm hands kneading her shoulders, strong but gentle)

—and she wanted to be as eager for him

(his beautiful mouth, so chiseled, so perfect)

—as he was for her

(hot and hungry on hers, taking her lips with a fierce, fiery need. She could feel her bones melting in the blaze of his desire, feel her own flare up to meet it. She'd so longed to touch him, to hold him—her warrior angel, her tall, beautiful brown-eyed stranger—)

"Wow," Rob murmured, breaking the kiss and leaning his forehead against hers. "That was sure as hell worth waiting for." His hands trembled as he slid them up and down her arms. "Who taught you how to kiss like that?"

Garland laughed shakily and turned her face away from him so that he couldn't see the stunned comprehension that surely must be there in her eyes. "A lady doesn't discuss those things."

Which, right now, was probably a good thing.

⁂

Alasdair turned from the kitchen doorway and crept back up the stairs, gently shepherding an indignant Conn up before him. He'd thought they would surprise Garland and come down to say hello to the healer because she'd seemed distressed at their refusal to join them. The healer *had* helped them, after all. They should at least show him gratitude—especially if it would please Garland, who'd given them so much.

So he'd checked himself in the mirror to make sure that his blue cloth shirt was buttoned properly, smoothed Conn's hair, and slowly descended to the ground floor, holding tight to the banister because stairs still made him nervous—there weren't many staircases in his world. He hadn't noticed that the low song of Garland and the healer's conversation had stopped as he crept down, so busily was he watching his footing.

He crossed the hall and stopped in the kitchen doorway, the greeting dying on his lips. Conn made a small, angry-sounding squeak and started forward, but Alasdair pulled him back.

Garland and the healer stood near the refrigerator, wrapped in each other's arms, engrossed in a kiss. The healer's hands moved restlessly over her curves, savoring them as he possessed her mouth like a starving man at a feast. Garland breathed a soft sound that made him ache with both anger and desire. How he wished he could be the one to draw such sounds from her!

Somehow he made it back up the stairs without stumbling and revealing that he'd seen them, keeping a firm grip on a wiggling Conn. Once safe in their room he threw himself onto his bed and stared at the ceiling above him. But for some reason his eyes wouldn't focus properly, and his throat burned.

What was wrong with him? Why shouldn't Garland kiss the healer if she wanted to? The healer certainly wanted to kiss her—Alasdair had seen that as soon as he'd had strength to notice more than his own injuries. The healer burned for Garland like the midsummer sun. Alasdair should be happy that she had found someone who wanted her so ardently.

So why had he felt like storming into the kitchen and snatching her out of the healer's arms?

He rolled over, not minding the twinges of discomfort from his deepest, not-yet-fully-healed wounds. At least it took his mind, however briefly, from the other pain.

Garland had all the right in the world to be loved. After the way her former mate had treated her, she deserved it. The healer could give her that love.

Except *he* wanted to be the one to give it to her.

Humans and selkies had often fallen in love over the centuries. But those pairings had never lasted: a human could not live among the waves and a selkie would not be happy away from them. He could never give Garland the love she deserved; he might not even be alive in a year's time.

But as the sun was his witness, he longed to try.

The doorknob clicked. Conn stood turning it the wrong way, a look of determination on his face. Alasdair rose and pulled him away from the door. "I know," he said gently, hugging the boy. "I don't like it either."

Conn looked at him "Want Garland," he whispered.

Alasdair held him tightly. Why should he be surprised that his son's first words in weeks were about her? "So do I," he muttered. "So do I."

⚘

"I think you were just fishing for compliments before. That was a delicious dinner," Rob said as they finished putting away the last of the dishes.

"You're just lucky my mother gives good instructions over the phone." Garland unobtrusively put away the plate and silverware she'd left out in case Alasdair and Conn had decided to come down for supper. In a way she was glad that they hadn't. She wasn't sure she could face both Rob and Alasdair at the same time.

"Nothing wrong with luck in my book. Shall we put the coffee on a tray and take it into the other room so I can corner you on the couch and see if my luck holds?" With a wolfish grin he used the kitchen dishtowel to rope her into his arms.

Garland laughed and squirmed away after giving him a quick kiss, but her laughter was forced. As large as the couch in the great room was she didn't think there would be room on it for three, even if that third person was only in her head.

What was wrong with her? Here was Rob—sweet, funny, intelligent, good-looking. He was exactly what she needed to teach her how to trust again. To love again.

So why couldn't she get Alasdair out of her head? Why had thoughts of him intruded when Rob kissed her? Why had she only been able to respond physically to Rob by pretending he was Alasdair?

Yes, okay, Alasdair was so beautiful that sometimes while she sat at her sewing machine her breath would catch and she would pause just to watch him—the endearing frown of concentration in his brow as he ironed her quilt pieces, his powerful frame bent to this careful, delicate task as if his life depended on it. As his wounds healed and his strength returned, the aura of power and grace that surrounded him seemed to increase daily. How could she not find him attractive? He was a like a fairy tale prince made flesh and blood.

On the other hand, he was a stranger—she had no idea who he was or where he was from. For all she knew, Rob and Kathy were right, and at the worst he was fleeing from some sinister past—taking advantage of her, using her.

Damn it all, prince charming or criminal, what was it about him that so stirred her to her very core?

She carried the coffee into the great room and set it down on the table. Rob went to the fire and tossed another log on it, then turned to her.

"Garland." He held out his hand.

The dancing firelight cast shadows over him but she could still see the serious set of his boyish face and the need in his slightly narrowed eyes. A shiver ran down her back. Was it of fear or desire? She swallowed and went slowly to him.

"Rob, it's—I—" she whispered as he pulled her to him. "Before, in the kitchen—"

"It's all right," he murmured, stroking her hair. "I'm out of practice, you know. One kiss like that in an evening is all my blood pressure can take at this point. I'm not going to rush you. It'll come. Will you just let me hold you?"

"Yes, that would be…thank you." She rested her head on his shoulder with a little sigh. She should have known better than to worry. Rob would never pressure her into anything she wasn't ready for. Sometime soon she'd kiss him again, and this time it would be *him* she kissed, not a fantasy man—

A sudden, shrill beep split the air. Garland started.

Rob swore under his breath. "It's my damned pager. I swear there's someone out there keeping track of exactly when not to have it go off." He fumbled at his belt and glanced at the pager's display. "Oh God, it's the police department. I'm sorry, Garland, but I have to take this one."

Garland led him into Derek's old office and went back to stand by the fire. But even down the short hallway and through the mostly closed door she heard Rob's exclamation of dismay. Evidently something bad had happened.

Rob reappeared a few minutes later. Garland could see by his shoulders, tight yet drooping, that maybe "bad" wasn't a strong enough word. She went to the table and said, "Do you have time for a quick cup of coffee before you go?"

"Yeah, I'd better. I'm going to need it." His voice was curt.

She looked up from pouring. "Do you want me to put it in a travel mug?"

"Don't bother. My signing the death certificate now or ten minutes from now won't make any difference. He's already been dead several hours."

Garland nearly dropped his cup. "Oh, no! What happened?"

"I'm not quite sure. The officer I spoke to wasn't terribly forthcoming. Something grisly on a fishing boat involving a slippery deck and the captain not realizing that what he'd hit with the propellers wasn't a sand bar, I gather." Rob gulped at his coffee as if the scalding liquid could remove the taste of his words from his mouth.

Garland's stomach clenched. "Who was it?"

"Young man, about nineteen. Just started fishing. It was his uncle's boat, which makes it worse. Dear God." He put his cup down and she saw that his hands shook. "I didn't think I'd have to do this sort of thing in Mattaquason. I hated my rotation in the ER. My job is to heal people, not declare hunks of meat that used to be human dead."

She put down her own cup and pulled him into her arms. "I'm sorry, Rob."

He hid his face against her hair and was silent for a moment. Then to her surprise he drew back and laughed a short, sharp laugh. "I suppose I should have known. It *is* March twenty-first, after all. Do me a favor, Garland. Remind me to make sure you're out of town come mid-September."

A chill prickled the back of Garland's neck. "What do you mean?"

He closed his eyes and sighed. "Nothing. Forget I said it."

"No. Tell me, Rob. I live here too. What's wrong with March and September?"

He opened his eyes and looked at her with a bleak expression. "I've lived in Mattaquason two years now. And for those past two years, some young person in town has died a violent death every March and every September, around the first day of spring and fall. If I weren't a rational man I'd begin to wonder just what the hell was going on here."

10

GARLAND FINISHED quilting the green forest quilt, machine-sewed the binding to it, and set it aside. Tonight she'd flip the binding over the raw edges of the quilt, hold it in place with the metal clips that looked like little girls' barrettes, and blind-stitch it to the quilt backing.

She could have done it all by machine. But somehow this little act of direct handwork, with nothing between her and the fabric but a silver sliver and a length of smooth cotton thread, was important to her. It was work that she liked to do right before she went to sleep because the rhythmic, repetitive motion of hand sewing cleared her mind almost like meditation. She always slept deeply and dreamlessly after binding a quilt.

Deep and dreamless sleep would be a refreshing change.

Ever since her dinner with Rob last week she'd had a hard time sleeping, her mind whirling through the same spirals of thought—the clammer…Mrs. Swain…the boy who'd died on the fishing boat, and the others before him that Rob told her about. Like the boy with a severe bee-sting allergy who'd gone for a walk in a grassy field full of blooming goldenrod on the edge of a salt marsh without his epi-pen kit in September. Or the girl whose car had skidded off an icy bridge into a tidal river last March. Or the surfer caught in an undertow in the aftermath of a nor'easter the September before that. The precision of the dates made it even more horrible, almost like a ritual. Suddenly Mattaquason did not seem like the safe, quiet refuge she'd pictured it as all the long months of hashing out her divorce from Derek with the lawyers. Life was just as ugly and unfair here as it was anywhere else.

But she didn't have the luxury of dwelling on any of this right now. She had to get busy and get another couple of quilts made. Kathy had asked for a new wall-sized quilt for the shop every month until July, not to mention the twelve or fifteen for the show in August. The green one would do for May but she needed April and June, and then more for the show. And the library quilt for September, too… Now let's see, what could she do for September? A nice pictorial quilt of a late season swimmer being attacked by a rogue shark? A skater falling through thin ice on a deserted pond? Why had she made Rob tell her about those deaths after all?

Only when she slipped into her color trance could she escape those worries. What could she do for an April quilt? To her, spring had always been about the return of light, the sun strengthening, the sky changing color. Flowers and birds were the last things to happen. First it was the light, the darkness of midwinter's night giving way—a bargello pattern, maybe, with a series of offset circles to represent the climbing sun, the colors subtly shifting from one end of the quilt to the other. She hefted boxes onto the floor to search through, grays and yellows and finally the palest of greens.

She was vaguely aware of Alasdair quietly picking up the fabrics she chose and pressing them smooth at her ironing board, arranging them on her cutting table so that she could begin to cut pieces as soon as she was ready. It was companionable without being intrusive—a warm, supportive feeling. And Conn—he had taken to curling up as close as possible to her while she looked through her fabrics, like a little cat. But unlike most small children, he didn't squirm or try to distract her. If anything, she could almost *feel* him—well, loving her, offering his snuggles up to her like a soft, supporting cushion.

When she'd accumulated a pile of fabrics, she stopped and scooped the little boy onto her lap. Knowing his mother was gone made her less hesitant to snuggle him, to give him what she no longer could. "Little limpet," she murmured into his dark hair. He smiled and nestled closer.

"How did you know that was his nickname?" Alasdair set down the iron and eased himself to the floor in front of her.

"I didn't. It just seemed—right."

"*Bàirneachag,*" he said softly. "That's how we say it."

"*Bàirneachag,*" she repeated. Conn twisted his head to grin up at her. "What language is that?" Maybe this was a clue, a lead to follow to find their home—

"I don't know what you call it. It's just what my people—" He stopped speaking and looked away.

"Alasdair—" Impulsively, Garland held out her hand to

him. She could almost feel his sudden pain—homesickness, perhaps? No, something deeper, more visceral than that. "I didn't mean to hurt you. I just thought maybe it might help you remember—"

Slowly, he reached out and took her hand in his. He gazed down at it for a long moment, his face thoughtful, then ran his fingers lightly over it and down each finger. When he turned it over and delicately traced the lines in her palm, she shivered. Still staring down at her hand, he said quietly, "I do not think this hand—or its owner—could ever do harm."

She laughed a little shakily. "You have no idea what things I've wished on Derek."

"And I know very well what you've done for Conn—and me," he added, more quietly. "What do your wishes matter, compared to your deeds?" He nodded toward Conn, who had closed his eyes and dozed off in her lap. "You've given us peace—more than he's ever known in his life. I only wish I could give you something half as precious in return."

They stared at each other for a long moment over their clasped hands. Something seemed to shift inside her, like a shoot bursting from its encasing seed and reaching toward the light. Like spring had come again inside her after a cold, bleak winter.

✵

The spring quilt almost seemed to make itself even though it ended up being slightly larger than any of her previous quilts. Even more surprisingly, she had all the colors she needed for it. Considering she used over sixty shades ranging from black to gray, then almost imperceptibly to gold and finally to green, it was nearly miraculous. She kept the quilting simple—this quilt was all about color—and bundled it up to bring it down to Kathy on Saturday morning.

Downtown Mattaquason was much livelier now than it had been just two weeks before. All the leftover Christmas decorations were gone and most of the stores had reopened, if only on weekends for the thin trickle of tourists that came down to take advantage of pre-season rates at the B&Bs.

Traffic had begun to pick up as well, and all the on-street parking near the Captain Hayes Gallery was taken. Garland finally found a place halfway up Main Street. She pulled into it, scooped up the quilt wrapped in a dry cleaning bag, and stepped out of her car into the street. May as well cross now, while there was a lull—

She was halfway across the street, trotting. There wasn't another moving car in sight when she started hardly a second before, but suddenly a large black car was zooming up the street toward her, driving at a speed that would have been more appropriate for the highway than for downtown Mattaquason.

Garland gasped and put on a burst of speed, clutching the quilt to her. But the car sped up too, following her diagonal path—good God, was it *trying* to hit her? She tried to get a look at the driver—was it a drunk or someone on a bad trip?—and just caught a glimpse of a elderly woman with blue-rinsed hair staring at her fixedly with bulging, terrified eyes, her mouth open in a scream even as she steered the car toward her—

☙❧ ❧☙

"Jesus Christ in a Jaguar!" someone said, too loudly. "What the hell happened? Garland, can you hear me? Someone call a doctor, fast."

Garland opened her eyes. She was lying on the ground,

surrounded by several wide-eyed people staring down at her, their hands hanging by their sides. Kathy Hayes knelt by her, looking positively ferocious.

What had happened? Why was she lying on—she squinted up and saw a bright pink and white striped awning—on the ground outside the Mattaquason Candy Castle?

Then she remembered—that car— "Wasn't a Jaguar," she muttered. She felt giddy and disoriented, as if she'd taken one too many breaths of laughing gas at the dentist's. "And Jesus doesn't try to mow down pedestrians, even ones not in the crosswalk."

Kathy's ferocity softened somewhat. "You're alive. Don't try to get up. Can you move your legs? What about your arms? I don't see any blood—"

Garland obediently moved her arms and legs—ohh, was she going to be sore later—then disobediently hitched herself up on her elbows to look at herself. Her vision wheeled for a few seconds and she feared she would throw up right there in front of the Candy Castle. Which surely would not be appreciated, even if there weren't any tourists in sight. Thankfully, the spinning slowed to a halt. "No blood. I'm okay, I think," she said, then remembered more. "Is the quilt all right?"

Kathy was staring at her, white-faced. "I'm still trying to figure out if *you're* all right. I just saw that damned car mow you down going forty. You flew like ten feet and hit the sidewalk. By all rights you ought to be dead or damned close to it. Did anyone get its number?" she demanded, glaring at the small knot of onlookers.

"Didn't have to," said a man. "I know that car. It was Ed Shirley's Lincoln. I almost bought it from him couple years ago until gas prices got so jeezly bad and I changed my mind."

Kathy frowned. "Ed Shirley? What the hell was he—"

"A woman was driving it," Garland said, feeling faint again. She'd thought the face she'd glimpsed through the windshield had been familiar, and she was right. It had been Shirley Shirley, the volunteer she'd met at the library. But why had the chatty, friendly old lady tried to run her down?

Run her down. Someone had just tried to kill her. She shivered and clutched at Kathy's hand.

Just then a police car careened past them down the street, lights and siren blaring, followed seconds later by a fire truck and an ambulance. The crowd watched them pass in silence, their faces curiously uncurious.

"Expect she crashed," another man finally said. A murmur of assent rose and ebbed away.

Good God. Was that all they could say? Garland struggled to sit up, ignoring the way the crowd suddenly seemed to be revolving around her again. "Poor Mrs. Shirley!" she cried. "Don't you care? How can you just stand there like this? Something must be wrong—she must be ill—"

"Garland." Kathy put her arms around her and dragged her to her feet. "That's enough. Come on, let's go. She's still stunned, everyone," she said in a louder voice to the crowd. "I'll take care of her. Sorry to trouble you."

"Trouble them? Kathy, what are you—"

"Here's your quilt, underneath you. It's fine." She handed it to Garland and propelled her the rest of the way down the street to the gallery, muttering to herself.

"Christ, Garland. I run out to the bank for a minute and get to see my best friend nearly..." She bit her lip, fumbling with the key to unlock the gallery's door, and opened it.

"Wait a minute. What about poor Mrs. Shirley?" Garland

tried to cling to the doorframe but Kathy was too fast for her.

"There isn't anything you can do about her," she said and shoved Garland inside. "Come on, sit down. You're whiter than a ghost."

Garland let her push her down on a bench. "Of course I am! A little old lady tries to run me over—I saw her, Kathy, she was aiming for me—and then crashes somewhere, and those people just stand there like it was a mildly interesting show on TV—"

"What did you want them to do? Somebody had obviously already called the police."

"But—"

"Garland, *shut up.*"

"Um...sure, Kathy." Her friend's voice had been so full of compressed anger and fright that there was nothing else she could say.

Kathy stared down at her for the space of several seconds, her face working, then closed her eyes. "I should call Rob Mowbray to have a look at you," she finally said. "Make sure you're all right..."

What if he's down trying to help poor Mrs. Shirley? she nearly said, but didn't. "You don't have to bother. There's nothing broken or anything. I just feel a bit bruised and dizzy, that's all."

Kathy looked relieved. "Are you sure?"

"I'll be seeing him tonight anyway. If something doesn't feel right I'll get him to check me over." Gingerly, she felt her head again. An icepack would be helpful but she didn't need Rob for that. "If anyone needs to see a doctor, it's that crowd out there. And anyway, don't you think it's the police we ought to be calling?"

Kathy didn't look at her. "And report what?" she asked

quietly.

"What do you think? That a car just tried to…" she trailed into silence. That a car driven by a woman who was probably critically injured or maybe even dead by now had tried to run her over? Was she *positive* that Mrs. Shirley had tried to hit her? What if she'd been having a heart attack and couldn't control the car?

"You're shivering. Reaction's setting in." Kathy snatched up a hand-woven Irish mohair throw from a pile and wrapped it around Garland's shoulders. "Stay there and I'll make you some tea."

Garland nodded and drew the blanket closer as Kathy disappeared in the back of the store. Her left hand had a nasty scrape across the back, her head pounded like a kettledrum, and she felt like she'd been tossed into a dryer with a couple of bowling balls, but other than that she'd survived being hit by a car unscathed. It seemed astounding. Completely beyond reason.

"Hey, no tears. You're all right now." Kathy came bustling back, holding out a steaming mug. "Drink some of this. It's sweeter than you like but you need the sugar. I wish I had some booze to put in it too but that can wait till you're home."

"I could have been k-*killed.*" Garland folded her cold fingers around the mug.

"But you weren't, were you?" Kathy's voice was cheerful, but Garland thought she saw a wariness in her eyes. "So what were you doing down here, anyway? A quilt? No, wait a minute. Drink some of that and then you can show me."

"It's the la-latest Garland Durrell Quilt of the Month." She took a gulp of tea and set it down next to her then unwrapped the package she realized she was still clutching and draped the quilt over her lap. "It's for April. I'm calling it 'Spring'."

Kathy didn't say anything.

"Kathy?"

Kathy used a word even more colorful than her usual repertoire. "Damn you for making this one, Garland Durrell, because I'm damned well going to have to blow all the damned commission I've earned from you and then some because I have to own this damned quilt. No one else is going to get their damned hands on it."

Garland laughed shakily. "Gee, I'm sorry you don't like it."

"It's one of the best damned quilts you've ever done!"

She folded it and held it up to Kathy. "If you like it that much, it's yours. I'm not going to sell it to you, of all people."

"Oh, I couldn't." But Kathy's eyes were gleaming as she reached for it.

"Yes you could. Take it." She chuckled weakly. "Though I don't know. Considering what just happened, maybe I should call it 'Equinox' rather than 'Spring'."

Kathy had been refolding the quilt. Now she nearly dropped it and stared in horror at Garland. "No. For Christ's sake, no. How did you—" She closed her mouth and set it in a thin line. "Spring. It'll be called Spring. Now come on. You need to get home and put your feet up."

∽ාⓔ ⓔා∽

Rob had already heard that someone had had a fatal accident downtown that day—a heart attack while driving—but he hadn't heard Garland's connection with it. He insisted on giving her an impromptu physical when she arrived at his house for drinks before their pizza-and-movie date and scolded her for not calling him immediately that afternoon.

"I didn't want to worry you," she protested. Good thing she hadn't told him what it seemed like—that poor Mrs. Shirley had been *trying* to hit her.

"Well, what do you think you've done right now? You're important to me, in case you hadn't noticed. If you ever get so much as a stubbed toe and don't call me, I'll…"

She grinned at him. "You'll what?"

He sighed and shook his head. "Tie you up and beat you with an ostrich plume, most likely."

"Ooh, I'm terrified."

"Good. Drink up—doctor's orders," he said, handing her a glass of wine.

Garland accepted it and wandered over to the sliding doors that led out to his deck. Below it spread one of the many small but deep glacial ponds that studded the Cape. A mist of green, like a gauze veil, hung over the trees and undergrowth around the edges of the pond, and she thought of her Spring quilt and smiled.

"This is a great location. You must love it here," she called over her shoulder.

"It is a pretty view." Rob stood behind her.

"Very pretty. Do you swim in the pond in summer?"

"I wasn't talking about the pond." He patted her bottom.

"Hey, watch it, Doc!" Garland tried to keep her discomfiture out of her voice. "That must be one of the oldest lines in the book."

"What can I say? Go with the tried and true. Besides, I have a strong appreciation for feminine loveliness. Especially yours." He slid one arm around her waist and pulled her against him.

Rob's embrace didn't feel all *that* strange…at least, it could have felt worse. Maybe the last few weeks of taking it slowly between them had begun to pay off. She took a breath and made herself relax against him. "Anyway, you've got a fabulous view. It's always been dark when I've been here before. I guess spring is finally getting here."

"Mm-hmm." He nuzzled her ear. "Do you realize it's been almost six weeks since I brought dinner to your house that night?"

"Is it six weeks? I hadn't really thought about it." Six weeks, then, that Alasdair had been with her. She tried to remember life before him and could only dredge up vague memories of the Chestnut Hill house and the interminable meetings with her lawyer. Alasdair and her new life here were inextricably bound together. "Poor Alasdair," she said aloud.

Rob stiffened. "I was thinking more about us having spent a lot of time together in these weeks," he said.

"Oh, yes, that too. It's been wonderful. I was so afraid that I'd be lonely these first months but I haven't been. Thank you," she added.

But Rob's mood seemed to have changed. They didn't say much in the car on the way to Gianni's pizzeria, which made her feel bad. Why had she immediately thought of Alasdair when it was Rob she should have been thinking of?

So when they arrived at Gianni's and Rob ordered them Chianti and a large "Kardashian" pizza—too much of everything—she laughed and tried to be light-hearted and cheerful. At the movie theater—an old one-screener with red velvet curtains and baroque ornamentation that showed classics and foreign films in the off-season—she snuggled close when he draped his arm around her shoulders. When they went back to his house after the movie and he invited her in for a nightcap, she smiled and said yes. And when their discussion of whether Cary Grant had been better at comedy or action drama had slowed and he took her glass of wine, set it on the coffee table, and kissed her, she closed her eyes and cooperated. Or so she thought.

But after a few minutes of soft, exploratory kisses, Rob pulled away from her and sat with slumped shoulders. "It's no use, is it?" he asked, not looking at her.

"What? What's wrong?"

"That. Kissing you. You don't pull away, but you're not really there, either. I've started feeling like I'm just kissing your body, and that you're somewhere else. And it's always me who starts it, too. I thought that maybe by now…"

"Six weeks," she said quietly.

He looked at her and his furrowed brow smoothed. "Yeah, six weeks. That's almost forever, isn't it?" He chuckled. "I'm sorry, Garland, I'm acting like a horny fourteen-year-old. Six weeks of closer proximity doesn't mean that you're as in love with me as I am with you."

There. He'd said it. Rob was in love with her. Here was validation that she was still attractive and desirable. She should be swooning in his arms, if only from sheer gratitude at his proving Derek Durrell wrong.

Instead she heard herself saying in a too-sincere voice, "It's not that I don't want to love you, Rob. It's…I'm not even formally divorced yet, you know. It's not final for another little while. So I guess it still feels strange…sort of not quite right…I don't know…"

He took her hand—her left hand—and stroked the ring finger. It still had a slight ridge from all those years of wearing Derek's rings—the plain gold wedding band and modest diamond engagement ring that had been replaced every few years with something larger and more ostentatious. They were all in her jewelry box now, their icy glitter forever muffled in a small manila envelope under a tangle of chains and baubles she never wore. She would sell them and give the money to a women's shelter.

"Is it Derek," Rob asked, "or is it something else?"

"Something else?"

"Like—" He met her eyes then looked away. "I'm sorry. I shouldn't jump to conclusions like that. So when is your divorce final?"

"May first." The date had been floating in the back of her mind, quiet but ever-present. After May she would be still be herself, and yet different.

"All right, Garland Durrell. I'll behave myself and back off until May first. But after that date you're fair game. And I'll have you in my sights." He put his arms around her and pulled her close. "Assuming that you don't tell me to get lost, it's going to be an all-out campaign. Just so you know."

Garland rested her forehead against his cheek. His arms felt strong and warm around her and she could sense his desire, held in check for now but very much there, simmering below the surface. She so wanted to respond to him, to give him what he wanted, to *want* what he wanted. To love him. When Alasdair left, maybe she would.

Because surely Alasdair wouldn't still be with her then. Most of the wounds on his body had closed and the worst ones on his feet were healing rapidly. He and Conn wouldn't stay with her forever, even if the thought of their leaving made her throat tight with sadness.

"I understand," she said.

HE HAD GUESSED THEY were looking for him. Now he was sure of it.

Alasdair sat chin in fist and watched the small group of seals swim back and forth in front of Garland's house, just as they had for days. Were they seals or selkies or something else? Mahtahdou's minions had been known to take on the shape of seals—his oldest brother had died when he mistook a group of Mahtahdou's creatures for his own warriors.

But he didn't dare step outside to have a closer look. If he left Garland's house he would be unprotected. And if those were Mahtahdou's creatures and not his folk…he shuddered and turned away, and hated himself for it. This was what he'd been reduced to: a cowering, craven shell of his former self. Torture and exhaustion and guilt had laid him low. While his body was almost healed, his spirit still languished. He needed to build it up again, to be a warrior again.

So why didn't he take his courage in hand and show himself to the seals? Most likely they were his folk: it was daylight, which Mahtahdou's creatures usually shunned. Were Ider and Dynas, his best fighters, among them? What would they do if he ran down the grass and onto the beach, splashing awkwardly into the water like a human rather than a true selkie?

No matter how healed his body was, he was still only half a selkie without his skin. Mahtahdou might as well hold his right arm hostage. How could he lead his people again without it?

His eyes swiveled from the window to Garland's design wall. A pattern of squares and triangles, from deepest indigo to palest turquoise, glowed there: his quilt, the one she'd promised him. The pieces were not all sewn together but he could sense the power already in them, a raw, swirling energy. Was it just the illusion of curves that the different angles gave it or was there something else—something deeper? He stared at it in puzzlement for several minutes then shook his head. Not all the pieces were up yet and the pattern was incomplete. Storm at Sea, she'd called it. With a name like that, he had better be careful with it when it was done.

And he hoped that would be shortly because healed or whole, courageous or cowering, he had to leave. Soon.

He had responsibilities to his people, a family to avenge. And he faced another danger, a danger that had blue eyes and gentle, capable hands, a danger he wanted to make love to for hours till he was exhausted and drunk with their shared pleasure.

But what kind of life could they have together, coming from two different worlds? Would she even believe him if he told her what he was? His only possible proof—his skin—was in Mahtahdou's hands, probably hanging like a trophy in his throne room.

Worse still, everyone he had ever loved had been destroyed by Mahtahdou. Father and Mother and his brothers—Finna—Conn, almost. He took a deep, ragged breath. He could not place Garland in danger just because he loved her. If she were to die at Mahtahdou's hands because of him, it would kill him too.

No, it would be far better if he left, because there was another who looked on her with hunger in his soul. A hollow ache filled him as he remembered the sight of Garland in the healer's arms but he ignored it. The healer would be a good mate for her, would love and care for—

The telephone rang, a new one that Garland had just put in the day before because she said it had a more pleasant sound. He thought it sounded just as bad as the old one but had nodded and agreed with her. He stared at it, then made up his mind and lifted the receiver. "Hello?" he said, just as he'd heard Garland do.

There was a pause. Then he heard the healer's voice say, "Uh…is Garland there?"

Did thinking about a person cause them to call on the telephone? "No, she's not. She went into town to have a mud bath, she said." He had thought about suggesting she have one on the clamming flats right in front of her house, but maybe there was some human rule that required going elsewhere to do it.

"Into town for a mud bath? What the…oh. I think I know what she meant." The healer chuckled, a much friendlier sound than his initial, rather suspicious tone of voice. "I'll bet she's at that new day spa that opened in the old Forrester house. Would you please ask her to call me? I was wondering if there was anything specific she wanted to do this weekend."

Alasdair fought down the impulse to shout, "No, she can't see you!" and throw the phone out the window. "I will tell her that you called," he said instead.

"Don't forget." Was that a note of sarcasm in his voice?

"I won't. Good-bye." Alasdair went to put the receiver back in its cradle.

"Wait a minute. I want to talk to you."

Alasdair paused. What could the healer want to talk to him about? "Yes?" he asked cautiously.

"How are you feeling? What about Conn? Stronger? Back to normal?"

"Conn is stronger. The wounds on my feet are closing well."

"That's great! So what do you think? Another week before you're ready to rejoin the world?" The eagerness was unmistakable.

"I don't know. I've never been hurt like this before."

"I should hope not." The healer chuckled again. The warmth was back in his voice, but it was a false warmth. Alasdair remembered how his father had sometimes sat with his eyes closed when judging quarrels, the better to listen for truth or falsehood in voices. Telephones did the eye-closing for you.

"It's just that…well, don't you think it's time you thought about moving along and getting on with your life? And letting Garland get on with hers before she…before she regrets having you in her house?" The healer sounded almost painfully sincere.

"Wouldn't she tell me if she were?"

"She might. But maybe she wouldn't. Garland is…sometimes I think she's too nice for her own good. I don't want to see her hurt because of it. I've come to care very deeply for her, and I can't help feeling protective of her. You understand, I'm sure."

Oh yes, he understood. He understood all too well. It was clear that the healer regarded him as a threat and wanted him gone. But he had walked in on Garland and the healer kissing, not the other way around. Why didn't the healer feel more secure about his place in Garland's affections?

"You don't have to decide anything this minute," the healer continued when Alasdair didn't reply. "Just think about what I've said. When the time comes, I'll be happy to help you settle elsewhere. Up closer to Boston, or anywhere else if there's something you'd like to get away from on Cape Cod."

There it was, the perfect escape. He could tell Garland the healer was helping him and Conn. Then, if they disappeared, maybe she would think that…but what did it matter what she thought? He would be gone.

"She's been under a lot of stress recently," the healer was saying. "Her divorce, and the accident—"

"What accident?" he interrupted.

"She didn't tell you? See, that's what I mean—she's too nice for her own—"

"*What accident?*" Alasdair didn't raise his voice. He didn't need to.

"Er…" For the first time the healer sounded unsure of himself. "It was the other day. She was hit by a car when she went to bring a quilt to her friend Kathy's—nothing serious, obviously—she didn't even call me when it first happened."

Alasdair couldn't help enjoying the hint of hurt in those last words. "Who did this to her?" he growled.

"An elderly lady—she suffered a heart attack and lost control of her car—she hit Garland, probably just a glancing blow, but still—"

A chill went down Alasdair's spine.

"—Garland's fine, obviously. Still, you see how stressful her life is right now—"

"Thank you," he said, keeping his voice as steady as he could. "I will think about what you have said. And I will tell Garland that you called." Before the healer could say anything else he pressed the button on the phone to turn it off and stared at it with a frown.

Why had Garland not told him about being struck by a car? Of course she had not been hurt. Not if she had one of her quilts with her. But who would have done such a thing to her? Why?

An old lady lost control of her car…she hit Garland… The words echoed in his mind like a frost-laden wind. He remembered the menacing, creeping fog that had tried to get into Garland's house and couldn't. Had Mahtahdou figured out whose house it was and guessed whom it might be sheltering? Blessed Lir, had he endangered her already?

He had hidden behind her long enough. She had given— healing, protection, nurturing for both him and his son—and he had taken. He looked across the room again at his quilt. Yet something else Garland was giving, something he had cold-bloodedly asked for. It was a wonder he wasn't choked by his own shame.

If he could not give her his love in return for all she had given him, then he could at least make sure that she could live her life unmolested by Mahtahdou. Once he had left her,

Mahtahdou would leave her and Mattaquason in peace.

⁂

Mermaids of Mattaquason was delightful. Garland liked the new day-spa's pale green and aqua underwater-themed décor and the heated massaging pedicure chairs and the sea mineral facial. She was less delighted with the musty-tasting detoxifying seaweed tea that the spa technician gently bullied her into drinking quarts of—Kathy kept pouring hers into a large potted *dracaena* when no one was looking—and with the lecture about Rob that Kathy had decided to give her while they were immobilized in their foot baths.

"He's crazy about you," she said. "I've never seen anyone fall so hard."

"And?"

"And?" mimicked Kathy. "And why, whenever we talk about him, don't I see the least hint of a sparkle in your eyes? He'd be good for you, Garland. Why aren't you giving him more of a chance?"

With some difficulty Garland kept her voice from being too defensive. "I am, Kathy. He and I have discussed it already. My divorce is final in May. I need till then to—I don't know. Belong to myself again."

Just then the spa technician came in with more tea and Kathy grumbled into silence. Garland was left in peace to think about what she'd just said. Was that what it was? Did she need to reclaim herself as Garland before she could think about letting anyone else lay claim to her?

She was still thinking about it while she drove home, pulled into the driveway and parked, and picked up the bag with the fish-shaped bath sponges she'd bought at the spa for Conn. She climbed out of the car and stopped in surprise. The front door was wide open.

Odd. She'd closed it when she'd left, hadn't she? She must have—ever since all the had vandalism started she'd been ultra-careful about locking doors just in case. She went inside, shut the door, and called, "I'm home," just as she always did. Usually Conn would come trotting out from wherever he'd holed up, usually with one of her collection of children's picture books, and hug her hello then investigate any bags she might have brought in with her.

But no Conn appeared.

Instead, Alasdair came to the head of the stairs and carefully descended, hanging on to the banister as he always did. "The healer called on the telephone," he said. There was an odd note in his voice that she couldn't quite decipher. "He asked that you call him back."

"Oh. Thank you for taking a message." Alasdair hadn't done that before. Maybe he was remembering how daily life worked. "Is Conn upstairs? I brought him something to play with in the tub." She set her foot on the bottom stair.

"No—he is down here with the books." He took a deep breath. "Garland, I have been thinking—"

"Conn? Yes, I'm listening, Alasdair—go on, what have you been thinking—*Conn!* Probably hiding, the little dickens. I guess *somebody* doesn't want to see what I brought him," she called in a louder voice.

"The healer told me that he could find a place for us to stay while I—while I get myself going again. So that we no longer must impose on you."

What *had* Rob said to him on the phone? "Impose? Don't be silly. You're not an imposition. I like having you and Conn here." She left the stair and went into the great room. "Conn, come out now. I have something for you."

Alasdair followed. "Please, Garland. We are grateful for what you have done for us. But it is time for us to go."

Garland stood still. She'd known it would happen sooner or later. And maybe it would be for the best if he left and she stopped pretending that he was hers. "I…I understand. You have your life to get on with," she said carefully, looking out the sliding doors at the dried brown lawn that hadn't yet wakened in this wet, chilly spring. She knew how it must feel.

He gripped her shoulder. "That's not what I meant—gods, if only I could stay here with you…if you and I could…"

If only he could stay…a sudden rush of warmth went through her. "If we could what?" she asked eagerly, turning to him. As she did, a movement outside the sliding doors caught her eye.

A small figure was running up the lawn from the beach. Its short arms and legs pumped frantically, and something purple billowed behind it like a superhero's cape: Conn, in her flannel shirt with the Compass Rose square over his clothes.

"What the…?" She reached for the nearest sliding door. "Did he tell you he was going out?" So that was why the front door had been open—Conn had evidently decided to go for a walk. If only he'd delayed his return another moment or two, until Alasdair had told her what it was he wished they could do. She unlocked and slid the door open a crack and turned back to him.

Alasdair was staring out at Conn with a look of deep horror on his face. For a moment she was sure he was about to collapse; then he pushed past her to the door and shoved it wide.

As Conn approached the terrace she saw that he wore an

expression almost identical to his father's, terror and loathing mingled. He was filthy, bedaubed with blackish slime and muck as if he'd been rolling in something unspeakable left by the tide, and a long, livid scratch ran down one cheek. In his hand he clutched a bunch of half-opened daffodils.

Garland ran out onto the terrace. "Conn! What happened?"

He launched himself at her, sobbing incoherently. She gathered him close despite the disgusting, putrid-smelling ooze that covered him and kissed him. "It's okay, honey. I'm here…you're all ri—"

"Inside!" Alasdair barked from the doorway. "Get inside, now!"

Garland lifted Conn onto her hip and looked back at him. "He's okay, Alasdair. What's wrong?"

"Garland, come in. Now. Please." Though his voice was calmer, he still wore that expression of fear.

"Come on, big boy," she murmured. "How about a nice warm bath? What were you doing, wandering off without telling anyone?" Still muttering soothing nothings, she carried him inside.

Alasdair nearly slammed the door shut after them, locked it, and yanked the curtains across it. Only then did he turn to her and Conn. "*Oganach*," he said softly, taking Conn from her. "Why did you go out there?"

Conn sniffled and hid his face, and shoved the flowers toward Garland.

"Thank you, Conn," she said. "They're beautiful." They were also probably from the Luffords' yard next door, but they were never around until June and wouldn't notice. "Did you fall down and hurt yourself?"

Alasdair's face tightened. "He should be cleaned. This—this

filth will burn if left on the skin.”

Garland opened her mouth to ask him how he knew and where Conn had been to get it on him, but his expression made her change his mind. At least until Conn was scrubbed.

They brought him upstairs and bathed him twice, and Garland ran the purple shirt through the wash so that he could have it back again. While she helped clean and comfort him, she watched Alasdair. He had been about to say something important when Conn came in, and then had reacted very strangely to Conn’s misadventure. Once the boy had fallen into an exhausted sleep on her bed, wrapped in her shirt and down comforter, she went in search of him.

He was standing in front of her design wall, staring at the Storm at Sea quilt as he often did. But she had the sense that he had been waiting for her, for he turned and looked at her without surprise. Before she could say a word, he spoke.

“I knew it before, but it is made clearer now by what happened to Conn. We must leave, and the sooner we co, the better it will be.”

She came to stand next to him by the design wall. “What’s made it clearer? What does a little boy wandering off to pick flowers have to do with it?” She looked down and almost whispered, “Why can’t you stay here with me?”

“Garland…” He touched her shoulder, and when she looked up at him he rested his hand against her cheek, as he had when they’d first met on the beach…but this time it *was* a caress. “I don’t want to leave. I—” he swallowed. “If I stay here, it will be bad for you.”

“Isn’t that up to me to decide?”

He smiled, but pain and longing dimmed his eyes. “No. In this instance, it is not.” He traced the line of her cheekbone then let his hand drift up into her hair. His fingers trembled. "But I would ask a favor of you. Will you finish the gift of your quilt to take with me when we leave?"

"But I don't want you to leave," she whispered, reaching for him. "I lo—"

He pressed his fingers against her lips, stopping the words. "Please, Garland. Don't make this any harder for me than it already is."

She took a breath, and another. "I'm sorry," she said against his fingers, and he let his hand fall.

"Then will you finish the quilt?" he asked gently.

She nodded.

She went back to work on Alasdair's quilt, standing at the cutting table so that she would not have to look at him. She picked up her rotary cutter then put it down again because her hands were shaking. She had been a heartbeat away from telling him that she loved him. The thing that had sprouted within her as he'd held her hand had come into leaf.

This was crazy. Rob was the one she was supposed to fall in love with. Rob, not Alasdair.

All right. So maybe she had a school-girlish crush on him. Or maybe something more, some deeper and richer emotion. And maybe he even felt the same for her.

But he was going to leave and return to his old life, wherever that was, and there wouldn't be room for her in that life. They both had to set aside whatever feelings they had, pick up their pieces, and go on.

She stared down at the piles of triangles and squares neatly stacked to one side of her cutting mat, all in shades of blue and turquoise. Storm at Sea. How appropriate this pattern had turned out to be, with storms within and without...

A memory came to her of a Storm at Sea quilt she'd seen a few years back in a quilting magazine, an otherwise-ordinary quilt with one difference. The quilt's maker had played with the angles that created the illusion of curves, and pieced a heart into her quilt, keeping the pattern and using only contrasting colors to form the design within the design.

Sorting through the cut fabric, she found pieces of the right shape and similar dark turquoise, and constructed a heart like the one in that other quilt. Then she fit it into the already laid-out pieces on the design wall. Surrounded by all the other shades of blue and green, it could only be seen if you knew where to look. The heart of the storm.

She stepped back to survey it. There. Schoolgirl crush or something more, she would still give Alasdair her love whether he knew it or not.

12

ON APRIL 29TH, Rob called.

It wasn't as if he hadn't been calling all along. She'd seen him several times since the night they went to the movie when he'd made his declaration. They'd gone out for brunch and to a fundraising dinner for the Historical Society and to a local quilt show up in Wellfleet. He had been much his usual self, smiling and pleasant if restrained, only giving her chaste pecks on the cheek when saying hello or goodbye. But as soon as she heard his voice this morning on the other end of the phone, she knew something had changed.

"Hi, Garland. So, uh, I was wondering…are you doing anything special for dinner the day after tomorrow?"

"Hmm. Would that be the evening of May first?" She stuck her needle into Alasdair's quilt and leaned back in her chair, trying to match his casual tone.

"As a matter of fact, it is."

"The first...yes, I think I'll be free."

He laughed. "I know you will. In all senses of the word. That's why I'm calling."

"You're not wasting any time."

"Why should I wait any longer than I have to? Actually," his voice sobered, "I'm not calling from entirely selfish motives. I thought you might like some company to mark the occasion. It's a milestone in your life, after all. The world makes a fuss over the start of a marriage but always turns its back on its ending. And anyway, it's as much a beginning as it is an ending. I'd like to celebrate your new beginning with you."

She felt teary-eyed all of a sudden. He was right. The quilt was nearly done, and Alasdair would leave. It was time to think about new beginnings. Especially with Rob.

She looked down at Alasdair's quilt, all pieced and sandwiched with its batting and backing fabric in her hand-quilting frame, a cross between an easel and a stretching rack. She supposed she could have quilted it by machine, which would have only taken a day or two. But machine quilting wouldn't have been right for this quilt. The fact that hand quilting took longer had nothing—nothing!—to do with it.

But she wondered if she shouldn't have compromised her artistic principles and quilted it on the machine. Then Alasdair and Conn would have left already and she could file these last weeks away as an interesting episode in her life, the Time I Found the Perfect Man On My Beach or something like that. More importantly, she could begin to recover for the second time in a year and a half from being left by a man she loved. May first would be the day she was officially free of Derek.

Maybe it ought to be the day she renounced Alasdair, too.

"Oh, Rob, that's really sweet," she said. "Thank you. I would like to have dinner with you."

"Then I'll come get you around quarter to seven. Love you, Garland." He hung up before she could respond.

Garland switched off her own phone and sat staring at it in her lap. Sweet, kind Rob. He would wipe away the memories of the other men who had so bruised her heart. She could start to forget, to pile the rest of her life on top of the memories the way an oyster secretes layers of mother-of-pearl around a grain of sand in its shell.

She picked up her needle once again, took a deep breath, and dove back into Alasdair's quilt. Storm at Sea. She'd always loved the pattern but had never made one. The time had just never been right, and other ideas and projects had clamored for her attention first. So when she'd decided to make it for Alasdair because of the manner of his appearance, she'd decided to make it as well as she could. All those blues and aquas that she'd loved and accumulated for years had been put into this quilt so that it was an ocean of color, of the sea in all its moods. When she'd laid out the fabrics for it she'd felt like a mermaid diving through endless indigo depths or frolicking in tropical turquoise surf.

And like King Midas whispering the secret of his donkey's ears to the reeds, she'd confided her feelings for Alasdair to the fabric, pouring into the quilt all the tenderness and passion and simple joy of being with him that she felt. But unlike the reeds in the legend, the quilt wouldn't tattle. No one would ever know what she felt for him except her and the quilt. It wasn't the most satisfactory confidant, but she felt better for it.

That was why she had to quilt it by hand and let the rest of her love get worked into it, stitch by tiny stitch. No simple echoing the seam lines or "stitching in the ditch" for this quilt. Instead, she was subtly outlining the heart she'd pieced into the pattern with swirls of silver thread, leaving it calm and unquilted—the heart of the storm. The silver thread would be storm winds and rain, and great sweeping curves of shaded blue thread would create waves. She smiled. Would Kathy complain of seasickness if she saw this quilt?

It felt strange not to be quilting a pattern in chalked or penciled lines, to just quilt where and how it seemed right. If she thought about what she was doing too much she would stop, feeling lost and confused. But if she half-closed her eyes as she worked her eleven stitches per inch, not looking exactly at what she was quilting at that moment but letting her mind range ahead, then the designs seemed to flow from her needle by themselves. It was like sitting down to draw with closed eyes and finding when you opened them that you'd made a perfect sketch of the Eiffel Tower.

After a while, she began to feel as if she were dreaming. A vision of being carried on the wind like a feather, swirling and pirouetting on the puffs and eddies of air, made her feel giddy. Yet all the while she could feel the needle in her fingers, the faint prick of its tip on her left index finger under the quilt as she stitched, the slightly rough silver thread no longer catching but gliding, flowing through the fabric. Then, changing to a length of blue thread, she felt as though she were dancing across the tops of storm-tossed waves, leaping from one foaming crest to another or rolling down the billows like a child on a snowy slope. Silver or blue, wind or water, she was reaching out to catch the essence of wild weather and capture it in patterns of thread.

֍

Rob was a few minutes early picking her up but she was ready.

"I made you and Conn tuna salad plates, and there's plenty of bread for toast. No knives in the toaster, please. And don't wait up. I'll probably be late," she said to Alasdair, who stood in the kitchen watching her.

"I…yes. Thank you for telling me." He did not meet her eyes. She'd not told him she was having dinner with Rob but he'd probably figured it out.

She and Alasdair had been even more distant with each other since the day Conn had gone flower-picking. Or maybe it would be more true to say that she had been more distant with him. Only when she'd been working on his quilt had she let her feelings for him out, like a prisoner let out of a cell for fresh air. But that morning, looking at the quilt, she'd realized she was nearly done. Another two days of work and the prisoner would be walled up in the cell forever. Alasdair would leave, and she could concentrate on falling properly in love with Rob.

The day had been bright and sunny, perfect May Day weather, and the evening still held some of the day's golden warmth. Garland wore a linen dress with a long jacquard shawl in shades of olive, rose, and amber. Rob's eyes gleamed as he opened the door for her. "You look incredible," he said, pausing for a kiss. "I wish we could just go home and have pizza delivered at some point."

"Aren't you hungry?" She returned his kiss, wondering if Alasdair was watching from the window.

"Oh, yeah. But I suppose we have to eat." Rob squeezed her arm and gave her a wicked, lop-sided grin.

At the Coq d'Or they had wine and an earthy tapenade spread on slices of toasted baguette at a table basking in the last of the rosy evening light, and a rich duck confit tart and bouillabaisse. Rob's eyes on her were almost as warm as the setting sun, and his hand kept straying to play with the fringe on her shawl.

"Would you like dessert?" he asked after their dinner plates were removed. "Or if you want, we can have coffee and whatever back at the house."

It wasn't hard to guess which alternative he preferred. It also wasn't hard to guess that coffee might not be all he wanted to have. She hesitated, then remembered that this was the night she was making herself begin to forget. "Let's do that."

They drove back to his house mostly in silence. Rob drove one-handed, holding her hand. He pulled into his driveway and turned off the car. "Well," he said, smiling at her. "Here we are."

She returned his smile and took a deep breath. "Here we are."

He watched her for a brief moment, then reached over with one hand and cupped the back of her head before leaning in to kiss her—not a peck this time, but a full-on, this-means-business kind of kiss. She closed her eyes and let him take her lips, resolutely shutting out all thoughts of another mouth, another man.

"Garland..." he murmured, dipping lower to kiss her neck then returning to her mouth. His breath was warm and quick. "Oh God, Garland, to hell with coffee. I want you."

She'd tried, all that evening. She'd tried very hard. But all at once knew she could not—*could not*—get out of his car and go inside with him. She disengaged as gently as she could. "Rob,

I—"

"Garland?" He drew back to look at her, still cupping her head.

"I—I think I'd better go home."

"Are you all right?" His voice was concerned. "Did something at dinner disagree with you?"

It was so tempting to say yes, to say that she suddenly felt sick to her stomach, that maybe she'd had a bad mussel in the bouillabaisse. But she couldn't lie. Not to Rob. "No, I'm all right. Physically, I mean. But I just…can't. I can't go inside with you."

"But…" His hand fell, and he slumped back into his seat. "I see. There aren't just two of us in this car, are there?"

She swallowed. "No."

He was silent for a moment, then hit the steering wheel. "Damn it!"

"Rob—"

"I've planned this evening for weeks, ever since you said you couldn't think about touching another man till your divorce was final. I made sure you had lots of time to absorb that you were through with your ex and would be officially and legally single. That's what you'd said—that you needed time to finish cleaning Derek out of your head, right? Maybe you did, but Alasdair moved right into his place."

"That's—I am not in love with Alasdair!"

"No? Do you swear that you aren't? Can you look me in the eye and say, 'I have no feelings whatsoever for Alasdair'? Can you?"

She looked down at her hands. They were gripping each other tightly. She forced them to relax and took a deep breath. "This is ridiculous."

"Is it? I've seen the two of you, you know. I've watched how he looks at you when you can't see him. And I've seen how you look at him, too. I've seen how you move near him and I've heard your voice when you talk to him. Do you even realize how you act around him?"

"No," she whispered.

"I only wish to God you were the same way with me."

"Rob, listen—it's—it's nothing. He won't stay forever—"

"So you figured that one out, did you? But not before he got what he wanted?"

"Rob!"

"Garland, what am I suppose to think? The first evening we spent together was wonderful. Then suddenly you retreated. It was like he was pulling you away from me, bit by bit. Christ, it's made me angry—you're so vulnerable, and he's been treating you like you're his private property, and you've been powerless to resist him." He started the car. "I'll take you home."

They were silent for most of the drive. Garland huddled in her seat, head bowed. Not until they came to Eldredge Point Road did Rob speak.

"So is he staying or leaving?"

"Leaving." She fought to keep her voice steady.

"When?"

"Another day or two, as soon as I finish making him his quilt."

"Nice of you to offer to make one for me."

She winced. "Rob."

He exhaled. "I'm sorry. That was unnecessary." They turned into her driveway. Rob pulled up to the front door but didn't take the car out of gear.

"You're home," he said pointedly.

She reached down for her purse and opened the door.

"Garland." Rob's voice stopped her.

"What?" She didn't look at him.

"I'm sorry if I said anything that hurt you, but I'm hurt too. Right now I feel like I've just had my skin peeled off. You know my phone number. When Alasdair is gone—*really* gone— you can call me if you want. I will be thrilled and make a complete fool of myself telling you in detail how much I love you and how I've missed you. But I don't want to hear from you until he's gone." His voice was low and steady.

She paused and stared at her feet, already out of the car. "I understand. And—I'm sorry. I truly am."

He didn't say anything more, so she climbed out and shut the door carefully. He did not wait while she fumbled for her keys and let herself into the house.

THE CLOCK IN the front hall said it was just under two and a half hours since Rob had picked her up. It had been a very long two and a half hours.

Garland dropped her purse on the table in the front hall and went into the kitchen. She'd make herself a cup of tea and then sit at the kitchen table and watch it steep itself into inky undrinkability while resting her head in her hands and feeling miserable—

No. No, she wouldn't sit and feel miserable. Rob had been right—she did need to get her past out of her head, the recent as well as the not-so-recent. It was too late to go upstairs and work on Alasdair's quilt, and Alasdair and Conn were probably already asleep. But she could go and clean out Derek's old office so that as soon as Alasdair left she could move the beds out of her quilt room and down here. Welcome to single womanhood, where you got to move your own furniture. Good thing she hadn't let Derek tease her out of taking strength-training classes at their sports club. "Are you trying to be stronger than me?" he'd once asked, pinching her biceps. "Why not just stick to aerobics classes and get some of those hot little thong leotards?"

She hadn't listened. Derek had met his new wife-to-be, Chelsee, not long after that conversation. She'd been a part-time aerobics instructor.

She tiptoed upstairs to change out of her dress and into a t-shirt and old running shorts, got a roll of trash bags from the kitchen cupboard, and flicked on the light of Derek's old office, determined not to think—just *do*.

It felt a little funny to stand in the doorway and look at the enormous desk and leather chairs and tall mahogany bookcases that seemed to scream A Very Successful Man owned them. With the exception of the bookcases and two leather wingbacks, she hated all of it. Nothing could have been more out of place in a seaside home. Kathy had said that her older brother was looking for a new desk for his office and would be happy to take it off her hands. He was welcome to it.

The bookcases would be easy to clear out. Derek had already taken the few things he'd wanted, and all that was left were knick-knacks and photographs. Most of those she unceremoniously dumped into a trash bag: a picture of Derek with a large dead fish at a fishing derby; a picture of Derek with some sports team owner at a play-off game; a picture of Derek presenting a large check to the Mattaquason Historical Society. A very ugly set of bull and bear bookends. A Tom Brady-autographed New England Patriots football helmet which she set aside to donate to the library's silent auction fundraiser in July. Dozens of back issues of *Barron's* and *Fortune*, interspersed with the odd copy of *Penthouse*. A decorative rack of antique golf balls that looked like a row of petrified kiwi fruit.

After a few minutes of sorting and tossing she realized she was humming. This had definitely been the right thing to do after the evening's fiasco. She was in control of her life. Taking this room apart proved it.

She tied up one bag, dragged it to the garage, then looked around the room. Those awful curtains had to go next. She pulled down the heavy maroon paisley chintz panels Derek had chosen and folded them to go to Goodwill. She'd move the bookcases into the great room and paint this room cream and pale sage green, and never let another copy of *Fortune* into the house again.

She double-checked the large credenza that concealed file drawers, but Derek had cleaned those out last fall. Good. She didn't want to have to deal with sending anything to him. So that just left the desk, and presumably he'd cleaned that out too.

Her presupposition seemed to be correct. The large middle drawer contained a few hundred paper clips—did they breed in drawers left unopened too long?—a letter opener shaped like a nine iron, and Derek's Waterman pen, which she tossed into the trash with glee. The two top drawers on either side held odd ends of stationery and ancient receipts from the lawn service and trash hauler. The other drawers held an equally uninteresting mix that also went directly into a trash bag.

Except for the lower right hand drawer.

Garland pulled out a stack of cardboard boxes and glanced inside the top one. Just more stationery with the Mattaquason address imprinted on it. Derek certainly wouldn't need that anymore. She started to dump them into a bag then paused. Might as well save the envelopes. She could put new address labels over Derek's name and use them for bill paying.

When she opened the last box she saw that the envelopes inside it were already addressed. To Derek, at his office. There were at least two dozen of them, and the top one was postmarked last year, just a few weeks before Derek had moved out. As she stared at the round, immature handwriting on the top envelope, she realized what these were: letters from his girlfriend.

Sense told her to return the letter to the box and bury the whole thing in the bottom of the recycling bin. Or better yet, burn it. But curiosity won. She pulled the pages—letterhead from the health club where they'd met—out of the topmost envelope and unfolded them.

And wished she hadn't. Detailed descriptions of ecstatic, juicy encounters in a broom closet at the health club were more than she could stomach, even if they were funny in a sick sort of way. But then from the bottom of a page she saw her own name leap out at her.

i just cant wait until you think its time to finally leive garlind and be with me. You poor baby how can you stand it, i know you married her to get your start in business and all and you have been so pashent and put up with so much all these years. Its about time you realy started living and having a real home life with someone who loves you. When you were saying those things about her the other day i felt so bad it must have been just a misrable life for you stuck in that big house with her and her not respecting you and not wanting to give you any children, i will give you as many as you want i love litle babies and want alot of them remember the docter we went to said i would be a baby machine. i'm counting the days until we can be together forever darling sweety so i can take care of you like you diserve.

Garland stared at the page with the lower case "i's" dotted with little hearts and wondered why all the air had been sucked out of the room, because suddenly she couldn't breathe.

"Garland?"

She realized that she was curled into a little ball on the floor behind Derek's desk, still clutching the letter. Alasdair stood over her looking puzzled, wrapped in Derek's *kanji* robe, and she also realized that he had called her name several times now. She opened her mouth to speak, but all that would come out was a rusty, wordless croak. She looked up at him again and his face blurred and fractured and finally dissolved in a wash of tears.

⁊⁊⁊

Alasdair had watched Garland go that evening feeling as if a battle were going on inside him. He knew from the hints she dropped that the healer had hoped to keep her with him late into the evening, which could only mean one thing. The rational side of him had pretended to be pleased—it would be good for Garland to find love in the healer's arms tonight. He'd felt her bewildered pain ever since he'd told her that he had to leave and it had been almost more than he could endure. But the rest of him had struggled not to keep her from going out to the healer's car and take her upstairs to make love to her himself. Being ripped at by Mahtahdou and his demons had not hurt more.

So when he heard the tires of a car and the sound of her key in the door as he lay abed, and a few minutes later her light tread up and then back down the stairs, he decided to stop pretending to sleep. He looked over at Conn, curled up in

Garland's purple shirt and sleeping soundly, then put on his robe and went downstairs after her.

He found her in the work room that had belonged to her husband. She had taken off the dress she'd worn earlier to dine with the healer and was in skimpy clothes that left her arms and legs bare. He hung back in the dark hall and watched her drop piles of papers into bags and sweep the coverings off the windows. Her movements were brisk and determined but there was a strange, unhappy expression on her face that puzzled him. Alasdair felt a sharp, gloating jab of satisfaction—so the healer hadn't been able to coax her into his bed after all. It was wrong of him to be so pleased at the fact. It was also impossible not to be.

Had something happened between them? Was that why she was cleaning this room now—because she was too upset to sleep? Maybe he should go back upstairs now and let her work out her feelings in peace…but no. If Garland was unhappy, he couldn't desert her. Even if she didn't know he was there.

When all the shelves and surfaces were bare she knelt on the floor behind the big desk, sorting through the papers in the drawers and emptying them into the bags. From where he stood he could just see part of her back and shoulders, hunched over her work. The clock in the front hall chimed eleven times. Would she stop cleaning when she'd finished the desk and go upstairs to her bed? If so, then he should go back up now so that she didn't see him. What would she say tomorrow when he asked her how her evening with the healer had been? Should he even ask her, or—

Garland suddenly vanished, undoubtedly bending over further to pick something up. But after five breaths she hadn't sat up again. He inched closer to the door, craning to see what she was doing, and heard a strange noise—a thin, high keening sound coming from behind the desk.

Before he could stop to think, he was striding into the room just as the sound deepened into a sob. Garland lay curled into herself on the floor, fists pressed into her forehead. Boxes and papers were strewn haphazardly around her, but she seemed to have forgotten they were there.

"Garland," he said, and dropped to his knees next to her. He worked his arms under and around her then heaved her rigid form onto his lap.

"It's all right, *ionmhuinn*," he crooned into her hair, rocking her gently.

At first she didn't seem to notice that he held her, or that he was even in the room. But gradually she turned and huddled against him, one hand reaching up to clutch the edge of his robe. Her thin shirt, damp with sweat, had rucked partway up her back and he traced slow circles on her exposed skin with his fingertips, still murmuring to her under his breath as she shook with the force of her sobs. His beautiful Garland—what could have done this to her? His own throat ached as he listened to the pain pouring out of her. If the healer had been the cause of this, that confident grin of his would be permanently missing after he'd gotten his hands on him.

He wasn't sure how much time passed until her sobs gradually subsided, leaving her limp against him, her face cemented by tears to the bare skin of his throat. He knew what he should do now: pat her shoulder and ask if she was all right, then gently put her off his lap and get her some water to drink and a wet cloth to wash her tears away. And he would do all those things in a few minutes. But this would be his last—his only—chance to hold her close to him, to smooth his face against her hair, to breathe in the scent of her. Once he let her out of his arms the barriers would come up again between them. Was he wrong to want to delay that for just a few more minutes?

He had stopped rocking but still stroked slow circles on the skin of her back and side. In the nighttime silence of the house, with his eyes closed, touch and scent suddenly seemed much bigger, more engrossing. Her skin was so soft under his hand…and her hair under his cheek was smooth and so redolent of her and—

She let go of his robe and slid her hand up his bare chest to his shoulder then slowly down again, but tentatively, as if she were afraid he might protest, and he realized she too knew that if they let go, the moment would pass and they would never touch again.

"Alasdair," she whispered, and he shivered as he felt her warm breath against the side of his throat. "Don't you dare let me go."

And then she reached up to turn his face to hers and kissed him.

He closed his eyes, the better to savor her. It would only be this once that he would feel the warm sweetness of her mouth—just once, in case he never knew love again. He tilted her back in his arms and kissed the last tears from her eyes, then found her mouth again and kissed her there too, not gently any more. If the healer had kissed her tonight he would wipe the touch of his lips from hers and make it so she would remember only *his* mouth on hers, *his* hands on her smooth warm skin—

Except that she was teasing him with her tongue so he groaned and could only kiss her deeper, and her hands were touching him, leaving trails of fire across his skin, and he knew that the tables had turned. As long as he lived it would only be *her* mouth that he wanted to taste, *her* body he wanted to touch and stroke and feel under him, around him. When her hand slid down his chest again and didn't stop at the belt loosely tied around his waist he knew he was lost, and could have wept for joy.

Her fingertips just brushed his hardening length, hesitating, questioning. He answered her unspoken question with a sudden, convulsive movement, sliding her onto the floor and stretching out over her. "*A chiall mo chridhe*," he whispered. His darling one. *His*. He kissed her and managed to remove all her clothes but the garment she wore over her breasts. Its resistance made him growl in frustration. He wanted her breasts *now*.

She laughed softly and arched against him, reaching beneath her, and then it was loose and he almost yanked it down her arms before tenderly cupping one rose-tipped breast, then the other. "So soft," he murmured, brushing his tongue over them.

She inhaled sharply through parted lips. "Ohh...don't stop."

"I've only just started," he whispered, and slid one hand down her warm belly to part her thighs.

⁙

"Did I seduce you, or you me?" Garland said, nuzzling his ear. "If it was me, I suppose I should be ashamed of myself."

But he could hear the smile in her voice, and the small motion she made with her hips against him was more shameless than ashamed. He met her motion with one of his own so that her breath caught in a moan—oh, gods, the feel of her enfolding him!—then kissed her hard.

"I asked you to—no, I was begging you to, in my mind." He shifted his weight onto his forearms so that he could look down at her. "You were more honest than I was. I thought I could pretend I didn't want you."

"No, I wasn't. I thought I could pretend I wanted someone else." For a few seconds her eyes dimmed. "But it didn't work."

The healer. Alasdair could think of him now without a jealous burn in the pit of his stomach. "I am sorry for him," he said. "But not very much."

She laughed and arched up to kiss him, and he knew that she belonged to him as much as he did to her. The thought was both exhilarating and terrifying. But he wouldn't—couldn't—think now. Not when she was cradling him between her long, lovely legs, moving against him just like *that*…

"Alasdair," she murmured into his mouth a few moments later. "You know that we could go up to my room and do this a lot more comfortably."

To her bed. They could make love again and fall asleep in each other's arms, and he could waken in the morning and see her face next to his, just as he'd longed to do—

No. No thoughts of morning. Not now. "Yes. Let's go."

They checked on the peacefully snoring Conn, and then Garland led him into her room and shut the door behind her. He watched while she lit a pair of candles on a bureau, then turned to him and took his hands.

"Make love to me again," she said softly, pulling him to the bed. Her skin gleamed golden in the candlelight, and her beautiful round breasts under his hands were so soft and inviting, drawing him in, and as he touched her she made little wordless sounds of pleasure that drove him wild with need. He could never have enough of her, not if he lived till the seas went dry.

"Why do you cry?" he asked afterward, brushing a tear from the corner of her eye with his thumb.

She reached up to touch his face. "Because I'm so happy. This is…I didn't know it would be like this." Her smile turned impish. "If I had, I might have done it a lot sooner."

"How much sooner?" He bent and nibbled the edge of her ear. "When did you decide you desired me?" He knew he shouldn't be playing this game, but he couldn't stop.

"Honestly? As soon as I saw you on the beach. But then I got wrapped up in taking care of you and Conn, so I pretended to myself that I didn't. And then there was Rob." She sighed.

Alasdair rolled onto his back and pulled her to lie against him, head pillowed on his shoulder. "Was he why you cried earlier?" he asked.

"Rob? Oh, no. Well, he had a little to do with it, but not really." She sighed, and he knew his guess that something unpleasant had passed between them was correct.

"Then what was it?"

"He never loved me, you know," she said quietly. "My husband, I mean. I didn't know that. It was all right there in a letter I found when I was cleaning out his desk. That's what made me cry."

Alasdair kissed her forehead. "Then he was a greater fool than I'd thought. But he's gone now. He can't trouble your life any more."

She was shaking her head. "You don't understand. I know marriages fall apart because people fall in love then eventually figure out that they're wrong for each other. I could handle that. But Derek never loved me at all. He was…he was using me. I never told you about how Derek and I met, did I?"

Using her. He shifted uneasily and said, "No. You don't have to."

"But I want to. I need to get this out." She propped herself up on one elbow and looked down at him. "He was one of my father's students. My father was a business management professor at the university where Derek was a scholarship student. He was also the head of the business liaison office that placed students in internships and jobs as part of their degree work—because of that, he knew absolutely everybody that mattered in the business world in Boston. We had CEOs and CFOs and presidents over for dinner or drinks all the time."

He nodded. Many of her words made no sense to him, but the basic meaning was clear. Her father had been a powerful man.

"My dad loved Derek, you know. He thought he was one of the best and brightest he'd ever taught. I met Derek when I came home from college one weekend and he was invited for dinner. I was dazzled, of course—this handsome junior being so attentive to humble little freshman me. And Dad was dazzled too—he started regarding Derek as the son he hadn't had. Derek and I started dating in November of my freshman year when I was home for Thanksgiving, and for the next three years he was absolutely devoted. He finished his BA but stayed at the university to get his MBA, and we graduated the same year. I'd planned to go on to graduate school but that summer he asked me to marry him. He needed me, he said. I really thought he loved me." She paused, then added quietly, "I know I loved him."

"What happened then?"

"My dad was thrilled. So happy to be able to introduce his go-getter of a son-in-law to all his CEO friends. I don't think

Derek ever had to write up a resume. He had his choice of positions."

She took a deep breath and went on. "I was devastated by not being able to give him children. Maybe if we'd had them things would have been different—I would have been busy with them, and Derek would have had his work. Lots of people live those sort of parallel lives. Then about three years ago Dad had a stroke. I think in his way Derek did love my father, because he'd never really had one—his father left when he was just a baby. It wasn't till after Dad had a second stroke and died that I think Derek started seriously looking at other women. He would never have tried to leave me while Dad was alive."

She chuckled, but he saw that there were tears in her eyes again. "It never occurred to me that Derek had used Dad. Had used me in order to use Dad. Somehow the divorce didn't hurt as much before as it does now. I could accept that Derek and I had made a mistake. But it wasn't a mistake on Derek's part, was it? He knew exactly what he was doing when he married me. And that's what hurts so badly now…the being used. I could have gone out and found the right man to love and had my babies if Derek hadn't decided that I was going to be his means for getting what he wanted."

That's what hurts…the being used. The words felt like an iceberg bearing down on him.

"I'm sorry," she said, resting her head back on his shoulder and taking a deep shuddering breath. "You probably didn't want to hear all that."

"No, you didn't…it was—" He swallowed again. "I needed to hear it."

"And I suppose I needed to get it out. It was just being hit with it like that, realizing how much of a lie I'd been living—"

He touched a finger to her lips. "You were young. And your father wished you to marry him. You cannot blame yourself."

"Yes I can. It was my life to screw up." She sighed. "And boy, didn't I."

"But you overcame him. You are stronger and wiser now."

She laughed gently, and it turned into a yawn. "I don't know about that. But just this minute I know I'm much happier."

He held her close, stroking her arm and shoulder until her breathing told him that she'd drifted into sleep. His own body longed to follow her there, but the thoughts whirling in his head would not let him.

Was he any better than Derek?

Yes! said one part of him. He would never have forced her to bottle up her power inside her for so many years till she nearly burned herself up, consumed by her own flame. He would never be like Derek and hold her back. Her success would bring him only joy.

But like Derek he was using her—first as a shield until he and Conn had healed, and now to give him a quilt for protection against Mahtahdou. And just like Derek, once he'd gotten what he wanted from her, he would leave her.

How could he do that to the woman he loved?

But he was a selkie and she was not. There could be no future for them together. And there was Mahtahdou to contend with as well. He had to leave her for her own protection. But would she see it that way? When he took his quilt and left her, all she would see was that she'd been abandoned once more. She would have given her love again, and would be left again.

Alasdair lay very still holding her and watched in despair as night slowly gave way to morning.

14

GARLAND AWOKE THE next morning with her head still resting on Alasdair's shoulder, encircled in his arms. She flexed her toes blissfully and smiled. Over the last weeks she'd wondered what it would be like to be in his arms, held firm against that broad chest. Now she knew. It was like being in a cross between an impregnable fortress and a silk cocoon.

When was the last time she'd been so...so content? Not for years, at least not since she and Derek had been newlyweds. She waited for the thought of Derek to hurt but it didn't. Not any more. As soon as Alasdair kissed her Derek had been banished. There was no room for anyone but Alasdair in her thoughts right now. Carefully, she turned her head and kissed the hollow of his throat and felt rather than heard him chuckle.

"I didn't know you were awake." She propped herself up on

her elbow and smiled down at him. He smiled back but there were shadows under his eyes. She touched one. "Didn't you sleep well?"

He shrugged. "I was too busy thinking about where I was."

"Good thoughts, I hope."

"There was no other place I wanted to be."

Had a certain darkness crossed his face? Well, it had been a satisfactory enough answer. Surely she'd imagined any hint of trouble in his eyes. She bent and gave him a long, slow kiss, exploring the contours of his lips with hers. How many times had she daydreamed about doing that? She felt as if she'd entered a color trance, only this time through her skin rather than through her eyes. To finally be able to touch him, to run her hands over him, to feel him pull her atop him and sheathe himself inside her with one primal, powerful movement, to feel him tremble and hear him whisper her name as his pleasure peaked, to follow him and gasp out her own...

She made him shower with her just so she could keep touching him under pretext of soaping him. Would she ever have enough of him?

She was combing out her wet hair, wrapped only in a towel, while Alasdair lay next to her on the bed watching, when a faint scratch at the door made her look up. It was open the merest crack, and an eye and small nose were visible at about doorknob level.

"Conn?" Alasdair sat up, not seeming to notice that he was naked.

Garland looked at herself in the mirror and saw she'd turned red. Conn was so young...would he understand that something had happened between her and his father? Would he be resentful or angry? Would he even notice?

Conn shuffled in, still in his pajamas and tousled with sleep. Garland held her breath as he climbed onto her bed and curled himself against Alasdair's stomach…and reached out to hold onto an edge of her towel. She glanced down at him and met his eyes, and saw him watching her with a slightly muddled but pleased expression.

"Are you okay?" she asked him gently.

He nodded. "Toast?"

Alasdair smiled. "We're hungry too, *gille mor*," he said to Conn. "Put on your clothes and we'll all have some."

Conn nodded again, still looking up at her, then rolled off her bed and shuffled back to his room.

Garland exhaled. "That seemed to go all right," she murmured to Alasdair.

He looked puzzled. "Why shouldn't it? Conn loves you. When the healer—" he checked himself and shrugged. "Conn loves you," he said again.

And what about you? Garland wanted to ask but didn't. Because she was afraid of what the answer would be. How would last night change things? Was he still intent on leaving now that they had slept together and at least tacitly admitted that there was something deep and compelling between them?

"I thought I'd get more work done on your quilt today," she said casually, standing up and going to her bureau so that she could see his reaction in her mirror.

But his face remained carefully composed. "Yes. Thank you," was all he said. "I'll dress too before Conn becomes impatient." He slid off the bed and padded to the other room.

⁂

She spent the day working on Alasdair's quilt and the night

in Alasdair's arms, and both of them in a strange state of immediacy, of living in the minute, so that each stitch and each kiss or caress had a life of its own, floating about like a soap bubble that would never pop but drift about forever.

Alasdair was quiet, sitting on the floor next to her quilting frame just touching her leg and threading needles for her as she needed them, but it was a tense quiet. Once or twice she thought he was about to say something, clearing his throat and sitting up straighter, but he never actually spoke. Only at night when they made love could she feel him relax and exist in the moment with her.

Remember this, she told herself. *Remember the feeling of his weight on you, the taste of his skin, the way he fills you as if you were his glove, his voice when he cries your name when he comes.* It would be her treasure to hide away and take out to remember, if he left. When he left.

Was Alasdair doing the same thing? Was he setting up a vault in his mind where their time together could always live, golden and beautiful?

Only Conn was himself, playing with his scraps of fabric or looking at his books, or coming now and again to hug her or sit on Alasdair's lap and stare up at her as she worked. He even sang sometimes, little wandering tunes burbled under his breath, which was something he'd never done before. What would he do if Alasdair decided that they must leave? The thought of losing him hurt almost as much as the thought of losing his father. Were she and Conn so drawn to each other because they recognized each other's unfulfilled needs—his for a mother and hers for a child?

The safest thing to do was lose herself in the quilting and not think because thought led too many places that could hurt.

In the quilt she was safe, awash in color and pattern. Sometimes she would wake up and realize she had quilted an entire section without really seeing what she had done. When she looked, silver thread glittered up at her.

"It's done," she said at sunset on the second day, weaving the tail end of her thread into the batting between the layers of the quilt and clipping it close, then sitting back in her chair with a sigh. She felt empty and limp, as if she'd just given birth "Or nearly done. I have to bind it, which won't take long."

"May I see it?" He rose and leaned over the frame, but she put her hands on top of it.

"Not yet. It's—I don't like showing things before they're done."

"But I've seen it already, while you were laying it out," he said, head to one side, wearing a puzzled air.

"I know. But this is different." How could she explain that this quilt was now more than just a bundle of sewn-together bits of fabric, that it was—it was *them*. Her and Alasdair. She glanced up at the window, lit obliquely by the setting sun.

By this time tomorrow, would he be gone?

∽◉⃝ ◉⃝∼

That night Alasdair's lovemaking was almost rough, with a hard desperate edge to it that was as exciting as it was enigmatic. After a while she felt herself almost disappear into it and dimly, when she could think at all, realized what he was doing—losing himself in it, just as she was.

When at last his passion was sated he still lay atop her with his head on her breast. She stroked his damp hair off his forehead and tried to catch her breath.

"Your heart beats so fast," he murmured.

"Should that be a surprise?"

He laughed and rolled onto his back, pulling her with him. "My Garland. You give me such…I'd nearly forgotten what it was like to be happy."

Nearly forgotten… "But you remember being happy once," she said. It wasn't a question.

He was silent for the space of three or four breaths. "I remember," he finally said. "Forgive me, Garland. When you found us, I was afraid. It was easier to say I didn't remember what had happened or who I was. Most of the time I didn't want to."

"I think I'd guessed that." She propped herself up on one elbow and traced the edge of his jaw with her finger, carefully not meeting his eyes. "Conn's mother—you remember her too?"

"Yes," he said quietly after another pause. "But she's dead. And I had planned to never love again."

Did that mean he loved her? "How long ago did it happen?"

He sighed. She saw the faint gleam of his eyes in the candlelight from her bureau. He was staring at the ceiling; there was a line between his brows as if he was trying to decide what to say. "Conn was only a few moons old," he finally replied.

A few moons…did he mean months? About three years ago, then. This time she met his eyes. "How did she die?"

Silence again. "Are you sure you want to know?"

"Yes."

He closed his eyes and remained silent. Then, just as she was about to prompt him, he spoke. "I failed her. She was still weak from bearing Conn and I did not protect her the way I should have. I left her to go on an attack, not realizing it was exactly what the enemy wanted me to do. Finna was taken along with three of her women. One of them managed to get away with Conn, but the others died later of their wounds."

Attack? Enemy? "What are you talking about?"

"He sent Finna's skin to me the next day, or what was left of it. It was still warm. He wanted me to understand exactly how long it had taken for her to die."

Her *skin*? "Alasdair—"

"Can you see why I'm afraid to love again? How could I do that to anyone else?" He was gripping her tightly, his fingers digging into her flesh. "That's why I have to leave. I couldn't stand it if he…if you—"

"Alasdair! What are you talking about?"

Without warning he turned again, pushing her down so that she was staring up at him. Even in the dimness of candlelight she could see the anguish in his eyes. "Garland—please, I hadn't planned on it being like this. In the old tales, he never has to tell her…she just seems to understand—"

"Who? Understand *what*?"

"That her lover is a selkie."

Garland lay still, trying to remember how to breathe. No. This was crazy. Or he was. Rob was right—Alasdair *had* suffered some brain damage. Selkies weren't real. They were creatures from folklore, from myth and legend, from her beautiful storybooks. They weren't men who came into your life and made you fall in love with them.

In the old tales she just seems to understand— "Alasdair, do you know how nutty this sounds?"

"It's true, my belov—" He closed his mouth, then went on. "It's true. I've lived all my life here in the waters near this house, as did my family and their family before them. We've been here for four hundred and fifty summers or more."

Dear God, he sounded serious. "Selkies," she heard herself say.

"Some of us came with the fishermen who sailed into the west, looking for new fishing grounds and new lands. They didn't stay, but we did. My fathers and mothers led them and became their lords. We've ruled the waters around your Cape Cod since then. At least until now," he added more quietly.

"You're telling me that you—that you and Conn—that you're some kind of magical—"

"Not magical. Just selkie. If we had the magic we needed, we wouldn't be in the trouble we are." He bent over her and stroked her face. "You're the one with magic."

She pushed his hand away. This has gone far enough. "I've been avoiding talking about us too, but I haven't resorted to fairy tales—"

"Not fairies. Selkies." He scowled. "How can I make you believe me?"

Clap your hands! said a mad little voice in her mind. *Clap your hands if you believe in selkies!* "Alasdair—"

"Why else do you think we were on your beach? Men don't wander unclothed on the shore in winter, do they?"

"Er, no, not usually—"

"Why do you think your healer couldn't find out who we are or where we come from?"

"I don't know. Maybe—"

"Maybe it's because we aren't part of man's world," he finished for her.

Not part of man's world. Which meant not knowing about telephones and toast and TVs. Or divorces or hospitals or *clothes*, for heaven's sake…"You really believe this, don't you?" she asked, more quietly.

He touched her face again. "It is not a matter of believing. It is a matter of truth."

She took his hand and held it against her cheek. And then remembered.

Dear God.

She raised his hand above her eyes, fingers spread, so that she could see the webs there. "Your hands…" she whispered.

He looked perplexed. "What about them?"

Webbed hands, just like the selkies had in her book. "Where's your skin, then? I thought selkies had sealskins to wear when they became seals."

Alasdair closed his eyes and frowned as if gripped by a sudden pain. "We do. When they're not stolen from us."

We do, he'd said. Not *they do*. "Stolen? By whom?"

He pressed his lips together for a moment, then opened his eyes. "Garland, there is no point in my telling you any more if you will not believe me. Will you accept that I am what I am?"

She lay very still and looked up at him. "How about I suspend judgment until I hear everything? Will that do?"

He returned her gaze steadily. "It will have to." His voice was low and even as he began—the coming of his ancestors from Scottish waters to this side of the Atlantic, until they reached Cape Cod. She heard his words and let them paint pictures in her mind like the illustrations in some of her books—the seal folk standing on a new shore, gentler and less rocky than their old Scottish isles, where the full moon rose out of the ocean for them to dance by.

But at Cape Cod they met something they'd never seen before.

"There were evils in our old waters. We knew them, and fought them when necessary. But what we found here was different."

Alasdair's voice shook slightly. He cleared his throat and went on. "The entity we met was younger and hungrier than what we'd known before. He wasn't content to lurk in deep places and be left alone. He wanted light even though he hated it, and he wanted to be known so he came forth and attacked men so that he could take delight in their fear and hatred. Most of all he longed to have substance, and hated men because they had what he never would—their own shapes, their own bodies. The men who lived here called him Mahtahdou."

Mahtahdou. "Does it mean anything? It sounds a little…"

"In their language it means 'Devil Bird.' He can summon storms and make the waves do as he wishes. If he wanted to, he could send a wave to destroy your house. Or all the houses here. If there is sea water, he or his creatures can travel through it and do as they wish. They liked to grab children who were digging for shellfish and drown them. Or smash the canoes of those who went out to fish. The men who lived here then relied on the sea for their living. Mahtahdou made it nearly impossible for them to live."

They liked to grab children digging for shellfish…did Alasdair know about the dead clammer? "What happened when your people first met him?"

"It is said that the men who lived here feared us when we first came. They were afraid we were Mahtahdou's allies, come to help him kill them. But we abhorred Mahtahdou and his creatures, and joined with the men to fight him so that we could both live in peace. We could fight him and his creatures in the water more easily than men could, so they were glad to accept our help. At that time Mahtahdou had found a body to inhabit—it was a shaman visiting from an inland tribe who did not understand what Mahtahdou was—and our battle with him was fierce. After a long struggle we destroyed his body and bound him, and the men gave us these waters as our home so long as we kept Mahtahdou enchained."

"Enchained how?"

"With magic. There have always been selkies among us who did have magic—it runs in my family, which is how we became guardians of Mahtahdou and lords of these waters, even after the men who were here were driven away by men from the old world who took their lands. My grandmother was a strong magic wielder and kept Mahtahdou well imprisoned. But none of her children had her strength. My father—" His voice caught again. "My father tried. For a while he succeeded, but he made a mistake. Instead of marrying one who did have the power to keep Mahtahdou chained, he fell in love with my mother. She was bright and strong and a brave warrior but not a magic wielder. And while they were happy and had five sons—my four older brothers and me—Mahtahdou was waiting and watching from his disintegrating prison.

"He escaped when I was young, when my voice was just starting to break. Father was killed almost immediately and the rest of my family fled. Our home—"

"Selkies have homes?" she interrupted.

"We did. It is an island, near to the place men call Monomoyick. But it's not on your charts and maps. We selkies know where it is but men almost never see it, and when they do, it's on a misty evening and no one believes them. We had a beautiful palace there, built of old sea-polished wood and roofed with shell so that it shone silver by sunlight and moonlight. At least it used to. Mahtahdou took it to live in— though he's a spirit and did not need an abode, he thirsted for what we had. Now it is so befouled—half of it is a fetid wreck—that I fear it can only be burned and rebuilt." A bitter smile twisted his face. "If any of us are left to rebuild it, that is."

Dear heaven, this was real. She didn't know how she knew that, but she did. "What about the rest of you? Your mother and your brothers?"

Alasdair rolled off the bed and began to pace at its foot. "Mother died trying to avenge my father and retake our home," he said. "My brothers, one by one, tried to defeat Mahtahdou and failed. Then there was only me. The last of the lords, ruling over a small fragment of what had once been a large people."

"And Conn," she said softly.

"And Conn." He stopped pacing. "Gods, Garland, what have I done, begetting a son? My people begged me—if I were to die, who would be lord after me? They needed someone to rally around, even if it were only a child. It didn't feel right to take a mate, but there was Finna."

He sat down on the end of the bed with his back to her and his head bowed. "She had always tagged after me when we were small," he said. "She was younger than I and so pretty. Her father had died alongside my mother, and I thought that by taking her as my wife I'd be giving back to her for that loss. I thought that she'd be safer because I'd be there to protect her. But I wasn't. Mahtahdou took her because she was mine and because she'd born me an heir. If she hadn't she might still live. I might as well have struck her down with my own hand. She would have suffered less if I had…" He trailed into silence.

She climbed down to the edge of the bed and touched his shoulder. "You couldn't have known."

"I *should* have known. I should have realized that Mahtahdou would use Finna to get at me. That was how he got

Mother out to fight…" He shuddered. "When we were taken that night before you found us, I very nearly did kill Conn to keep him from being touched by Mahtahdou. But I was too late. They took us and three of my warriors and I had to watch while Mahtahdou gave them to his creatures to play with. It took a very long time for them to tire of their sport." He swallowed. "And then they started on us. I expected far worse than what my warriors had been through, but Mahtahdou wouldn't let any touch us but himself. And in the end he chose not to kill us outright. He wanted us to die slowly and be conscious of death as it took us. Too much torture doesn't permit that, you see. He said he was taking our sealskins to hang on the wall of his hall that used to belong to my family so that he could look at them and gloat over his victory, and he cut us until we were bleeding from many wounds. He licked at my wounds and said that I was delicious and he wished he could eat the rest of us. And then he had us bound and dragged to the water and thrown into the storm."

She remembered the eerie shouts and screams in the wind that night, her first in Mattaquason, and Rob examining their wrists and ankles the morning after, and shivered. "How did you get free?"

"I don't remember," he said slowly. "When I hit the water I screamed as the salt of it touched my wounds, and then I blacked out. No selkies would have dared to be near, but our little brothers the seals might have been there. The only thing I can guess is that they bit away our ties so that we wouldn't drown. I don't know if they brought us to your beach or not, but the next thing I knew I was lying on the sand in the sun, and a beautiful woman was holding my son wrapped in a magic skin, and—"

She stopped him. "Wait—that's the second time you've said something about magic—what are you talking about?"

"Garland." He turned and touched her face gently. "I know you don't know it. I don't understand why you don't, but your quilts—they're magic. Very magic. When I touched your shirt that you put around Conn that morning—you had sewn a piece of your quilts—"

"A block," she said. "A Compass Rose block."

"Yes. Whatever it is, it is like—like a cloak of protection. Why do you think Conn never wants to take it off? Why do you think that he wasn't killed when he wandered out of your house the other day?"

"That scratch on his cheek—"

"One of Mahtahdou's creatures found him, I think. But it couldn't take him, or even hurt him much, because of your shirt."

Her head was spinning. Selkies and demons and quilts—

"And the robe that you gave me to wear—the one you made for your husband—" His expression softened. "I was so jealous when I felt it, wondering what perfect man had merited that robe. There was such love in it—"

And Derek could barely stand to touch it when she'd given it to him. "But I don't *do* anything to them. I just make them."

"It is *because* you make them that they have magic," he said. "The first thing I thought of when I touched your shirt was my grandmother. Do you know how she kept Mahtahdou bound all those years? With a braided circlet of beach grass. Something that anyone could make. But when she made it, it could keep Mahtahdou restrained and powerless. Think, Garland! What else has happened with your quilts?"

This was ridiculous. "Nothing," she said. "Yes, people like

them—"

"Being struck by a car while you held a quilt that told of the return of life to the land and being unhurt—is that nothing? Catching Conn's fingers in your fishnet quilt is nothing?"

She was silent. He nodded and went on.

"After I felt your power and understood that you meant us no harm—that you would take care of us—it was the first time I'd had any hope in years. My people are scattered and my—my skin is in Mahtahdou's hands. But if you were helping me, with your power... There was only one problem. You were kind and gentle with my son, and strong and caring to help us heal...and so beautiful, like summer fruit ripening in the sun..." He leaned toward her and kissed her, letting his lips linger on hers.

"I ached with wanting you," he murmured. "But I have to leave you, before I can't. I thought the healer loved you—that he would take care of you—"

She held his face between her hands so that he couldn't look away. "But why do you have to leave?"

His eyes were dark and sad. "Why else? I killed Finna with my love. I will not kill you the same way. Listen to me. Mahtahdou knows I am alive and that I'm here with you. He must have guessed when my body was never found. He tried to get into your house but couldn't—remember how all the other houses here have been damaged, with their windows broken? His creatures found Conn but could not take him. And I think your accident with the car was a test, to see how strong your magic was—"

"Wait—a test? How could he have—"

"I told you that Mahtahdou can inhabit a human body when he needs to. I think he used the body of that woman to see if he could kill you. If he could not, then he would know you were out of the ordinary." He put his hands over hers. "If we don't leave soon, something worse will happen. Your magic may be able to keep his creatures from breaking windows, but will it be strong enough to withstand a mountain of water flung at your house? All I ask is that you give me the quilt you have made me—it may keep me safe long enough to gather my people together and rescue my skin, and then—"

"And then what?"

"I don't know," he said softly. "But I'll know that you'll no longer be his quarry. I need to make sure you're safe. And I"—he took a deep breath—"I will not hide behind you any longer. I am not a Derek. I have used you, and I am not proud of that. If matters were different—" He broke off, shaking his head. "I owe you my life, beloved. Now I must protect yours."

She jerked her hands away and pounded the bed in frustration. "But you and Conn won't be safe. Alasdair, if this is real, I—I don't want to lose you now. Either to this Mahtahdou or to anyone else."

"Then you do believe me?"

Did she? His story accounted for so much—his otherworldliness, his injuries, his fear of leaving the house—but demons and magic quilts? "I don't know. I think I do, but parts of it…I just don't…" She exhaled, and met his eyes. "But I know this. I love you."

"Garland—" He reached for her.

"I don't care who you are or where you came from. I want to be with you always, and I want to be a mother for Conn. I *love* you," she whispered.

He didn't reply but pushed her down and kissed her hard, and then made love to her, and she stopped thinking again and let her body say everything that could not be said in words.

15

Garland looked through half-opened eyes at the sleeping Alasdair who lay on his stomach next to her, one arm flung possessively across her. Aragorn. She had called him that once, hadn't she? It had been a more apt nickname than she'd guessed for her dark, beautiful, dispossessed lord.

Dispossessed lord…what did she think about his tale? Impossible—and yet it had been impossible not to believe him last night, watching the emotions that had chased each other across his face as he spoke. Did she believe him now, in the cool light of day?

She stroked the hand that lay atop her breast and touched the webs between his fingers. Selkie hands. He hadn't even thought of using them as proof last night—she'd been the one to remember. But was that proof enough?

What if he *were* a selkie, working to defeat this Mahtahdou-thing? Did he really plan to leave her and go fight it—him—just when they had found each other? She rested her cheek against the top of his head and remembered their lovemaking last night. He had touched her, held her, loved her like a man who knew it might be his last time.

And if Mahtahdou were real and Alasdair defeated him, then what? Alasdair had mentioned the old stories of human and selkie lovers. In most of them the selkie lovers stayed on land for a while, long enough sometimes to beget families. But in the end they always returned to the sea. Was that how it would be for them? Would she have him for a year or two or ten and then be forced to watch him leave her, just as Derek had? Would that be any better than watching him leave now? Her hand tightened on his convulsively.

Alasdair stirred. Garland cursed herself for waking him and lay still so that he would drift off again. But instead he groaned and lifted his head.

"Garland, I…there's something wrong." He seemed to find it difficult to focus on her face. "It hurts, like it did—" With an effort that made him groan again and his face contort, he rolled onto his side.

The sheet below him was soaked with blood.

⁂

Garland tried to take deep, calming breaths while she dialed Rob's cell phone number.

How had Alasdair's wounds reopened? They'd been healing well, with fresh, pink scar tissue emerging from under the scabs. Yes, their lovemaking last night had been gloriously bruising, but surely not enough to—

Five rings…six… "Come on, Rob!" she muttered.

But no one picked up the phone, not even voicemail. Fine, then. She'd try him at the office. She punched in the first digits, but Alasdair reached out and touched her hand.

"Do you think it wise to call him?" he asked, speaking as if it were an effort to get the words out.

"Why shouldn't I? He's a doctor."

"He's also in love with you and sees me as a rival."

She felt a warm flush rise up her neck. "How did you know?"

Alasdair's mouth twisted in a faint, crooked smile. "I may not be human, but I am male. I know how he feels about you. Will he want to help me?"

"Of course he will," she said, hoping she sounded surer than she felt. "Doctors have to help—they take a vow, to 'ease suffering and to harm none' or something like that. Personal feelings aren't allowed to come into it." She finished tapping the number in and waited.

"Dr. Mowbray's office. This is Stacy. How can I help you?" Rob's receptionist's warm, calm voice had never sounded so welcoming.

"Stacy! Thank God you're there. It's Garland Durrell. Is Rob there?"

There was a pause. When Stacy spoke again, the warmth and calm had vanished. "Mrs. Durrell. Oh no, he's not. It's so strange—I found a message this morning that he'd been called out of town unexpectedly."

Garland was glad she was sitting down. "Gone? Are you sure?"

"I tried calling him at home but there was no answer. I have to call all the appointments he had today and reschedule—"

"Did he say when he'd be back?"

"Well, it wasn't very clear—he left a note stuck in the office door, and it was sort of scrawled, like he was in a hurry—"

He hadn't even bothered unlocking the door and putting it on Stacy's desk? What could have driven the usually careful and courteous Rob into such a rush? And what would have dragged him away from his patients?

"—but it looks like it says 'a while.' I'm sorry, that isn't very helpful, is it?" Stacy sounded flustered and apologetic. But under the surface emotions Garland heard something else, too. Was it fear?

"Stacy, are you—are you sure you don't know where Rob is?" she asked, very gently. "Is there something wrong? Did he tell you not to talk to me? I need him badly—my friend here is hurt agai—"

"Oh, I've got another call coming in. Can I put you on hold? Maybe it'll be him." Stacy cut her off so abruptly that it took Garland a few seconds to realize what had happened.

"Stacy put me on hold," she murmured to Alasdair. "She thinks Rob might be on the other line." She sat with the phone glued to her ear for several minutes, listening to a Mozart string quartet and thinking about when she'd tried calling 911 the day she'd found Alasdair. The similarities were disquieting.

"Always hated Mozart," she said in explanation as she slammed the phone back into its cradle. "Stacy must've forgotten about me."

Alasdair didn't reply but the furrows in his brow deepened. "Do you really think the healer is gone?"

"I don't know." She was already hitting the redial button. A loud, obnoxious busy signal sounded in her ear. "Damn," she muttered, hung up, and turned back to him, hoping she looked and sounded more confident than she felt. "I'll try her again in a few minutes. You rest while I'll make you some toast. Are you hungry?"

"Hungry for you, but I'll settle for toast," he said, with a ghost of his old smile.

"Incorrigible." She bent to kiss him gently then looked at his torso. Fortunately she still had some of the Teflon pads and bandaging from when he'd first been injured, but she'd have to run out to the pharmacy for more if she didn't get hold of Rob soon.

While waiting for Alasdair's toast she tried calling Rob's office again. The line was still busy. Stacy had said she'd have to make a lot of calls to cancel Rob's appointments, but the blaring busy signal made her uneasy.

She stared out the window at the beach. Yesterday had been golden and glorious, but overnight the weather had done a complete about-face. Sullen gray clouds hung low in the sky, and tendrils of fog reached and withdrew across the sand like groping hands. The very air felt heavy and foreboding, as if a storm were lurking offshore, waiting to pounce. She turned away with a little shiver, finished buttering Alasdair's toast, and brought it upstairs.

Alasdair lay as she'd left him, his eyes closed and his mouth tight as if he were holding back a grimace of pain. She set down her tray and dragged up a chair beside him. "Do you want to eat now?" she asked.

He opened his eyes. "Toast. I'd been thinking how much I was going to miss toast when I left."

"You're not going anywhere for now, so you might as well enjoy it." She helped him sit higher in the bed then peered at his side again. The bandaging would need changing by lunchtime if his wound were still oozing at the same rate.

Alasdair managed a slice of toast and some tea but shook his head when she offered more. "Maybe later," he said, and closed his eyes. "Tired."

"I'm not surprised. You had a busy night," she teased.

"I had the best night of my life," he murmured with a smile, but his eyes stayed closed.

"Sleep, then. I'll keep trying to get hold of Rob. If I can't, maybe we ought to bring you to the hospital in Hyannis."

"I—maybe. Not sure that's good…idea." He turned his head slightly, and after a minute she realized he'd drifted off to sleep.

She sat watching him, noticing that his forehead was still creased. Even asleep he was in pain. This shouldn't be happening. There was no logical reason for it. Yesterday he'd been whole and strong. What could have made his wounds reopen?

The door creaked slightly, and she saw Conn peering around it. She held a finger to her lips and motioned him to come in. He tiptoed over to her and looked down at Alasdair. "Daddy," he whispered.

"Daddy isn't feeling well today. Why don't we let him rest for a bit and I'll make you breakfast."

She shepherded him down the stairs, made him pancakes with strawberry jam, and settled him at Derek's old desk with a box of crayons and a pile of old stationery. "I'm going to check on Daddy. I'll be upstairs if you need me," she told him.

He nodded, then looked up at her and held his arms out. She knelt next to his chair and hugged him hard. "Everything will be all right," she whispered. "I'll make sure of it, I promise. You and Daddy—you're important to me. Okay?"

" 'Kay," he whispered back.

Alasdair hadn't moved. She bent over his face to listen for his breathing, and a loud ring behind her nearly launched her across the bed. She snatched at the phone with shaking hands. "Rob, where have you been? You've got to—"

"This is Elizabeth Souza, from the Friends of the Library. Might I speak with Mrs. Durrell, please?"

Garland paused. Elizabeth? It wasn't supposed to be Elizabeth calling right now. Then she collected herself. "Oh, Elizabeth, it's me. I'm sorry, I was expecting—"

"I apologize for calling at such an early hour, but we only thought it fair to contact you as soon as the decision had been made. The Board of the Friends of the Library has asked me to inform you that it is withdrawing its commission for a quilt commemorating the library's anniversary." Elizabeth's voice was flat and emotionless.

"What?" Whatever she'd been expecting, it hadn't been this.

"The Board of the Friends of the Library has asked me to inform—"

"I think I heard you the first time, Elizabeth." Garland tried desperately to shift gears. "I'm just trying to understand—is there something wrong? Has the celebration been cancelled?"

"The celebration will go on as scheduled. However, it has been decided to withdraw—"

"Was it the fee? I'm happy to waive that if—"

For the first time, some emotion crept into Elizabeth's voice. "That is kind of you, Mrs. Durrell, but it will not be necessary. The Board thanks you for your time. Good morning."

"Elizabeth, wait—"

But she'd already hung up. Garland turned the phone off and stared at it.

What had that been about? Something didn't feel right about the whole phone call—the message itself as well as Elizabeth's delivery of it. Why were the Friends changing their mind? Elizabeth had called just last week to remind her about presenting some preliminary design ideas at the Celebration Committee meeting later in the month. And why the cold manner? Elizabeth had never called her Mrs. Durrell before. Ever. Had she unwittingly offended someone on the board? A chill went up her spine. Rob was on the board, wasn't he? Could he be behind this as a way to get back at her for the other evening?

A soft groan interrupted her thoughts. Alasdair's eyes were still shut but he was moving his head from side to side and shifting restlessly. She reached under the blankets and took his hand, just as she had when he was first injured. The furrows in his brow smoothed somewhat but did not entirely go away.

She put the phone back on the bedside table and held Alasdair's hand in both of hers. Elizabeth's call had been distressing, but Alasdair was far more important. The Friends of the Library could wait.

☙❧ ☙❧

After Alasdair had stopped tossing and slipped more deeply into sleep, Garland took the phone with her into the bathroom while she took a quick shower.

But the phone didn't ring.

She tried Rob's office again but the line was still busy. After a moment of wrestling with herself she called Dr. Phelps' office. Even if he was older than the dinosaurs, surely if she begged him he'd stop by.

His number was busy too.

She spent the next hours dialing each number in turn every five minutes. The busy signals never wavered. Between calls, she stitched the binding to Alasdair's quilt. It might have seemed like a triviality at a time like this, but snatching a few stitches when she could helped keep her from sobbing uncontrollably as she gazed down at the lines of weakness and pain etched on either side of Alasdair's beautiful mouth.

At lunch Alasdair refused the toast and tomato soup she made him.

"What happened to my champion toast eater?" she scolded him gently.

"Not hungry," he said, turning away.

She set the tray on the floor beside the bed and bent to look at him. His eyes were unnaturally bright. She placed her hand lightly on his forehead. "You're hot. Do you feel feverish?"

"No. Yes. I don't know." He closed his eyes again.

"Let me check your bandages and then you can rest some more, all right?" She forced cheerfulness into her voice that she was miles from feeling.

He nodded without opening his eyes.

She peeled the sheets back so that she could examine the pads on his torso and nearly screamed. His arms and legs were covered with ugly, oozing welts, as if he'd been flogged with barbed wire.

This was impossible. It was one thing for his old wounds to reopen. It was another for new cuts to appear.

She knelt at his side. There was nowhere on his arms or shoulder that she could touch that wasn't criss-crossed by cuts.

"Alasdair, how did this happen?" she asked, trying to keep her voice steady.

"What?" But he didn't even open his eyes.

"Listen to me. If I can't get hold of Rob or Dr. Phelps in another few minutes, I'm going to take you into the hospital in Hyannis. Do you understand?"

"No," he said, looking up at her through the merest slits.

"Why not? There's something seriously wrong here—an infection or something. We've got to get you to where there are doctors and medicine—"

He swallowed. "I know what's wrong with me. It is nothing the healers can help."

"What? What is it?"

He barely moved his lips. "Mahtahdou."

She sat back in her chair and stared at him.

"He knows I'm alive," he whispered. "At least it's me he's attacking, not you or Conn."

"Alasdair." She spoke carefully. "Are you *sure?*"

He sighed. "You didn't believe me last night—"

"I don't know!" she burst out. "Everything you told me is so far beyond anything I've even imagined. Selkies with magical skins and evil demons living on islands that sometimes aren't there. I have no way to know if that's real, but I do know that this blood and pain in front of me is real."

"He has my skin. He's using it to try to kill me again. What else could cause this?"

"I don't know!" she said again, helplessly. "But I love you, dammit, and I'm not going to let anything happen to you." She rose and pulled the blankets back up over him. "I'm going to get you cleaned up and then I'm going to go try Rob again."

It was almost a relief to leave her room and go to his and Conn's to use the phone there. The dull, hopeless look in Alasdair's eyes before he closed them was almost more worrying than his bizarre physical symptoms. She sighed and picked up the phone. It rang as she held it in her hand, making her jump.

"This had *so* better be Rob," she muttered, then turned it on. "Hello?"

"Garland."

"Kathy?" She let out her breath. "Oh, hi. Could I call you back? I'm waiting—"

"I've cancelled the show in August. I would appreciate it if you could come down at your earliest convenience and get your quilts from the shop." Kathy sounded strained and hoarse.

Garland felt as if she'd been punched in the stomach. It was like Elizabeth's call all over again but a hundred times worse. "What?" she gasped.

"Today, if you don't mind." Kathy's voice caught slightly on the 'today', but the controlled monotone didn't go away.

Garland took a deep breath but it was impossible to speak without her voice shaking. "Kathy, what's going on here? What's wrong with my quilts all of a sudden? What's wrong with Mattaquason? Is this town going crazy?"

A faint sound, rather like a sob, reached her ear. "I'm sorry, Garland," Kathy whispered. "I wish I could...come and get your quilts. Right away. *Please.*"

The line went dead.

LESS THAN TEN minutes later Garland was speeding toward town. Alasdair was asleep when she went to check on him and Conn had curled up on the couch and dozed off over a book. They didn't need to know she was gone; with any luck she'd be back in half an hour.

Downtown was almost deserted. Several shops were dark, as if closed, and even the windows at the Captain's Bridge were unlit. As she drove slowly down the street she saw the lights in two shops turn off abruptly as she passed. The first pharmacy she drove by was dark and deserted-looking, but the larger chain store at the end of Main was still lit. Gratefully she pulled into a parking spot and hurried in before it too could close.

Only a couple of customers were in the store. They studiously looked at their shoes or at items on display even when she brushed by close enough to touch them. She nearly met the eyes of one woman whom she knew slightly from the Historical Society. But when she smiled, the woman stared through her as if she weren't there. Garland straightened her shoulders and pretended she hadn't noticed anything amiss.

But something was very amiss in the first aid aisle. The shelves were empty.

She stared at them in shock. Were the first aid supplies being moved to another section? But no, there were all the little unit pricing stickers indicating where bandages and pads and tape had been. The panicky, angry feeling she'd had in the street began to creep back in. She stalked to the checkout counter at the front of the store. No one stood behind any of the registers there.

"Hello?" she called, feeling slightly foolish.

There was no response.

On impulse she craned her neck and bent to peer over the counter. Hunched in the far corner, hidden behind a stack of cardboard boxes, was an elderly salesclerk. Garland felt a temporary alarm—was he all right? But then she saw that he had his hands clamped firmly over his ears.

She marched down the counter, bent over it, and tapped the man's bald head. "Excuse me," she said loudly. "Could you help me, please?"

The clerk shuddered and buried his face against his knees.

"I said, excuse me!"

"Go away," the clerk mumbled.

"I need to buy some first aid supplies, but the shelves are empty. Do you have any more?"

"I won't help you. Go away."

"Listen to me!" she shouted. "I need bandages!" Her voice

sounded desperate, even in her own ears.

The clerk didn't bother answering this time.

Garland thought for a second about launching herself over the counter, grabbing the man by the scruff of the neck, and shaking him. But then she realized that he already was shaking like someone in the grip of a fever—or of mortal fear.

"Go away, Mrs. Durrell," someone said behind her. She turned. It was Sandy, the waitress from the Captain's Bridge. She wore a grim scowl in place of her usual gap-toothed smile. "You're not wanted in this town."

At least someone would finally talk to her. "Why not? What did I do? A few days ago you all liked me."

"If you hadn't come to Mattaquason, five of our people would still be alive. Their blood's on your hands. Now go, before we lose anyone else."

"What are you talking about?" Garland grabbed the counter behind her for much-needed support. "I haven't hurt anyone."

Another woman came up behind Sandy, one Garland didn't know, and pulled her back a few paces. "Don't talk to her," she muttered. "You don't want to get yourself in trouble, now."

"Gina was my sister's girl," Sandy said to her, her face crumpling. "Now she's dead because of this bitch. Go on," she shouted at Garland. "Get out of here or we'll do it for you! Next time He should take you! I don't know why He hasn't already!"

"Sandy!" the woman gasped. She took her arm and propelled her out of the store, still holding a basket of merchandise on her arm. The anti-theft alarm at the door buzzed loudly but no one seemed to notice.

⚜

Garland had to lean against her car for a full five minutes before her shaking calmed enough to let her even think about opening the door and starting the engine. What had happened to everyone in town? And what had Sandy been talking about? Five deaths…

Next time He should take you. A shiver went down her back as she remembered Sandy's words. Who was "He?" And why did the way Sandy said it remind her of—

A car pulled up behind her. She looked up and saw that it was a police cruiser. As she straightened, the driver's side window rolled down. Captain Howe looked out at her.

"Please go home, Mrs. Durrell," he called.

She took a few steps toward the cruiser. "No. I want to know what is going on in this town. Where is everyone? Why is everything closed on a Tuesday afternoon in May? Why are all my friends running away from me?"

Captain Howe jabbed at the window button as she approached till there was only an inch open for him to speak through. "Go home now, Mrs. Durrell. Please. There's nothing here for you."

"Why not?" She moved closer and saw his eyes widen as she approached. His face was white and strained.

"Good God," she said, more to herself than to him. "You're afraid of me. Why?"

"Please. Go." he said in a strangled voice.

"I'm part of this town too. What is going on here? Why won't you tell me?"

Captain Howe opened his mouth but no sound came out. Without even glancing behind him he pulled back into the street and floored the gas, tires squealing. A gust of wind blew down the empty street in his wake, cold and salt-smelling. It struck the tears on her cheeks, chilling them, as she stared at his retreating taillights.

"This isn't real. I'm dreaming it," she muttered. But Kathy's phone call had been real enough. It was time to go to the Captain Hayes Gallery and see if she could get some answers.

No cars were on the road and she was able to park directly in front of Kathy's shop. But her windows, too, were dark. So how was she supposed to get her quilts?

Then she saw the large black garbage bag sitting on the sidewalk in front of the door. A flash of pale yellow-green showed at the top where the wind fluttered the plastic. She walked up to it and peered inside.

It was the Spring quilt that Kathy had loved so much and that she'd given to her, bundled in, *crammed* into the bag without even an attempt at folding. Under it she saw a wrinkled fold of green and magenta batik, and a flash of a red fish covered by gold net. Here were her quilts. Stuffed in a bag like trash.

She stalked up to Kathy's door and pounded on it with her fists. "Kathy Hayes, open this door and tell me what the hell is going on here!" she shouted. "Now!"

The street was silent behind her under the low gray clouds and creeping tendrils of fog. A few streetlights had already turned on because it had grown so dark. Not even a shadow moved within the shop, but somehow Garland knew Kathy was in there, cowering in the back room, fists pressed to her mouth to keep from responding.

"Open it!" she yelled. "I know you're in there."
Nothing.
"Kathy, one more time. Do I have to kick the glass in?"
Still nothing.

Garland paused. "All right, best friend," she said more quietly. "If that's how it is…you know, if it hadn't been for your cajoling I might not have moved down here after the divorce. But I guess that doesn't matter much to you, does—"

A flash of light from the back of the shop stopped her. A few seconds later Kathy herself came into view, clutching a flashlight. She unlocked the door, grabbed Garland's arm, and pulled her inside.

"God damn it, Garland, do you have to make so much noise?" she almost moaned, propelling her toward the shop's back office. "Come on. We might be safe in here."

"If you'd opened your door like a civilized person I wouldn't have had to pound on it. And what do you mean, safe? What's going on?" Garland staggered slightly as Kathy pulled her along because her knees felt weak with relief. *Someone* was still talking to her.

Kathy shut the office door and turned the flashlight back on, then tucked her jacket against the crack at the bottom of the door. "There. That ought to keep anyone from seeing the light," she murmured to herself, and looked up at Garland. The beam from the flashlight cast weird shadows on her face. "You *don't* know, do you?" she asked.

Garland stared as she sank to the floor next to her. "All I know is that everyone in this town is going insane, and that includes you."

Kathy sighed. "We're not insane. We're just trying to stay alive."

"Kathy—"

"And I shouldn't be talking to you like this. But I don't think Lord Mahtahdou will—"

"Wait—did I just hear you say Mahtahdou?" Dear God, if

Kathy of all people—Captain Kathryn Hayes, USA—was talking about Mahtahdou too… Alasdair had spoken the truth. He was real. And so were the selkies.

"*Lord* Mahtahdou," Kathy corrected. "So you *have* heard." Her mouth tightened in a grim line. "Your selkie must have told you, I suppose. Oh, Garland, why didn't you listen to me when I first told you to get rid of him? None of this would be happening now if you had."

Garland ignored a twinge of guilt. "Why didn't you tell me why I should?" she demanded.

"Would you have believed me if I had? What if I'd said to you that Mattaquason had been more or less controlled for the last twenty-five years by a—a bodiless entity that can call up storms and killer waves and demands our absolute obedience if we want to live here? Would you have believed me?"

Garland pressed her lips together. Would she?

"Anyway, we don't tell anyone until they've been here for a while…and then only if we think they have to know," Kathy went on. "We hadn't even told Rob Mowbray yet, though I'd already decided I should after I saw him the other day—"

"What about Rob? I've been trying to call him all day."

For a moment Kathy looked abashed. "I bumped into him in the market a couple of days ago. He was looking pretty down and I asked him what was wrong, and he said you two had had a bit of a disagreement…jeez, Garland, he's head over heels for you and all you can see is that damned selkie." She shook her head. "Rob asked if I could exert any influence I had over you to get you to get this Alasdair out because he was worried you'd be hurt. I nearly had a heart attack on the spot. You've had him with you all this time…Garland, do you know how Lord Mahtahdou feels about the selkies?"

"I'd guessed," she said shortly.

"Your Alasdair is a dead man—or selkie or whatever. I'm just afraid you'll be a dead woman, too, for helping him. Do you understand the power Lord Mahtahdou holds over this town? The things I've seen—" Kathy shuddered. "If he wanted to, he could wipe half of Mattaquason off the map with a careless swipe. Who do you think is responsible for all the…the incidents recently? Did you know there were at least another two this morning? A girl who worked at the fish market on Ladd's Wharf—they said an arm of water reached up and pulled her off the dock while she was on break. She disappeared without a trace. The other was another house on the beach up in the north part of town. It just collapsed into the marsh at high tide. The owners are missing. Lord Mahtahdou is *very* angry."

Garland thought of Sandy's anguish. No wonder everyone in town had been so hostile if they knew about this…but— "If Mahtahdou's quarrel is with Alasdair, why hurt the town? Why doesn't he come after him?" Except he already had. "Or after me, for that matter?"

"I don't know. If Lord Mahtahdou wanted to, he would have—"

"Stop calling him 'Lord'. He's evil and a thug. He killed Alasdair's family, and he's trying—"

Kathy clapped a trembling hand to her mouth. "For chrissakes, don't say things like that!"

Garland pushed her hand away. "How could he hear us?"

"You don't know how powerful he is. Don't you understand? He owns this town. The houses he's destroyed— the people he's taken…I told you, he can control the weather and the waves and whether the fisherman catch any fish and…had you heard about the—er, occurrences at the equinoxes?"

"You mean the deaths?"

Kathy looked nervously around again. "They were tributes to him. Tithes, sort of. Look, Garland. The bottom line is if you don't give the selkie to Lord Mahtahdou, more people in town will die until you do. And I can't promise *you* won't either. He…" she licked her lips. "He's interested in you."

"How do you know? Have you chatted with him recently?" Garland couldn't help asking sarcastically.

She hesitated then said, quietly. "Yes. Yesterday."

"Kathy—"

"He summoned me to visit him on his island—"

"The selkies' island." She remembered Alasdair's face when he spoke of it.

"Well, it's his now. He…I've never had to go see him there before. Fred Barlow brought me there in his lobster boat. It was…it was the damned weirdest thing I've ever seen. He cut the motor about a hundred feet off…and when I looked the water between the boat and the island had divided. There was a corridor of sand, with the water on either side of it like walls. Lord Mahtahdou called to me then—that voice…I've been trying to forget it." She wrapped her arms around herself. "It was so cold. Icy cold. It sounded like one of those computer-generated voices that pronounce everything correctly but still don't sound quite human. So I climbed out of the boat and walked along that path. It scared the crap out of me. I kept waiting for the water on either side of me to start behaving like water again, not like…like whatever. I could see into it like I was looking in an aquarium—there were fish, and seaweed, and the usual things you see. But there were other things, too—they squirmed and swam in the water, but they weren't fish. They were all looking at me and grinning. Their teeth—" She shuddered and fell silent.

"Did you see Mahtahdou? What did he look like?"

She took a breath. "He looked…like you."

"Like me." A dark, jagged nausea prevented her from saying anything more. Mahtahdou's stealing her appearance felt almost like being violated in some subtly obscene way.

"For some of the time." Kathy didn't look at her. "He can take any appearance he wants, I think, though it's only an image. He doesn't seem to have his own body, though sometimes he's borrowed them."

"Borrowed them?"

"He—he takes people. Possesses them and uses them when he needs a physical presence. I think that's what happened with Mrs. Shirley and the car…but he can only do it for a little while. Being…*inhabited* like that…it burns people up, in just hours sometimes. They either go crazy or die…can I finish telling you what happened?"

Garland swallowed the sour saliva that filled her mouth. Poor Shirley Shirley—the horror she'd seen in her face in that instant before the car bore down on her— "Go on."

"We talked. Lord Mahtahdou said he'd made a mistake by dumping the selkie and his kid in the water to bleed out rather than killing them outright. He was very angry—Mattaquason is damned lucky that he didn't throw a tsunami at it."

"He can do that?" A cold hand seemed to touch her neck.

Kathy laughed mirthlessly. "Do you know about the storm that destroyed part of Monomoyick back twenty years or so and rearranged the harbor? Where do you think that came from?"

She shivered but would not let Kathy see it. "So this is why everyone in town has been so strange to me today. Because of Mahtahdou."

"Yes."

"And back when I first found Alasdair and Conn…you and Captain Howe already knew."

"I didn't know specifically who they were. It's safer not to know things. But finding them on a beach in their condition—we knew it had to be someone who'd angered Lord Mahtahdou, and we didn't want to have anything to do with them. Now will you let me finish?"

Garland nodded.

"Thank you. Lord Mahtahdou told me he'd thought about destroying Eldredge Point to get at him but decided there were better methods. He's very interested in you. In fact, the reason he didn't destroy Eldredge Point was you."

"Was that all?"

"No." Kathy set the flashlight on the floor next to her, leaned forward, and put her hands on Garland's arms. "Garland, no matter what you might think, I'm your friend. And right now, as a friend, I'm telling you to get in your car and leave Mattaquason. Now."

"Leave Alasdair and Conn to Mahtahdou?" Garland heard the outrage in her voice but didn't try to temper it.

"Yes," Kathy said steadily. "I don't give a damn about them, but I do about you. Go far away—somewhere inland—and don't ever come back. Forget about Mattaquason. I'll see that your house gets packed up and sold and send everything to you. It might be too late but if you leave right now—"

"I can't do that!"

Kathy shook her a little. "Listen to me. The reason Lord

Mahtahdou summoned me was to tell me to find a way to bring you to him."

Garland felt herself grow very still. "Why?"

"I don't know. Do you know what I'm risking by tell you to run away instead? If he were to find out—"

"So why haven't you left too?"

"This is my home, Garland. How long has my family lived here? But I'd already decided I was going to as soon as I turn fifty-five. No one can blame me for wanting to retire somewhere warm, can they? Why do you think I was so happy to sell your quilts for all that dosh?"

Her quilts. "Why the garbage bag, Kathy? That really hurt."

Kathy dropped her hands. "Lord Mahtahdou wanted me to destroy them. He hates them for some reason. But I thought…if you left now, you could take them away with you and sell them—it would give you enough to go on until we got your house sold for you—" She picked up the flashlight and pointed it at her watch. "You should probably go. You've been here for a while, and if someone notices your car out there—"

Garland climbed to her feet. "I understand," she said quietly, and opened the door. "Thank you for telling me all this."

"Will you go? Will you leave town?" Kathy called after her as she walked through the echoing gallery to the shop's door. "I promise I'll make sure your things are safely taken care of for you…it's the least I can do—"

Garland slipped through the door without replying. Awkwardly, she hoisted the garbage bag full of her quilts and wrestled it into the trunk of her car. Then she climbed behind the wheel.

So Mahtahdou was "interested" in her and had a problem

with her quilts? She shook her head. Right now she needed to do something about Alasdair. She could run to the pharmacy up in Orleans…but that would take too long. Maybe she could stop at Rob's office…but no. There was no way to know if he was there. And if he was, she didn't need him to treat her the way the rest of Mattaquason had—

Her cell phone rang. She fumbled for her handbag and found it, not even stopping to look at the ID. "Hello?"

"Garland?"

"Rob!" At least *he* hadn't called her "Mrs. Durrell." For a moment she couldn't see through the tears that came to her eyes. She wiped them away with her sleeve. "Oh my God, I've been trying to call you—where were you?"

"Out. I came straight over to your house when I got your messages but you weren't here."

Rob's calm, competent voice sounded wonderful, if a little strained. "You're at my house? How is Alasdair?"

There was a pause. "I've seen him," he finally said. "I've done what needed doing, but I think you'd better come back here quickly."

A cold weight seemed to settle on her chest. "What's wrong? Is he worse?"

"He's sleeping. But I need to talk to you, and it's pretty urgent."

"I'm on my way. Oh—Rob?"

"Yes?"

"Thank you. I know we…that I…thank you. You don't know what this means to me."

Another pause. "Just come home, Garland. Okay?" He clicked off.

Garland put away her phone. At least Rob wasn't behaving

like the rest of the town and shunning her the way she'd begun to fear he would—he hadn't sounded quite like his usual self, but at least he'd come. She started the car and pulled onto the deserted Main Street. Behind her the town was dark and still under the lowering, swirling fog.

ROB WAS JUST descending the stairs as Garland came through the front door. He hadn't shaved today, and his face was pale under the shadow of stubble. As he stepped under the light in the front hall she saw his that his eyes were glittering and glassy. Was he ill? But if he was, why the mysterious note for Stacy? Why not just call in sick?

"Garland." He put his medical bag down and pulled her against him, holding her tightly. She stiffened at first, then relaxed and hugged him back. Rob was so *good*. She regretted not being able to love him.

"Thank you for coming." She stepped away and turned toward the stairs. "How's Alasdair? Do you—" She looked back at him and realized he was watching her intently. "Rob? Is there something wrong?"

He looked at her and swallowed, and she was struck anew by his pallor. She touched his forehead. It was cold and clammy. "You *are* sick, aren't you?"

"No," he said brusquely. "Just tired. Come in here. I need to talk to you about him." He took her arm and propelled her toward the great room.

"Not there," she murmured, holding a finger to her lips. "Conn's asleep on the c—"

A cold, damp breeze struck her face, stopping her words. One of the great room's sliding doors to the lawn overlooking the beach was wide open, and an unpleasant, salty smell filled the room.

"Conn!" She ran to the couch. A picture book lay abandoned on the floor, its pages riffling in the breeze from the open door. The couch itself was empty.

No! Had he gone outside to look for flowers again? But after what had happened to him the last time he'd gone out of the house alone…she whirled back to Rob.

"Conn was asleep on the couch when I left. Did you see him when you came in?" she demanded.

He shook his head. "I didn't look. I noticed the door was open, but I assumed you'd left it that way on purpose so I left it alone and went straight upstairs."

Her heart was thudding in her chest. This wasn't happening. Conn had opened the door for some reason and then left the room…he was probably back at Derek's desk, coloring—

"Conn," she called, hating the quaver that shook her voice, and sprinted to the office. But the room was empty…and if Rob hadn't seen him upstairs…

"Where are you going?" Rob called as she pushed past him.

She ignored him and dashed out the slider toward the

beach. Oh, why had she left Conn alone? She should have woken him up and brought him with her downtown. But he'd been sleeping so peacefully, and she'd locked the doors—

More fog billowed up the lawn from the water, blown in eerie puffs like smoke from a forest fire, only cold and wet instead of acrid and burning. She almost didn't want to breathe it in, but forced herself to fill her lungs as she ran and shouted, "Conn!"

Only the sound of the wind in her ears and the slap of waves on the shore broke the silence.

In the damp, tide-smoothed sand past the tangle of beach plum and bayberry bushes she found footprints leading down to the water…if whatever had made the oddly-shaped prints possessed something that could be called feet. But no little boy prints punctuated the bizarre, uneven depressions in the sand. Could it be that he hadn't come down here after all? Maybe he *had* gone over to the Luffords' again to pick flowers—

At the very edge of the water, a puddle of color caught her eye. A purple puddle.

No. Oh, no.

But even before she'd reached it she knew what it was. She picked up Conn's beloved shirt, tears burning on her cold cheeks, and shook the sand carefully from it. The collar was ripped almost fully away from its band, and a long gash ran down one arm, but the Compass Rose that she'd pieced on it in rose and pale blue and violet still seemed to glow slightly in the dim, foggy air.

•••

When she returned to the house Rob still stood where she'd left him in the doorway to the great room, looking faintly dazed.

"Rob," she said, and he jumped.

"Garland," he said, straightening. His left eye twitched. If the man wasn't sick, he was certainly doing a good imitation of it. "Did you find him?"

"No. Only this." Her voice trembled as she held up the purple flannel shirt, and she steadied it. This was no time to go to pieces. Conn and Alasdair needed her. "I need to know—Kathy said she was going to tell you but maybe someone else already did—do you know about Mahtahdou? And what Alasdair and Conn are?"

He nodded. "Yes, they…yes, I know now."

Good, then she wouldn't have to explain. "I'm afraid that Mahtahdou has kidnapped Conn, and that he's the one making Alasdair sick. Is that what you think too? You saw him."

"Yes."

She took a deep breath. "So what about you? Are you going to fall at Mahtahdou's feet the way the rest of this town has?"

His eye twitched again "Why do you ask?"

"Because *I* won't." They didn't have much time. "Rob, I'm sorry—I tried to love you, I really did. But Alasdair—"

"I understand," he said quietly.

Relief flooded through her. He was taking this so well. "I love him. And I'm not going to let Mahtahdou destroy him and Conn. He seems to think I have this power—that Mahtahdou can't touch me—and if that's true, then I have to try to save Conn and get Alasdair's skin to stop him from hurting him any further. Will you help me?"

Rob was staring at the floor. She anxiously watched the top of his head and held her breath.

"You want to find Mahtahdou?" he finally said. "Where?

How?"

"Alasdair told me—he's taken the selkies' island for his own. I've got my boat, and it'll only take me a few minutes to pull it down to the beach and get it rigged. It's the only thing I can do. I can't let him hurt Conn again. Will you…" She paused, then said quickly, "Will you stay here with Alasdair while I go? I know that's a lot to ask—"

He looked up at her. "No. There's nothing I can do medically for Alasdair, but I can help you. Why don't I go with you?"

"With me?" She frowned at him. "Rob, I don't think—I mean, you don't look very healthy yourself right now." The last thing she needed was Rob collapsing when she was trying to help Conn.

"I'm fine. Just tired. But Conn may not be." Some of his weariness seemed to leave him, and he stood straighter. "If he's injured again, I can help him while you deal with Mahtahdou."

She hadn't thought of that. "Are you sure? This is going to be dangerous—"

He stepped toward her and put a finger to her lips. "I know. Do you think I'd let you go alone?"

Oh, Rob. Tears welled up in her eyes before she could stop them. "I don't know what I did to deserve your friendship." She took both of his hands in hers and squeezed them. They were icy cold and clammy, but his return grip was strong.

"You're the most important thing in the world to me," he said softly, and smiled. "So let's go."

⁂

The mid-afternoon light was gray and evening-like and the fog as thick as ever as they rolled her little sailboat on its dolly out of the garage and down the lawn to the beach. She set the mast in its step and raised the triangular sail, clicked the rudder pins into place in their loops, and slid the daggerboard into its slot. A fitful breeze had risen and was blowing the mist about in puffs and tendrils. It seemed to rake cold, wet hands through her hair and she wished she'd thought to grab a hat before she left. But she didn't want to go back to the house to get one now—the sooner they got going, the less time Mahtahdou would have to hurt Conn…and the less time she'd have to ask herself what the hell she'd do, once she found Mahtahdou. If she found him.

"Rob, I think you need to know…I have no idea what I'm doing. I don't know where we're going, apart from south toward Monomoyick." She swallowed. "You can change your mind and stay here, you know."

Rob squeezed her shoulder. "No, I can't. You'll find him. I know you will."

They pushed the little boat into knee-deep water and clambered onto it. Garland took the tiller and glanced back at her house, its lines half-obscured by the blowing fog. While Rob had tried on lifejackets in the garage she'd run upstairs to check on Alasdair. His face was almost gray and his breath came in short, shallow pants. She couldn't leave him like this. But she had to.

She'd tenderly wiped the sheen of sweat from his forehead and bent to kiss him. "I'm going to find Conn and your skin, because…because there's nothing I can do to help you here," she whispered, gazing down at his drawn face through a film of tears. "You've got to hang on while I'm gone, do you hear? I know that you told me the truth about the selkies, and I don't care if you'll leave me some day. At least you'd be alive and well. But if you leave me right now because Mahtahdou's killed you, I—I'll—" One of her tears fell on his cheek. He didn't move as she brushed it away, then kissed him again. "I'll be back."

As she straightened, her eyes fell on his quilt, still folded next to her chair where she'd left it while stitching on the binding. She picked it up.

"It's not quite finished, but I'll give it to you anyway," she murmured, draping it over his still form. "You said you felt safer when you had one of my quilts."

A fleeting tremor—so swift that she was almost sure she'd imagined it, ran over his body. Would he sleep more easily now? Would his pain lessen? She could only hope—

"Garland?" Rob called from downstairs.

With a last touch on his cheek, she'd left the room.

⋘ ❧ ❧ ⋙

At first Garland hoped that maybe the selkies would appear to help her find their—Mahtahdou's—island. She pictured ten or twelve dark seal heads suddenly appearing in the water around her boat, guiding her there then shucking off their sealskins and turning into a group of tall, dark-haired warriors, ready to defend her and Rob as they marched on the captured palace to find Conn.

But no sleek heads poked up around her. Not even a gull was to be seen—only the gray water and fog billowing in the chill wind.

Next to her, Rob shuddered. She glanced at him with concern. "Cold?"

"Hmm? No. I'm quite comfortable."

How could he be, barefoot and in a pair of light khakis

soaked to the knees and a dress shirt? Darn it, she should have grabbed a fleece for him to wear but she'd been so intent on getting going that she hadn't thought of it. Not that she was terribly comfortable either—wet jeans were not good sailing attire—but she was more used to it.

"Here." She held onto the mainsheet with her foot, unzipped her lifejacket part way with her free hand, and started to pull out Conn's purple shirt that she'd tucked inside it for safekeeping. "You can wear this—it'll break the wind a bit—"

"I'm fine." Rob snapped, then shuddered again.

"Uh…okay." She tucked the shirt back inside her lifejacket. That wasn't very like Rob. But maybe his nerves were starting to get rattled. She knew hers were.

Ordinary fog was white. Sometimes when it drifted past a tall dune or some other large object, a faint shadow would appear in it—a darker shade of white, more or less. Ordinary fog did not swirl and flash in dull green, or yellow brown, or maroon or purple. But for the last twenty minutes she'd been catching hints of color from the corners of her eyes, as if the world wasn't obscured by fog but by smoke from a burning chemical plant—

A long, scraping sound suddenly issued from underneath the hull of the boat.

"Damn! Hold on." Garland let out the sail, reached across Rob to yank up the daggerboard, and braced her feet, waiting for the sudden jolt of running aground. Where had a sandbar come from? At this tide there should be ten or fifteen feet of water here—

But the impact never came. The boat slowed and turned slightly into the wind, its sail swinging loose.

"Why are we stopping? Is something wrong?" Rob asked,

looking back at her.

"No." She pulled the mainsheet back in and the sail caught the wind again. "That scraping noise—I thought we were about to run aground."

"What scraping noise?"

"Didn't you hear it?"

"I didn't hear anything." He turned and gazed ahead into the fog.

She gaped at his turned head. How had he not heard that? It had sounded like giant fingernails rasping beneath them.

Then again, the wind might have drowned out the sound. She glanced up at the sail and tightened her grip on the mainsheet. The wind had been moaning with increasing strength since they'd pushed off her beach. Darn it, the last thing she needed was to capsize in icy water with a non-sailor on board.

But after a few minutes she realized that the boat was not behaving as it usually did when a gust of stronger wind hit it— no heeling, no bursts of speed. For some reason, the wind sounded as if it were rising to gale force—but it was only sound.

She shivered, but not from cold. There was something uncanny going on here, but she couldn't let it get to her. So far it was all illusion, sound and no substance. She was stronger than that. After Derek she knew all about dealing with illusion.

"What's that?" Rob pointed to something off the bow of the boat. She followed his pointing finger to a calm place a few feet across that had appeared in the choppy water ahead. As she squinted at it, it began to seethe and bubble as if a scuba diver were below, about to surface. The bubbles grew larger— from ping-pong ball- to baseball-sized. Then as they drew abreast she saw that each had a faint vertical line, almost like a pupil on an eye…and that they were looking at her, swiveling as they sailed past—

"Garland?"

The bubbles popped all at once. She stifled a gasp.

"What was it?" Rob was looking at her curiously.

"Nothing. Just…it was nothing. Don't worry." But she glanced back at the water where the bubbles had been, now as choppy and restless as everywhere else. What had that been? She could have sworn those were eyes…but it was no use dwelling on it lest she frighten Rob…or herself.

The fog deepened, with an occasional ugly yellow-brown or greenish tinge to its billows, and the wind-that-wasn't wailed eerily around them. More patches of bizarre eye-like bubbles that seemed to stare at her knowingly appeared, and she watched them with growing apprehension. Did all these strange phenomena mean that Mahtahdou knew she was coming? Or was Mattaquason so tight in his grasp that this was just the way things were now? She shivered again.

"What will you do when we find Mahtahdou?" Rob asked suddenly. His blue eyes were dark in the gloomy light.

That was precisely what she wanted to know, too. How could she challenge a being that could summon storms and inhabit the bodies of innocent humans in order to kill? At least she knew he wouldn't try to kill her on the spot. But what was it about her that had sparked his interest enough that he wanted to see her?

The scraping sound along the bottom of her hull was getting on her nerves. She leaned back and peered into the dark water, trying to see if something had caught on her daggerboard.

A long, thin, greenish limb erupted out of the water a foot from her face. She gasped and nearly fell backwards off the boat. Four equally long, thin, greenish fingers waggled madly at her in a parody of greeting—fingers that ended in three-inch-long claws. The wind howled again, and this time it sounded distinctly like a dirty, crazed laugh. Then the hand plunged back below the surface.

Her heart beat wildly. Kathy's tale of the things she'd seen in the water near Mahtahdou's island hadn't been an exaggeration, had it? Evidently they had claws to match their teeth. What weapons did she have against creatures like that?

But it had just been that, something briefly seen and then gone. Mahtahdou was trying to scare them. "Thank you," she called, hoping her voice didn't tremble. "I wondered what was making that noise."

The wind-sound paused as if uncertain then broke into sniggering laughter that sent fresh shivers down her back. Or was it getting colder out here? She glanced at the low mass of Monomoyick Island, trying to gauge how far south they'd come. But the fog rendered the scrubby dunes even more featureless than they already were.

She sighed, then straightened as something caught her eye. Off to her right, away from Monomoyick…was that a shadow in the fog?

"Rob—over there—do you see? Is that an island?" She gestured with her chin.

He peered dutifully into the fog. "It could be."

She stared at the shadow. The fog thinned for a few seconds, revealing a low, sandy beach. It looked like an island…but could she be sure? If she sailed off in that direction, she would lose sight of the only physical reference point she had. But if it were Mahtahdou's island…she bit her lip, then eased the sail out and pulled the tiller toward her, aiming the little boat toward where the shadow lay—

And knew, with an uncanny certainty, that it wasn't her destination. She shoved the tiller back and pulled in the sail, and after a moment the shore of Monomoyick came reassuringly back into view.

For a while she was content to hold her course while her heartbeat returned to normal. It had looked like an island…she'd seen it. But something had felt wrong as soon as she turned toward it. Was Mahtahdou trying to trick her into losing herself in the fog? For now, while Monomoyick was in view, she was safe. But when she came to its end there would be nothing to tell her whether or not she was sailing toward his island or off into the open Atlantic.

Twice more Garland thought she saw islands…and twice more she knew that something was wrong. It was starting to get to her after all—the swirling, malevolently teasing fog, the howling wind that wasn't really there, the intermittent scratching and tapping on the hull of her boat, the things that looked like eyes watching them. What weapons did she have to counteract Mahtahdou's illusions?

"Wish I'd brought a quilt," she muttered. "That would have shown—"

Wait a minute. She *had* brought a quilt, hadn't she? She patted the bulge of Conn's purple shirt tucked in her lifejacket—the shirt with the Compass Rose square sewn on it—and actually laughed aloud. Was it just a coincidence, or could it be what was keeping her from getting lost?

"It's not your round yet, Mahtahdou whatever-you-are," she called.

Rob looked at her oddly, and as if in answer the wind moaned. But this time it really was wind. It blew her damp hair off her forehead and cooled the nervous sweat that had broken out there. Heartened, she took a firmer grip on the tiller and continued to gaze out into the fog.

Whether it was the freshening wind or her own bolstered courage, the fog seemed to thin after that. The sight of the squat lighthouse that marked the end of Monomoyick Island heartened her further. Alasdair had said the selkies' island was somewhere near here, if you knew where to look—

This time, the scratching noise under her hull really was sand. She gasped and nearly fell off the boat as it ran aground, forcing the daggerboard and rudder up.

Rob grunted and grabbed for her. "Careful!"

"I'm all right...." She blinked at the misty air, but only gray water met her puzzled eyes. Then slowly, as if revealed by an opening curtain, the mist drew aside. For a moment the water and mist wavered, then vanished. A sandy beach, rising to low, grass-covered dunes, took their place.

This was it. She had found Alasdair's—and Mahtahdou's— island.

18

GARLAND LEAPT into the shallow water, leaned past Rob, and let down her sail. "Come on," she said. "Help me pull the boat up the beach."

He stared up at it. "Are you sure this is it?"

Garland followed his gaze. It looked like a normal Cape Cod beach: fine creamy-white glacial sand with coarse dune grass swaying in the rising wind. To their right, the beach quickly curved and bent out of view. On their left it went on at least a quarter-mile before vanishing into the thinning fog. This was no sandbar but a substantial island. But was it really the home of supernatural beings?

A gust of wind spattered a fine spray of raindrops across her face. She looked up and saw that as the increasing wind blew the fog into threads the sky was darkening to an ominous steel gray. She remembered the storm that struck the night before she found Alasdair. Was Mahtahdou brewing up some foul weather for their benefit? But why had he waited until they'd found the island? Surely he would have tried to blow them out to sea before they even made it here?

"I don't know," she answered. "But I'm willing to bet it is. Let's explore."

At her direction, Rob grabbed the boat's bow and helped her pull it above the tide line—or at least tried to. His hands seemed clumsy, as if he couldn't control them—Rob, whose hands she had watched in admiration deftly binding up Conn's wounds not so long ago. But maybe they were stiff from chill or nerves. Hers certainly were.

She glanced back up at the darkening sky and took down the mast, lashing it to the bundle of sail and spars on top of the dinghy's hull. It would make getting the boat ready to leave again take longer, but they wouldn't get anywhere if the mast were bent in a storm. She started to take off her lifejacket, then after a pause zipped it up again. It made her feel a little more secure to have an extra layer between her and whatever it was they were about to confront.

Now all they had to do was find Mahtahdou.

The bank under which they'd dragged the boat stretched the length of the beach as far as she could see, forming the leading edge of a high dune. It reminded her of a defensive earthwork, like the ones around the ancient hill-forts in England. Ignoring the shocked voice in her head that reminded her that dunes were fragile and should never be climbed on, she clambered up it. From its crest she saw that another, taller dune sat beyond it.

She also had the distinct feeling that they were being watched, and not by an outraged beach ecologist, either. A chill ran down her back, one not born of her damp clothes and the increasing wind. But no other living creature could be seen—and no footprints were visible anywhere around her. She shrugged her shoulders and doggedly climbed the high sandy slope, Rob scrambling after her.

"There, I told you so," she said quietly as they peered over the top of the dune.

A large, low, sprawling building nestled in a broad circular hollow below them, glowing faintly in the dimming light. Clumps of beach-rose shrubs and scrubby cedars grew around it in artistic carelessness.

Or at least, they once had. Now the cedars were lacy skeletons, and the roses, though still alive, looked yellowed and diseased. Even the waving dune grass here looked stunted and sickly. It might have been beautiful, once. Was Mahtahdou's presence so noxious that even sturdy shore plants shriveled in it?

Rob swayed slightly and grabbed her arm for balance. His fingers dug into her flesh. "Now what?"

Good question. She squinted down at the clearing. Marching up to the door when she had no idea what might be inside it seemed foolhardy. Yet the dead cedars would provide little cover for a more stealthy approach. Perhaps they should circle round it and decide then…but the thought that Conn might be in there with—with *things* like they'd seen on the way here decided her. "We're going in."

"You sound so confident."

Was that amusement in his voice? But no, his face was sober and if anything paler and more drawn. "I'm not. But we don't have much choice, do we?"

They edged gingerly down the slope and approached the

building. It too had not fared well under its present tenant. Unidentifiable filth daubed its surfaces and an almost palpable aura of dereliction hung about it. Here and there holes had been punched in the walls that the wind whistled eerily through.

But even in the dull gray light of the lowering clouds, even through the depredations of Mahtahdou and his creatures, it was beautiful. Flowing, sinuous lengths of driftwood formed its structural beams, their curving lines dictating the shapes and planes of the walls: little alcoves, and gables, and covered porticoes paved with beach cobbles. And the walls themselves…it was as if some underwater smith had taken shells—silvery, iridescent abalone and mussel—and hammered them in an impossible forge into planks and sheets. The effect of the whole was swirling and hypnotic yet coherent, as if this place were the discarded shell of some deep-sea god. If it was still this beautiful now, what must it have been like when the selkies held it? Garland reminded herself to breathe, wishing she could try to make a quilt of it.

Something poked the backs of her knee.

She didn't quite scream, but she did make a wild, muffled squeaking sound as she whirled around. A sudden metallic taste in her mouth told her she'd bitten her tongue. Beside her, Rob inhaled sharply and grabbed her arm again.

A small and greenish *thing* stood there, somewhere at knee level. It had three rubbery, boneless-looking legs ending in clawed toes, one of which clutched a short stick which it flourished at her and had evidently just used to get her attention. It had no discernible head but a wide grinning mouth full of neatly pointed teeth, and little else. As she stared at it, it swept her a deep, courtly bow, then ruined the effect by sniggering unpleasantly.

"What is it?" Rob whispered.

"I don't know." She blinked, hoping it would disappear. It didn't. Nor did it attack them. It just stood there, as if waiting. A faint, unpleasant odor like a mixture of burned sugar and rotting fish wafted up from it. Anything that smelled like that was, unfortunately, probably not a figment of her imagination.

There was a small popping noise, and another one appeared next to it. Then another. And another. She cringed, waiting to see what they would do. She and Rob could maybe take on one or two of them, but four…no, five…no…

As she watched, an entire line of the strange three-legged creatures appeared, varying from one another in height or shading—some were nearly black, and a few tended to purple. They jostled and grunted to one another but stood in place, and suddenly she realized they formed a line leading around the side of the palace.

"What is this—Mahtahdou's version of a red carpet?" she muttered to Rob.

"I don't know," he answered hoarsely. "Should we follow them?"

The first thing sniggered again and scratched itself with a clawed foot, then made a wet, explosive sort of noise, not from its mouth.

Garland grimaced and took a step back. "I'll guess that was a yes. Though I must say if that is the best Mahtahdou can do, I'm not very impressed."

A ripple of motion ran through the line, and a second later she wished she hadn't spoken. The three-legged things were now at least eight feet tall.

"Jesus!" Rob gaped up at them.

Garland bit back a cry of alarm. From now on, she'd keep her mouth shut. "Let's go," she said, and reached for Rob's cold, sweaty hand.

They walked down the line. She felt ludicrously like a colonel on a parade ground reviewing her troops, and tried not to flinch when they shifted and twitched. After a few yards, they began falling in after them so that she and Rob marched at the head of a snorting, cavorting line. It made her feel uneasy and also faintly ridiculous, which was probably exactly what Mahtahdou wanted. Fine. If he wanted to play games, they'd play along. Squaring her shoulders, she held tight to Rob's hand.

A line of seventy-four things had formed behind them by the time they came to the door—she'd found herself counting them with a sort of horrified fascination as she and Rob passed. But as they walked she wondered what would be on guard at the entrance. Hopefully not something that made these things look cute and friendly.

But no clawed, fanged, toothed, horned, or other creatures were waiting for them. In fact, the double doors—made of more of that amazing shell material, inset with what looked like polished quartz pebbles—stood open. Some sort of translucent curtain hung before it, obscuring the view in.

Garland reached out a hand to push it aside, but something—some instinct—made her hesitate. It was an odd reddish-gray color, shiny and wet-looking, like a very ugly vinyl shower curtain. But shower curtains didn't pulsate or generate long strings of slime, like a salivating dog. "I don't like the look of that," she said. Rob leaned forward, but didn't answer.

As they stared at the faintly throbbing thing a split suddenly appeared at its bottom and worked its slow way up, like a curtain opening on a stage. Oh God, did they really have to walk past this disgusting thing?

Beside her, Rob stirred. "Do you want me to go in first?"

"No." This was her business—hers and Mahtahdou's. She took a deep breath, as if to make herself as thin as possible, and stepped across the threshold of the palace.

❧ ❧ ❧

Garland found herself in a long, high hall, dimly lit with a cool silvery light that seemed to come from the pearly shell walls. Slender arching beams of driftwood lined the walls, their branching ends forming a ceiling that looked almost like it belonged in a fan-vaulted medieval church. Like the outside of the palace, this too once must have been exquisitely beautiful.

It wasn't anymore. Whatever filth daubed the exterior walls positively encrusted the interior. It took all of her willpower not to gag and cover her mouth and nose: the faint nasty smell of the first creature they'd met was concentrated and augmented with other, even nastier odors inside here. Not even the many jagged holes ripped in the walls allowed enough of the rising wind in to dissipate the stench. She shuddered and tried to breathe lightly. It wouldn't do to let Mahtahdou see how close to being overcome she was. Though it might be a nice gesture to throw up on his feet.

Except that Mahtahdou didn't seem to be here.

She took another step into the room. At its far end was a raised dais, and on it was a chair—a throne of what looked like crystal—massive and beautiful, carved with delicate ripples and wavelets as though it had been hewn from a block of water. The chair was empty. The room was empty, too—none of the three-legged abominations danced and cavorted here, as she'd expected they would. The only sound was the wind, whistling in the walls—

No, not quite empty. There was something lying at the foot of the throne—a small, dark-haired something wearing navy blue sweatpants and an incongruously cheery yellow "Mattaquason, MA" t-shirt.

"Conn," she whispered, and then she was there beside him, turning him over. He was filthy, wet, and unconscious but seemed otherwise unharmed. She unzipped her lifejacket and pulled out the purple shirt and bundled him into it. Now he would have some protection—at least, she hoped so. She lifted him—not an easy thing to do when wearing a lifejacket—and tried to balance him on her hip as she looked around the shadowy hall.

"Rob," she called quietly. "It's okay—no one's here. Come help me." If their luck held, they could find Conn's and Alasdair's sealskins as easily as she'd found Conn and get out of here before Mahtahdou returned.

A pair of hands grasped her shoulders, and someone kissed the back of her neck.

"Rob!" she gasped. "Oh my God, you scared the heck out of me." The last thing she needed right now was him getting romantic again.

She squirmed away from his hands and turned to face him. But the gleam that shone in his eyes was not amorous—if anything, it was amused. And cold—so inhumanly cold—

"Welcome to my hall, Garland. I've been looking forward to this moment," he said, and smiled.

19

Garland took a step back as understanding washed over her in a sickening flood. "No," she whispered, and held Conn more tightly. Not Rob…not sweet, kind Rob—

"Why not?"

Mahtahdou grinned at her with Rob's mouth, but it wasn't Rob's boyish, forever-seventeen grin. She'd seen sharks in TV documentaries that smiled like that. How could his mouth twist into such an expression?

"Surprised to see me?" he continued conversationally. "I don't know why. It *is* my home, at least for now. You did well not to touch my doorkeeper, by the way. Isn't it charming? But coming into contact with it can be an *absorbing* experience, if you know what I mean."

He leaned toward her, swaying, and blinked as if he couldn't focus Rob's eyes properly. "Damned human bodies. They're like your tissues that you humans blow your noses on. Useful for a few seconds and that's it. Into the trash." He waved his hand.

Was it shock or the cold that now seemed to flow off him in waves that was making it so hard to breathe? Oh, Rob. When had Mahtahdou taken him?

A strangled howl sounded outside, followed by another and then by dozens more. Mahtahdou glanced behind him toward the door. "My friends want to come in and play with you. Shall I let them?"

He made a similar call, and all at once the three-legged, rubbery things came swarming in, most of them shrunk back down to knee-height. But other creatures had joined them— some with more or fewer legs, or with long snouts or blunt, lamprey-like mouths, or with trailing tentacles ending in squinting, malevolent eyes. They capered and leapt with a motion somewhere between a dance and a stagger. Some clustered around Mahtahdou's feet like obscene pets. They glared up at her and bared long, needle-like teeth. She remembered the clammer who'd vanished. No wonder Officer Moniz had said they'd needed bags to bring him home in.

"There we go," Mahtahdou almost crooned. "No, behave yourselves. Mrs. Durrell is our guest—our *very* special guest."

Garland swallowed the lump of fear that arose in her throat. "Why use Rob Mowbray? Why not face me yourself?"

"Because the good doctor came in very handy. I knew he might someday, but I never guessed just how useful he would be. He got you here, which is where I wanted you." He smiled again but only half of Rob's face moved this time, as if it would no longer work properly. Garland remembered Kathy's explanation of what happened when Mahtahdou used someone as he had poor Mrs. Shirley. *It burns people up in just hours sometimes*, Kathy had said. *They either go crazy or die.*

"How long have you been using Rob?" she demanded.

"Why? Want him for something yourself?" Mahtahdou leered. "Though last I'd heard, you didn't. You were sating yourself with someone else's body." He turned and staggered toward the throne then sank down onto it.

"The little selkie lord," he continued, leaning against the throne's carved back. "Did you like my handiwork this morning? I must say, I enjoyed myself. *Very* much." He gestured at one of his creatures. It scuttled behind the throne and came back dragging a limp length of something sleek and brown and finely furred. Another three-leg followed, gripping a black-hilted dagger in its teeth.

Mahtahdou took both objects and held them up in front of him as if inspecting them. Garland stared at the soft brown thing and her mouth went dry.

"Do you like my pretty toys?" Mahtahdou flapped the brown length of fur at her then delicately, like a carver finishing a statue, inflicted a series of long, precisely-spaced slashes across it with the dagger. She winced with every stroke. "This knife is far too sharp," he confided. "A duller blade is much more amusing."

The creatures crouched around him howled with laughter.

She couldn't help it—she had to turn away. What was Alasdair feeling right now as he lay on her bed? And she was here having to watch and think about it—

"Oh, does this bother you?" He licked the blade lasciviously. "But he tastes so *goooood*. You know that. You've tasted him yourself, haven't you?"

"Stop that." The sight of him running his—Rob's—tongue along the blade was nauseating.

"Why should I? Or are you going to try to stop me?" He went back to cutting slits in Alasdair's skin but his movements were less coordinated, less controlled. "If so, I should like to know how. You weren't very forthcoming on our trip over here." The knife slipped and gashed Rob's arm. He frowned down at it, then resumed his mutilation.

Dear God. Mahtahdou hadn't told her how long he'd been using Rob, but if he kept up at this rate Rob's body would be destroyed soon. She had to save not only herself and Conn and Alasdair's sealskin but also figure out how to get Mahtahdou out of him. Conn was temporarily safe in her purple shirt but she herself was unguarded. Could she snatch the skin from Mahtahdou and run? But that would leave poor Rob to melt under the strain of hosting Mahtahdou.

"Give me that skin," she said, lifting her chin. "And Conn's. And then get the hell out of my friend. You had no right to do this to him."

"I had the best right in the world—the fact that I could." Mahtahdou leaned forward and tried to look at her but Rob's eyes veered crazily in different directions.

A distant peal of thunder rumbled in the silence. The weather was worsening. If she was going to get away from here on her little boat she'd have to do it soon. "What has taking him gained you? Rob's falling apart around you. Let him go."

"W-e-ell…" Mahtahdou drawled out the word. "Maybe I'll consider it. But you'll have to give me something in return."

She only just managed not to let her jaw drop in surprise. What did she have that he could possibly want? For a second, a vision of her quilts danced in her mind. Kathy had said he hated them…did he want her to hand them over to him?

"What?"

He smiled. "Yourself."

A gust of wind whistled loudly in the ruined walls but she only half heard it. The chill that gripped her had nothing to do with the weather. "What are you talking about?"

Mahtahdou let the dagger clatter from his fingers. "This body got me here with you but it won't last me long. Yours, on the other hand…" His face creased into an almost dreamy smile. "I had a body once, many years ago. It belonged to a shaman of the humans who lived here. He was powerful for a human…until the family of your selkie lover destroyed it and caught me in a trap."

He gazed contemptuously down at Rob's once-supple hands, now trembling badly. "You can see that I can inhabit the bodies of normal humans for only a few hours before they fall apart. But the bodies of magic-users like that shaman…and like yourself…those bodies can endure me quite well. Indefinitely, in fact."

Garland hoped her voice would not shake. "I can't help you. I don't know how to use magic."

"No?" Mahtahdou heaved himself up from the throne and staggered toward her. "Then what is this?" He flicked a finger at, but did not quite touch, Conn's purple shirt with her quilt square on it.

"I didn't do anything to it. I just…made it," she said in a small voice. Had Alasdair been right after all? *Did* she somehow sew magic into her quilts?

"Even better. It will be that much easier to take your power if you haven't already turned it to your own use." He smiled unpleasantly. "Bodies…lovely bodies. With a body, my scope of activities can be much broader. With a body, I can go into the human world and influence it directly. I can wrap my hands around some poor human's throat and savor the aroma of life oozing out of him, or I can set whole groups at war and enjoy watching them tear each other apart. I can maim and kill and destroy with my own hands, and make others do so for me. But it's even better now. Back when I had that shaman's body, humans were few. Now there are thousands of you. Millions, if what I've heard is true. So much blood to spill. So much destruction and pain…" He shivered ecstatically.

Her horror was giving way to anger. "And I'm supposed to want to voluntarily hand myself over to you?" She held Conn closer to her as Mahtahdou whirled and stumbled toward her. But instead of attacking her he smiled again.

"That all depends on whether or not you would like to watch while I use this body to kill the selkie whelp you're clutching," he almost purred. "It's already served me well enough to give the selkie lord a dose of that lovely slime you saw oozing from my doorkeeper…not easy to inject through a needle, but the results were most gratifying. He'll be dead inside of an hour if he isn't alrea—"

"You lie!" she shouted, backing away from him. Dear God, he had to be! But she remembered with sickening clarity the gray cast to Alasdair's face and his uneven, almost panting breathing when she'd left him.

"You know I don't," Mahtahdou said. "Admit it, human. You are trapped."

She averted her eyes from his gloating face and tried to think. Only two choices were left to her: she could attempt to flee for home (*in a thunderstorm?* asked a small, rational voice in her head as another peal of thunder, closer now, echoed through the hall) in order to keep Conn safe and to try to help Alasdair (*how?*) But that would doom innocent Rob to death, consumed by Mahtahdou.

Or she could stay here and try to defeat him somehow, guaranteeing that Alasdair would die alone…and that Conn might follow if she failed.

The only circumstance she could see in her favor was that Mahtahdou would not, if he could possibly help it, harm her— she was too important to him. He might try to trick her or frighten her, yes. But physically, at least, she was safe. For now.

Why wasn't that thought more comforting?

"I see wheels turning in those eyes," Mahtahdou whispered in Rob's voice. "Do you think that you can outwit me, little human?"

He began to circle her, leaning toward her at an awkward angle. "A female. My last body was male. I enjoyed it very much. The sensations were quite entertaining." He rubbed lasciviously at Rob's groin. "It will be even more intriguing to use a female's body and see which I prefer."

How was she supposed to think when he said things like that? "Will you be quiet?"

"Why should I? You have no choice, you know." He stopped circling and stood before her. "Surely you've worked that out by now. Even if this body dies in a minute, I've still half-won already. The selkie lord will be dead. And even without a body I can still force you to my will in other ways. Mattaquason will still be there for me to play with. Hmm." He tried to fold Rob's arms on his chest and look thoughtful but only one arm obeyed. "Whom next could I inhabit? Perhaps your friend Kathy Hayes would like to see what it is like to drive her car off a cliff into the water. Do you think she would enjoy that? I liked playing with cars that other time."

He grinned, and the creatures crouching around the room chortled too. Even the growing wind seemed to join in, blowing in abrupt gusts through the holes in the walls.

"Come, human. I grow tired of this conversation. Give yourself to me." He licked Rob's lips.

In her arms Conn stirred. She stroked his head. Please don't let him wake up right now! "Conn would be safe?" she asked, almost whispering. "You'd let him go unharmed? And Rob? You'd let them both go?"

Mahtahdou's eyes gleamed and he stepped even closer. "Of course," he said at once. "Put the whelp down over there and we can—"

She recoiled. "I didn't say yes yet," she snapped. Time, time—what could she do to play for time? Or did she even want to play for time? With each passing second both Rob and Alasdair died a little more. "You haven't said why I should want to do this. What's in it for me? Why should I let you take over my body?"

Mahtahdou looked puzzled for a moment then smiled. "Ah. Now we're talking. I had begun to think you were simple-minded, with all your concern for others. There is a straightforward answer to that. It's power.

"Occupying you will be different from what I do with this body." He flapped one of Rob's hands as if it were an ill-fitting glove. "You will still remain conscious with me inside you, even though I'll be the one in control. But I'll be happy to fulfill any little jobs you might have left undone, hampered by your human rules. Surely there are some loose ends in your life you'd like to see tied up?"

He pointed at one of his creatures. It shuffled forward on

its three clawed feet, but as she watched it began to change. The three legs melded into two, the squat body elongated and divided into a head and two arms…and there was Derek in one of his three-piece suits, the charcoal gray Brooks Brothers one he'd always worn when he had an appointment with one of his more conservative clients, looking at her with his old grin. She gasped. She couldn't help it.

"Hey, Gar," he said, looking her insolently up and down. "Jesus, you haven't changed much. Still the same old cow. I'd love to know what Alasdair saw in you—no, wait, I do know. He wanted to use you. Just like I did. He thought he could get you to help him with his stupid cause. Do you think he liked shagging you? Hell, no! What was it those tight-assed British ladies used to say? 'Lie back and think of England?'"

The Derek-thing advanced and she found herself backing away from it. This was crazy and impossible. How had Mahtahdou known?

"Don't you know he was laughing at you the entire time?" Another rumble of thunder accompanied its words. "I suppose I have to admire someone as devious and underhanded as me. He's been hiding behind you all these weeks, playing you like a violin, teasing you till you were so hot for him you'd do whatever he asked. It's what I would have done in the same situation—"

"Stop it!" she shouted.

The Derek-thing grinned at her again, and his head exploded into greenish flames. A foul odor of rotten fish and burning rubber filled the hall as he was quickly consumed, leaving only a greasy smear of ash on the floor.

"There," Mahtahdou whispered in her ear from directly behind her. "Wouldn't you love to be able to do that? I could make it happen. I could make a lot of things happen. Anyone who's gotten in your way…anyone who's held you back. Your ex-husband—we can come up with something delightful for him, something lingering and unpleasant so that he'll suffer as much as you did—"

She flinched away from him but his words niggled at her. Did Mahtahdou know her better than she did herself? Was that what she really wanted—revenge on Derek, to see him suffer the way she had?

Mahtahdou was still talking, Rob's voice sounding both oily and hoarse. "What else do you have here to cling to? Don't you understand that you had no future with the selkie lord? One day he would've grown tired of you and returned to the sea to find some selkie female to give his seed to. That's what always happens."

That's what always happens…Mahtahdou's words echoed the ones she herself had thought a few days before. In the old stories the selkie always left his or her human lover to return to the sea. Even if Alasdair survived what Mahtahdou had done to him he would leave her as soon as he had his skin again—

"You were going to lose him no matter what. You have no other choice," the low, insinuating voice murmured. "Time grows short, magic-user. Soon this human's body will be useless and I will have to toss it aside. If you let me in now, he might survive."

Rob's life was in her hands…Conn's too. Was her life worth more than theirs? It wasn't as if she'd actually be dead…

"Think of what we can do together," Mahtahdou whispered. "No one will be able to stop us, selkie or human. No one will stand in my—in *our* way."

Garland's arms ached from carrying the limp Conn, and

Mahtahdou's words echoed in her mind. No one would stand in his way…but someone could—and she was holding him. Someday Conn would grow to adulthood and try to claim his heritage. Surely Mahtahdou knew that.

Which meant that Conn would probably not live to see the sun set today if she let Mahtahdou inside her.

She glanced toward the door of the hall. Could she run for it? But the doorkeeper hung there in a solid sheet once more—

Something—an unconscious movement or her darting eyes—must have given her away. Mahtahdou snarled and lunged at her, his movement jerky and uncoordinated but swift. She saw that he'd retrieved the dagger he'd used to cut Alasdair's skin.

"It's too late—I'm deciding for you," he snarled, and grabbed at her arm as he brought the dagger down. But it was aimed at Conn, not her.

"No!" she shouted, and wrenched her arm out of his grip. The motion over-balanced him and he fell over. The three-legs and other creatures shrieked in rage, but even through the din she heard the wet, ugly snap of Rob's arm breaking as Mahtahdou hit the floor. The dagger clattered from his fingers onto the scarred mosaic floor.

"Rob!" She stared at him through the hot tears that had sprung to her eyes.

Rob's body shuddered and twitched, and a cloud seemed to gather over it. The cloud grew darker then coalesced into a dark column of shadow that rose to man height. It bent over slightly to look down at Rob's once-again unmoving body, then turned away.

"*Gah!*" said a voice in her head. "*Useless human. I should eat him.*" The shadow moved away from Rob and loomed over her.

"Leave him be!" She shifted Conn onto her hip to kneel at Rob's side. Should she turn him over, off the broken arm? He was still breathing, thank God, but in the rapidly dimming light from the windows she couldn't see much else. Had Mahtahdou left him in time or was he damaged beyond repair? It was a blessing in disguise that his arm had broken or Mahtahdou never would have let him go until it was too late.

Well, he had. And Rob was as safe as he could be, for now. She'd won the time she'd longed for. The thought gave her courage.

"You've lost your tool," she said to the shadow. "What will you do?"

"Do not make the mistake of underestimating me just because that"—he gestured contemptuously at Rob—*"is broken. I have far better ones at my disposal."* Mahtahdou flowed into a man-shape so that he looked like a huge, animated silhouette. He gestured at Alasdair's skin, lying not far from Rob. *"Shall I put on the selkie's skin and become him for you? I will take his form and you will desire me and beg for my touch on your soft, vulnerable places, and you will be mine."*

A horrible picture rose in Garland's mind of Alasdair, strong and beautiful as he had been just a few days before, making love to her. But when she looked into his eyes they were a dead black, and when he smiled his teeth were long and pointed. She squirmed to get away from him as he kissed her neck then bit savagely into her throat. "Get out of my head!" she shouted.

A flash of lightning illuminated the hall with acid light. The things around the room stared up at Mahtahdou, their eyes wide, as thunder drummed around them.

"What if I did? Do you forget that there are still plenty of weapons I can wield against you? Remember what I can do to your friend Kathy or

anyone else I choose. And what if you leave here now? Can you take that with you?" He motioned at Rob again, then pretended to study his fingernails. *"If poor Dr. Mowbray washes up on your beach dead, I should hate to think of the dim view the Mattaquason police will take of that."*

"What?" She stared up at him.

"Especially after they find that note saying that he's gone to Garland Durrell's house—" He made a gesture and the three-legs began to creep toward them, surrounding her and Rob as they bared their pointed teeth. A wave of their horrible stench washed over her and she nearly gagged.

"And the condition they'll find him in…" Mahtahdou murmured inside her head. *"Who would have thought that nice Mrs. Durrell was capable of such a horrible act?"*

One of the three-legs gave its nasty snigger. Another bent over Rob's neck, mouth gaping. A flash of lightning glittered on its teeth.

"Don't you dare touch him!" she cried, trying to kick it away. As she did, another grabbed at Conn and snatched him out of her arms. But it dropped him after only a few feet, whining. Garland launched herself at Conn as the thing tried to grab him again, and she realized that the touch of the purple shirt had hurt it.

Mahtahdou flowed toward her, thick and dark and almost solid-looking, barring her way to Conn. But her outstretched hands plunged *through* him, through a cold stickiness that made her shudder even though she knew there was no substance to it.

"How dare you touch me?" Mahtahdou shrieked in her head and jerked aside.

Garland winced—it hurt almost as much as if he'd shouted

in her real ear—but didn't take her eyes off Conn. Her momentum carried her right to him, and she snatched him against her and rolled, glad for the cushioning effect of the life jacket she still wore. She came up into a crouch, scrambled back to where Rob lay a few feet away, and squinted down at Conn's upper arm where the three-leg had bitten him. Was that blood?

Mahtahdou growled, a wordless, inhuman sound. He'd grown till his head almost touched the high ceiling, and he loomed over her and Rob and Conn.

Another bolt of lightning made her gasp again and shield her eyes. Thunder cracked overhead with a sound like breaking bones, and above it wind roared angrily.

And a flood of icy sea water gushed through the doors of the hall.

20

A THIN, TEARING squeal abruptly cut off as the doorkeeper disintegrated in the frigid flood. Mahtahdou's creatures scrambled frantically to escape it, screeching in panic. Garland beat them back and gripped Conn, then just managed to grab onto Rob's belt as the water swept toward them.

The surge slammed her into the wall back first. She gasped, winded, but again her lifejacket cushioned her against the blow. The cold water almost instantly numbed her hands but she kept her grasp on both Rob and Conn, and their combined weight and mass kept them from being tumbled in the flow.

"Unhh…" Conn stiffened in her arms, then gasped and grabbed at her neck.

"I've got you," she said to him over the roar of the rising water. "Hold on tight."

He didn't answer, but she felt his legs clamp around her waist below the jacket. Now if only Rob would wake up—she couldn't be sure she could keep his head above water—

There was barely time for her to gulp a lungful of air before the flood washed over her head. She tried to kick up toward the surface but it was impossible to tell if she was aiming in the right direction. The rushing water pulled and tossed and nearly yanked Rob from her unfeeling fingers but she hung grimly on, and Conn's arms around her neck would have choked her if there'd been air for her to breathe. If they didn't let go, maybe their bodies would be found together—

Then she was above the water, and it was pulling the other way. As quickly as it had come the water was receding, pouring out through the doors at an unnatural speed. She drew as much breath as Conn's death-grip would allow, then let go of him and grabbed at a beam of wood in the wall to keep from being sucked out of the hall. The three-legs had tried to escape by making themselves tall again, but the relentless rush of water pulled them through the door and out into the darkness of the storm.

She clung to the beam—the water had dragged her farther than she'd guessed and she was only a few yards from the door—and watched them go. What was Mahtahdou doing? Had his fury made him create a storm so strong that it had escaped even his control?

"Conn, you can let go a little," she murmured to him as the water level dropped to knee depth. Rob still hung from her grip like a dead weight—no, *not* dead, please not dead—and she wouldn't be able to hang on to him much longer. She eased him down to the floor then dropped beside him, trying to hold his head out of the last of the flood. She was still alive and unhurt, and so was Conn. Had Rob survived as well? Or had both men in her life been destroyed by Mahtahdou? Oh, Alasdair…grief sharp as Mahtahdou's knife sliced through her. She did her best to swallow it back. Right now she had to keep Alasdair's son from suffering his father's fate.

She flexed feeling back into her cramped fingers and reached for Rob's throat. A thin pulse beat there, to her enormous relief. Rob's body, at least, was alive. Whether his mind had survived Mahtahdou was another question.

Where was Mahtahdou? She stood up and surveyed the hall. The deluge had done more than purge it of Mahtahdou's creatures. It had scoured their filth from the walls so that they glowed with a pearly light visible even in the dimness of the storm-darkened afternoon. The last of the water had drained away, leaving behind it the clean, fresh tang of the open ocean.

A scream that managed to be both deep and shrill, like all the notes on a pipe organ played at once, split through her mind. Across the room the black shadow of Mahtahdou cowered behind the selkie throne. Fear radiated from him in almost visible waves, and all at once Garland understood. This hadn't been his storm.

But if it wasn't his, then whose was it?

As if in answer to her question something slammed against the outside wall of the hall. Another gush of water, driven on a blast of wind, burst through the doors. She grabbed for Rob's belt again and clamped her arm around Conn, but instead of flooding the room the water rushed up in a column, shaped by the wind. The column grew and broadened till it reached the roof of the hall, then swirled and began to change. Two immense legs appeared at its base, and two equally mighty arms rose and flexed. At the top of the column a pair of narrow, glowing eyes, lit with cold lightning, searched the room. The figure opened its mouth, and thunder rolled through the hall. Conn whimpered and burrowed against her, letting go to clap his hands over his ears.

For a few seconds the enormous figure towered over them, surveying the newly cleaned walls, the throne behind which Mahtahdou cowered…and her. She pressed Conn's head against her and shrank away as the figure took one enormous step across the room and bent toward her. A gust of wet wind whipped her hair back from her face. This was it. They would drown after all, she and Conn and Rob—

But the wind and water that swirled past her were warm, not icy. And the glowing eyes focused on her were wild and elemental, but not malevolent.

And then she saw that the huge figure held something— something limp that glittered here and there. It hurtled out of the air and splatted in a sodden heap against Conn, then fell to the floor. She stared down at it and saw another flash of gold. It was their fishnet quilt, the one that she and Conn had made together, the one that had so captivated Mattaquason's fishermen a million years ago in the window of Kathy's shop.

⁓∘⊙∘⁓

'*NO!*' Mahtahdou shrieked.

"Damn," she muttered under her breath. He hadn't forgotten about them after all. The pain of his cry in her head made her close her eyes. But when she opened them again, she saw that Mahtahdou hadn't moved.

"Conn," she said, pulling his hands from over his ears. "Can you stand?"

He let his legs relax from around her waist and set his feet to the floor. After a second, he nodded.

"Good. Get ready to run when I say so. Run to the beach if you can and look for seals. They'll take care of you."

"Not leave," he whispered.

"Yes leave. It will only be for a little bit." Just because the storm-thing seemed hostile to Mahtahdou didn't necessarily mean that it would be friendly to them.

But where had it come from? And how had it gotten hold of one of her quilts? A mental picture of her cedar-shingled roof flying into Nantucket Sound flashed through her mind, and she flinched.

A gust of wind blew into her face, and she looked up. The enormous tempest was looking at her, and she saw the purpose in its eyes. Whatever it was, it seemed to know exactly what it was doing. Somehow it had gotten hold of one of the quilts Kathy had made her take back and had brought it to her. And whatever it was, Mahtahdou feared it. The question was, what did it want her to do with it?

She picked up the sodden quilt, wrung the water from it and inspected it swiftly, one eye on Mahtahdou and the storm. The gold cord she'd so carefully knotted into a net with real fishing net knots and sewn into place over the fish was still intact. Of course it was. She didn't do shoddy work.

But *why* had it been brought to her?

"*NO!*" Mahtahdou shrieked again. The storm had turned away from her and was reaching for him.

But Mahtahdou would not go down without a fight. With a whoosh of displaced air he shot upwards, as tall as the storm-figure and as terrifying. The two figures circled one another and then grappled, wet wind and black smoke surging and rolling above her. Conn cowered against her, clutching her purple shirt around him.

Then it hit her. Alasdair's skin lay forgotten on the floor where the flood had washed it, directly across the chamber from her. Could she get to it and run while Mahtahdou was distracted? Not that Alasdair needed it anymore—the thought cut like a knife—but it didn't seem right to leave it here. And she had to try to find Conn's as well.

"Get ready to run, Conn," she murmured. "Stick close to the wall."

Slowly, cautiously, she inched around the edge of the room. She kept her head down, hoping that the enormous grappling figures wouldn't notice her slow progress or step on Rob's limp form, and cringed when a limb of wind or smoke crashed into a wall with as much force as one of flesh.

When she'd reached the wall closest to where the skin lay, she looked up once more. Above her Mahtahdou roared as the storm seemed to get a grip on him, but in the next second he'd squirmed free and they circled each other once more. She resisted the urge to yell encouragement to the storm thing and darted across the hall. Alasdair's skin was just a few feet behind the throne, a tumbled brown heap. Ten more feet…five…

"No you don't, human!" roared a voice.

Just as her fingertips brushed short sleek softness, something slammed into her. She grunted and grabbed, and was rewarded with a handful of fur before the momentum of whatever had knocked into her sent her sprawling. She heard Conn scream somewhere across the room and tried to shout to him to run, but the blow had winded her.

Mahtahdou had wrenched away from the storm and stood over her, reaching. She held Alasdair's skin closer to her and scrambled up into a crouch. He wouldn't get it. Not without a fight.

Then another voice spoke. But it whispered, not roared, and Garland wondered for a split second if it had spoken aloud, or only in her head.

Garland. The quilt. Use it.

The quilt? Then she realized that she still clutched the golden fishnet quilt in her other hand. Use it *how*? What could a small, wet quilt do against Mahtahdou's huge surging, chaotic power? And who had spoken to her?

The storm leaned forward and grabbed Mahtahdou from behind even as the threatening shadow bent toward her. She rose and held the quilt up and stared wildly from it to Mahtahdou writhing in the storm's grip, imprisoned for a few precious seconds. The golden grid of the fishnet sparkled, even in the gray storm-light.

Net. For trapping things. Could that be it? Was that why the storm had brought it to her?

Muttering a silent apology to Alasdair she dropped his skin, and with both hands, flung the small quilt over a flailing, billowing piece of Mahtahdou.

Instantly the quilt became even heavier. She hung onto it desperately as it drew the thick, roiling smoky figure into itself as if it were a sponge soaking up water. Mahtahdou screamed again, but this time his screech was hollow in her mind, receding like a train hurtling down a track. He shrank, sucked into the quilt, and it writhed horribly in her hands as he struggled to escape the pattern that was entrapping him.

And then he was gone.

The quilt in her hands rippled, then fell limp as anything made of fabric should.

She couldn't take her eyes off it. Was Mahtahdou inside it?

Would his shadow roil out of it once again if she moved? After a long moment of hardly daring to breathe she shook it a little.

Nothing.

She shook it a little harder. Still nothing.

With careful, deliberate movements she folded the quilt into a square, then rolled it. Some cord to tie it might be nice just now. Even nicer would be to drop it and run, find Conn, and sail home…if her dinghy hadn't been swept out to sea by the storm.

Something sidled up behind her. Conn held onto the back of her shirt and peered around her side at the bundled quilt. He was pale and there were scratches on his cheeks, but he was otherwise unhurt, thank heavens. "He's gone," he said.

"He's gone," she agreed, and hugged him against her side with her free hand. "Are you all right?" And Rob—she had to check on him—

A gust of wind hit them, and then another and another, in a strange sort of rhythm. The storm-figure—she'd forgotten about the storm. She looked up at it and realized what the odd, rhythmic puffs of wind were.

It was laughing.

It was standing over them in a nimbus of flying rain and wind, and it was laughing.

Then suddenly, it too was gone. She blinked and stared up toward the rafters where its head had been. A small movement at the bottom of her field of vision drew her eyes down.

Another figure, man-shaped and this time man-sized, stood about twenty feet from her and Conn. It was sliding some sort of cloak from its shoulders, a cloak made up of sea-colors, deep blue and limpid turquoise and pale frosty green the color of foam on the crests of waves…a cloak made of triangles and diamonds and squares, set in a pattern of curves.

Her knees gave out then. But Alasdair was across the room and pulling her into his arms before she touched the floor.

"You did it!" he muttered fiercely into her ear, holding her so tightly that she could barely breathe. "Grandmother couldn't have done it better." He hugged her even more tightly until she coughed in protest, then held her away from him to look at her with shining eyes.

She clutched at his forearms because her knees still didn't seem to be capable of holding her up. Joy and vitality radiated from him in an almost visible glow. Yet a few hours ago he had been gray and almost lifeless.

"Mahtahdou said you were dead." She touched his bare chest, crisscrossed with scars. "But you're alive."

"Because you healed me." He glanced behind him at the Storm at Sea quilt, lying where he'd shed it. "I woke up and you were gone, but the quilt…with it around me I…." He squeezed her shoulders. "You saw. I am alive and Mahtahdou is gone. Now do you believe me about your quilts?"

"I still don't understand—"

He was smiling and shaking his head. "The net. Do you remember how it trapped Conn's fingers? It caught Mahtahdou as well, but it took all of him. Just like my grandmother's woven band, but stronger. I don't think there is any way he'll be able to escape your magic." His face grew solemn. "You did this, Garland. You gave me back my life, my home—"

Conn suddenly appeared under Alasdair's arm, peering up at them. Alasdair pulled him into their embrace. "And my son. You saved my son."

"Bad gone," Conn said again, nodding at the quilt she still held.

"Bad gone," Alasdair agreed. He took the quilt from her and set it carefully on the floor, then looked around the room. "And we're home. This is your home, Conn. We can return to it now." He turned back to her. "Garland gave it to us," he said softly.

Garland looked away, not sure of what to say, and her eyes fell on Alasdair's sealskin, lying where she'd dropped it before casting the quilt at Mahtahdou. There was one more thing she needed to give him. She detached herself from his arms and bent to retrieve it then stood for a moment, her back to him and Conn. In a moment she would turn and give Alasdair his skin. He would be complete again, free to return to his world. The selkie world.

Where there wouldn't be any room for her.

The thought nearly crushed her but she couldn't let the pain stop her. She'd known what would happen if she rescued his skin. He would take it and be a selkie once more, and life would go back to the way it was before. Only now she'd be even lonelier, because she'd learned what it was like to be truly loved.

The skin was heavy in her hands. She smoothed her hand over its sleekness. Behind her Alasdair made a soft sound.

"This is why I came out here in the first place. This and Conn." She swallowed hard at the sight of the slashes Mahtahdou had made in it and ran a finger along one. A strange tingle ran through her hand and into her finger, and the slit closed as she traced its length.

"Garland..." Alasdair said.

Hardly daring to breathe, she touched another cut. It too closed.

She touched them all though she could barely seen them through the tears that ran unchecked down her cheeks. Her arm felt as though it were glowing white hot. How she did it was almost beside the point. She could give Alasdair back his world. All of it.

"I said I'd get your skin and bring it back to you. Here." She turned and held it out to him, sniffing fiercely. Powerful magic-women shouldn't cry in public. "You can be a selkie again. You and Conn. His skin is here somewhere. I'll find it and make it whole again." She'd be losing Conn, too, wouldn't she? Her little limpet. Her almost-child.

Alasdair was silent. The hissing crash of waves on the beach and the sigh of the wind in the broken windows were the only sounds she heard. Then he reached out and took it from her. There was an expression on his face that she wasn't sure she understood—or that any human could understand. Would it be comparable to returning a lost limb to an amputee, or sight to a blind person? He ran his hand over its length, feeling its wholeness, and finally looked up at her with blazing eyes.

Then, without a word, he strode out of the throne room.

Conn looked up at her, opened his mouth, then turned and ran after his father.

21

GARLAND STOOD still, staring after them, then around her at the pearly walls of the room. The clouds and fog had lifted and the setting sun illuminated them with soft golden light so that they almost glowed. She bent and picked up the still-folded fishnet quilt then found a length of the cord that had bound Conn and tied it snugly around the quilt. There. She didn't know if it was necessary, but it made her feel better.

It was nice that *something* could make her feel better.

She'd known it would happen. Of course Alasdair had gone back to the sea, and Conn had gone with him. That was what selkies did. It didn't matter that she loved him more deeply than the deepest ocean, or that he loved her too…she knew he did. Nature was still stronger.

Still, he could at least have said goodbye.

But maybe it was better this way. What good would words be at a time like this? Could they make it easier for her to let him go?

She rubbed her face on her damp sleeve, making it damper. She was safe and so was Mattaquason. She could go home now and try to be glad that this had happened. Without Alasdair she wouldn't have learned what she was capable of. If she worked to focus her new-found power, what could she do with it? Could she make quilts that healed the sick or eased grief and pain?

But in the meanwhile, what was she supposed to do with Mahtahdou's quilt? Was she stuck being his guardian now, just as Alasdair's grandmother had been? Somehow the thought of drying out the quilt with Mahtahdou inside it, wrapping it in acid-free tissue paper, putting it away a lignin-free cardboard quilt storage box in her cedar closet, and checking it for moths periodically seemed anticlimactic. Would her homeowner's insurance cover it in case of theft or—she shook her head. Being giddy wouldn't help now. Surely she could find a way to give it to the selkies to guard. And maybe Kathy would be her friend again, and Sandy and Elizabeth and the rest of them in town. And Rob—if he survived, would he be her friend again too? They could never be lovers—probably neither of them could face that now—but maybe they'd be able at least to nod and smile politely at each other at Friends of the Library and Historical Society events—

She would go home and find out if she could only stop crying.

Rob still lay where she'd left him, his broken arm straight beside him. At least it was a clean break and hadn't poked through his skin; getting him home was going to be hard enough as it was. Or maybe she should leave him here and go for help? But there was no guarantee she'd be able to come back again. No, she'd have to bring him now. Somehow. First she had to find her boat.

She zipped off her lifejacket and slid it under his head and whispered, "I'll be back," then rose and looked around the room. The selkies would restore it and rebuild the damaged parts of their hall. Alasdair would sit here in his rightful place again and Conn would come after him. Maybe Alasdair would take another wife and they would give Conn brothers and sisters. He would love that.

And maybe sometime, when she was sailing her boat on a perfect, hazy summer day, she would catch a glimpse of this island hanging between the worlds. But she wouldn't try to land on it. Not again.

In a corner she found another length of fur, smaller than Alasdair's and lighter in color, with spots dappling it like a fawn's coat. Of course. Conn was still a baby, wasn't he? She healed the cuts Mahtahdou had made in it—it was plusher than Alasdair's sleek fur, almost like a stuffed animal's—and held it to her cheek for a moment. Would Conn be as happy to see his skin again? Would he gaze up at her with his large, wondering eyes for a moment before disappearing into the water after his father? Would he try to wear her purple shirt over his sealskin? She smiled, but it felt more like a grimace of pain.

Then she picked up the fishnet quilt again—much as she hated to touch it, she wasn't going to let it out of her sight until its final prison had been decided—and turned to the door. She paused next to the Storm at Sea quilt where it still lay on the floor in a puddle of seawater. Alasdair had no need of it now that Mahtahdou was chained and he had his own skin back.

But it wasn't hers anymore either, even if she'd sewn her heart into it. It had served its purpose. She stepped past it and out the door.

♦

The sinking sun edged the wrack of dark blue clouds near the horizon with shining silvery orange, and a soft breeze rustled the beach grass at her feet as she ascended the first dune. Just enough wind to carry her home, assuming Alasdair hadn't blown her boat away. Spending the night on this island was simply more than she could face.

A small, purple-clad figure appeared in front of her just before she crested the dune. "Hi!" it said, and launched itself at her.

"Conn! Don't startle me like that." She caught him and held him tightly, just for a minute. Then she let go and knelt beside him. "I need to leave soon. But take this." She put his sealskin into his hands. "It's all better now. You can use it again."

He took it from her but barely looked at it. "Come on," he said, pulling at her arm.

"Oh, Conn, I can't. It's getting dark and I need to get Dr. Mowbray home because he's hurt. But I'm glad I saw you so I could say good-bye." She brushed his hair off his forehead, then leaned forward and kissed it. "I'm going to miss my little limpet," she whispered. "Be a good boy for your Daddy, all right?"

"No. Come on." He dropped his skin and tugged at her arm with both hands.

She sighed and rose, brushing sand off her knees. Maybe he'd found her boat. That would be helpful. "All right. I was going there anyway. Take your skin, honey. I don't think selkies are supposed to leave them lying around."

He bent obediently and picked up the fur, then seized her hand again and tugged. "Come *on!*"

She let him lead her down the dune, pausing to look back across the short plain dotted with yellowed rose and beach plum bushes and skeletal cedars and dune grass. Would they grow strong and green again now that Mahtahdou was gone? Did Alasdair know that beach plums made a delicious jelly that was considered a delicacy on Cape Cod? Not that he'd be able to have toast anymore...oh God, she *had* to stop thinking about him. He was no longer part of her life.

Conn let go of her hand to run ahead of her and scramble up the high bank above the beach. "Come on!" he said.

She clambered up the steep face of the dune—not as easily as she had earlier, what with trying to hold the fishnet quilt as carefully as possible...and *damn*, but she was tired. "What, Conn?" she asked.

He pointed down at the dark surface of the water. She squinted into the setting sun.

Seals, dozens of them, swam toward the shore below where she stood. Some had already inch-wormed their way up onto the beach in their oddly boneless wiggle. They snorted soft whoofling sounds through their noses or made quiet, low-pitched groans to one another, and she couldn't help wondering what they were saying...if seals could talk, that was.

But one of them, a large, strongly-built one, had reared up on its flippers as if standing to attention. The air around it seemed to change, to grow hazy and indistinct, like the rising waves of heat seen over a desert. The squat figure inside it lengthened— she couldn't quite see in the dusky light—

"Garland."

Alasdair stood silhouetted in the dark golden light, gazing up at her where she stood on the peak of the dune. He was shrugging something off his shoulders, something sleek and dark. His skin, that she'd made whole again. Her heart gave an almost painful thump.

"Alasdair," she said, and swallowed. "I was just—"

Before she could finish her sentence, another seal next to him faded into that strange mistiness and someone—a woman—appeared beside him in its place, tall and dark-haired with shining eyes. Ah. Yes, of course.

But then another woman joined him, and then a man. As she watched, thirty or so—men and women and children—wiggled from the water and *changed*, and clustered around her and Conn in a wide semi-circle at the foot of the dune. They held their sealskins over their arms or draped casually over shoulders, and they were tall and beautifully formed and totally careless of their nudity, so that she felt not only shabby in her rumpled wet shirt and jeans but overdressed as well.

Alasdair stepped through the crowd. "Here she is," he said over his shoulder. "This is she who bound Mahtahdou."

Conn grabbed her hand. "Come on," he said once again and pulled. She was tempted to dig her heals into the sand and resist, but Conn's determination was going to land her on her backside if she didn't follow.

Alasdair was waiting for them at the bottom of the high bank. He took her arm and raised it so that the fishnet quilt was in plain sight.

A murmur rose among the gathered selkies, and one by one they stepped closer, reaching out to touch it with nervous fingers. Someone took Conn's sealskin and it was passed from to hand to hand as they stroked it and looked at her. She could see the wonder in their eyes and hear it in their subdued whispers to one another. Then an older woman very gently reached out and touched her arm. *"Tapadh leibh, laidire boireannach,"* she said softly. "Thank you."

"Oh…uh, you're welcome," she replied. That seemed to give the others courage; now they touched her too, sometimes saying words she couldn't understand, sometimes just smiling and nodding. Next to her Conn bobbed up and down on his toes, grinning proprietarily as if she were his show-and-tell object on the first day of school.

Alasdair watched as well, just to her right where she couldn't see his face without turning. When the selkies around her seemed to have satisfied their curiosity and had fallen back into a semi-circle once more, he spoke. "It's getting dark. Where were you going just now?"

Darn it, the sun had touched the horizon while the selkies had been inspecting her. Would she be able to make it home all right? Twilight would linger for at least another forty-five minutes at this time of year, but she still had to figure out how to get Rob out. Maybe the selkies would help her since she'd helped them.

"I—" Her voice came out in a rasp. She cleared her throat and continued. "I was going home. But I'm glad I saw you before…before I left. Here." She held Mahtahdou's quilt out to him.

He shook his head. "I can't take it. You bound him. You're his guardian now."

Oh, *splendid.* "I was afraid you'd say that. Well, uh…good-bye. I hope—"

"Good-bye?" He shook his head again. "No, Garland. I don't think so."

"What do you mean?" Why was there a smile lurking in the corners of his mouth?

"You must consider my position," he said, eyes wide and innocent. "You're the most powerful magic-wielder we've seen since my grandmother's day. You were the one to enchain Mahtahdou. If you were me, would you let the person who had control of your deepest enemy out of your sight? It would be most unwise, I think."

"Alasdair! Are you saying that you don't trust—"

The smile she'd seen blossomed into a laugh, and through her indignation she realized she'd never heard him laugh before—a rich, deep, *happy* sound. Then he caught her in his arms and brushed his lips across her ear.

"Mahtahdou is gone and I can love again. You've given everything back to me except for one thing—my heart. I love you, Garland. I don't want my heart to be anywhere else but with you. You can't leave me."

The world spun around her, balancing delicately like a gossamer top on his words. "But…I'm human. You—"

Instead of whirling to a crash, the world lifted and filled with light as he spoke. "Yes, you're human, and I'm a selkie. You weave magic and I don't. What does it matter? I love you and I can't live without you." He blew gently in her ear. "Be my wife, beautiful lady."

She clung to him, trying to make sense of what he was saying. "Are you *sure*?"

Someone tugged on her shirt. She looked down and saw Conn staring up at her hopefully.

"Please?" he asked, and wrapped his arms around her leg.

Joy in the form of laughter bubbled up inside her. She pulled Conn into their embrace. "I was right when I called you 'little limpet', wasn't I?"

"Limpets know where it's safe to cling," Alasdair said. "But I'm still waiting for an answer."

"You know what my answer is. You knew all along. I don't know how we'll do it, but I'm yours." She laughed shakily. "Will they make a song about us? The human who gave a selkie back his skin, and he stayed with her instead of leaving?"

"They'll make songs about more than that. What about one with the blue-eyed lady who trapped Mahtahdou in her golden net? But we're going to prove those old stories wrong. Neither of us has to choose one world over another. In summer we'll live here with the selkies, and in the winter I'll help you make your quilts. We can have both."

She touched his cheek where a smile had banished his old stern expression. If she had anything to say about it, it would never return. "Ha. You and Conn just don't want to have to completely give up toast."

His eyes gleamed warm gold. "I'd thought of that. But more importantly, we won't have to give up *you*."

22

A year later...

FROM THE *June 5 Mattaquason* Mariner, *"Mattaquason Faces and Places" column by Jim Barnes:*

Fans of local quilt artist Garland Durrell held their collective breath as the gavel went down on an extraordinary auction of her quilts last weekend, held to benefit local conservation efforts by Cape Cod Preservation (CCP).

The glittering evening, held at Ms. Durrell's home on Eldredge Point, featured food, music, and twelve of her fabric creations. The guests, both local and from off-Cape, were spellbound as each quilt was presented for bidding. A bank of phones was brought in for call-in bids from as far away as London and Los Angeles, and altogether close to $75,000 were raised for the CCP, a not-for-profit group that works with the National Park Service to preserve and protect the natural resources and habitats on and around Cape Cod, especially for the marine mammals that call the waters of the Cape home.

A radiant Ms. Durrell, who is expecting her first child next month, presented a ceremonial check for the amount to Henry Bard, the CCP's executive director, supported by her husband and stepson.

Ms. Durrell is well known for her exquisite quilts, a favorite of both locals and summer visitors. Examples of her work can be seen in both the library and town hall as well as in private collections around town and around the country...

From the "Mattaquason Faces and Places" column, same issue:
Dr. Sidney Phelps is pleased to announce that Drs. Chandra and Mahdavi Ram will be joining his practice as internists. The husband-and-wife team will be welcome additions to Mattaquason, short on local medical practitioners since Dr. Robert Mowbray returned last year to his native Iowa to practice medicine with his uncle. Existing and new patients are welcome to stop in to the office next week and meet the new physicians, who are both graduates of...

From the "Upcoming in Town" notices, same issue:
Plans are underway for the Equinox Extravaganza to take place on September 21, starting at 5pm and featuring two local bands, a bonfire and cookout, and ending with fireworks at 9 pm on the Town Beach. All Mattaquason residents and their guests will be invited to attend.

"We had such a great time at our Equinox Extravaganza last March that we decided we needed a fall one, too," says organizer Kathy Hayes, one of the event's business sponsors. "We have a lot to celebrate in Mattaquason, don't you think?"

ఌఁ౿ఙ

ACKNOWLEDGEMENTS

Writing a story is a solitary endeavor. Creating a book, on the other hand, is usually the work of many. I'd like to thank the many who helped SKIN DEEP see the light of day:

My critique partners Janet Halpin and Doreen Rebh, who read early versions of this story.

E of Aquila Editing, who kindly but firmly pointed out what needed fixing and made it a much better story.

Judy of Judicious Revisions, who polished off the rough edges. Any remaining infelicities and errors are purely mine.

And for various forms of support, encouragement, and shenaniganizing, thank you to my dear friend and blogging partner Regina Scott, to Janet Halpin for years of slogging along in the trenches with me, and to my fellow Moderators and Administrators of the SCBWI Blueboard who keep me sane and laughing and aren't scandalized when I write books for grown-ups on the side. I love you guys!

ఌఁ౿ఙ

BY JOVE

For Theodora Fairchild, returning to graduate school after three years of teaching Latin to unenthusiastic middle-schoolers is a dream come true. The professors in the Classics Department at John Winthrop University in Boston are the best in their field; the classes are varied and intellectually stimulating…and she meets brilliant, sweetly nerdy post-doc Grant Proctor.

As she gives in to her feelings for Grant, someone seems determined to keep them apart—no matter the consequences. Things are not quite what they seem in the Classics Department, and someone there has plans for Theo that don't include Grant. When Grant disappears, surviving the semester becomes only one of Theo's worries; her wits and wisdom may be the only things that can save the man she loves.

The Leland Sisters series (young adult)

BEWITCHING SEASON

In 1837 London, young daughters of viscounts pined for handsome, titled husbands, not careers. And certainly not careers in magic. At least, most of them didn't.

Shy, studious Persephone Leland would far rather devote herself to her secret magic studies than enter society and look for a suitable husband. But right as the inevitable season for "coming out" is about to begin, Persy and her twin sister Pen discover that their governess in magic has been kidnapped as part of a plot to gain control of the soon-to-be Queen Victoria. Racing through Mayfair ballrooms and royal palaces, the sisters overcome bad millinery, shady royal spinsters, and a mysterious Irish wizard. And along the way, Persy learns that husband hunting isn't such an odious task after all, if you can find the right quarry.

BETRAYING SEASON

Penelope (Pen) Leland has come to Ireland to study magic and prove to herself that she is as good a witch as her twin sister, Persy. But when the dashing Niall Keating begins to pay her court, she can't help being distracted from her studies.

Little does Pen know, Niall is acting upon orders from his sorceress mother. And although it starts as a sham, Niall actually falls deeply in love with Pen, and she with him. But even if he halts his mother's evil plan, will Pen be able to forgive him for trying to seduce her into a plot? And what of Pen's magic, which seems to be increasingly powerful?

COURTSHIP AND CURSES

Sophie's entrance into London society isn't what she thought it would be: Mama isn't there to guide her. Papa is buried in his work fighting Napoleon. And worst of all, the illness that left her with a limp, unable to dance at the Season's balls, also took away her magic. When the dashing Lord Woodbridge starts showing an interest in Sophie, she wants to believe it's genuine, but she can't be sure he's feeling anything more than pity.

Sophie's problems escalate when someone uses magic to attack Papa at the Whistons' ball and it soon becomes clear that all the members of the War Office are being targeted. Can Sophie regain her own powers, find her balance, make a match--and save England?

CHARLES BEWITCHED (novella)

In this novella follow-up to Bewitching Season and Betraying Season, sixteen-year-old Charles Leland is not looking forward to his summer holidays from Eton—not when he has to spend them studying history to make up for a less-than-stellar grade last term. Even the thought of staying with his sister Persy and her husband Lochinvar while his parents are in Ireland can't cheer him up.

But cramming history quickly takes a back seat to finding out what has happened to Persy, who disappears from home the day he arrives. All signs indicate that she's been abducted by gypsies--but a gypsy boy named Nando convinces Charles that her disappearance has a much more otherworldly explanation.

Now Charles must brave the perils and sheer strangeness of the fairy lands to try to rescue his sister from being forcibly married to a powerful fairy lord, with the help of the fairy lord's own very insistent younger sister, a copy of History and Policy of the Norman and Angevin Kings that he must read before September, and Her Majesty Queen Victoria. But will he also be able to rescue himself?